BTR   2/21

This book should be returned/renewed by the
latest date shown above. Overdue items incur
charges which prevent self-service renewals.
Please contact the library.

Wandsworth Libraries
24 hour Renewal Hotline
01159 293388
www.wandsworth.gov.uk

Wandsworth

D1349440

POST MORTEM

GARY BELL QC
AND
SCOTT KERSHAW

R A V E N 🐦 B O O K S
LONDON · OXFORD · NEW YORK · NEW DELHI · SYDNEY

BLOOMSBURY, RAVEN BOOKS and the Raven Books logo are trademarks
of Bloomsbury Publishing Plc

First published in Great Britain 2021

ISBN: HB: 978-1-5266-1240-3; TPB: 978-1-5266-1239-7;
eBook: 978-1-5266-1238-0

2 4 6 8 10 9 7 5 3 1

Typeset by Integra Software Services Pvt. Ltd.
Printed and bound in Great Britain by CPI Group (UK) Ltd, Croydon CR0 4YY

MIX
Paper from
responsible sources
FSC www.fsc.org FSC® C020471

To find out more about our authors and books visit www.bloomsbury.com
and sign up for our newsletters

Winter nights are hard in prison. Hours dilate and darkness is absolute.

On Tuesday 9 January the sun set over London at 16.11.

Children were walking home from schools; parents had welcomed in the final hour of the working day. For all inmates at Wormwood Scrubs, association time had been cancelled after a fatal stabbing at the weekend. The cells were bolted at sundown, and they didn't open again for sixteen hours.

No disturbance was reported in the night. No sounds of distress echoed between bars. Even the rats, it was later said, made themselves scarce.

At dawn, they found the bodies.

Thirteen men had died in their cells.

Some had choked. Others had bled. It wasn't long before rumours spread through the wings. Whispers of suicide pacts. The governor called it a tragic coincidence, a bizarre succession of unfortunate accidents. The coroner reported death by misadventure.

Nobody at the prison dared to call it what it was until the tabloids did it for them.

The Prison Service was facing a locked-room mystery spread out across three impenetrable wings. Thirteen bodies in a single winter night.

What happened should've been impossible.

Somehow, it was murder.

PART ONE

OLD DOGS

1

It took me a few minutes to force the door, levering a length of pipe back and forth against the lock, but I could already smell them from the other side: urine and faeces, dank fur, sour blood like old copper coins. When the lock finally gave, and the door sprang wide open, I had to hoist my collar up over my mouth to keep from gagging.

Inside, the animals went berserk.

I entered the building slowly, cutting through shadows with a torch in one hand, brandishing the pipe I'd used to jemmy the door with the other. There were nine dogs, I counted, each bashing itself against the confines of its pen, jaws snapping, desperate to rip and tear at me – the trespasser, the criminal.

I paused, anxiously watching for any buckling in their cages.

These were game dogs. Killers in training. I might've been on the hefty side, but up against one of these I didn't fancy my chances.

The baying was constant, but any chance of alerting a passer-by was slim. This building, a former launderette stripped of all but the bolts of its former mechanical guts, was tucked away on an industrial estate in Croydon, neighbour only to desolate factories and waste-processing plants.

The dogs' cages were spaced along the back wall in a row, each no larger than three square feet with muck piled in every corner. Five of the nine were American pit bull terriers. They weren't fully grown, and the stumps of their ears and tails hadn't healed since being sheared off at the bases, but already they were fearsome enough. Inching further into the building, my torchlight picked up a pair of secateurs on a workbench stained with old blood and the sight redoubled my queasiness.

Alongside the five pit bulls, separated by an empty tenth cage, were four of the dogs I'd come looking for: Dogo Argentinos, each around a hundred pounds of muscle under pure white fur. They butted the steel with lunatic aggression, and my mind couldn't help but go back to the case I'd worked on months before, which had focused on a similar white aggressor by the name of Billy Barber. He was, in some way, responsible for me coming here.

While serving time on remand, Billy had recommended my services to Isaac Reid, a drug dealer who now wanted me to appeal his own conviction for double murder. Reid's case had been one of almost mathematical simplicity: business rivals had moved into a house in Margate, quaint seaside town on the Kentish coast and alleged territory of Reid's criminal organisation; into this equation a so-called zombie knife was introduced, the newcomers were hacked to death, and Isaac Reid was sent down for life.

The key to his appeal was a Dogo Argentino that had belonged to the dead dealers. It was Reid's argument that, since the dog had been standing guard over the property that night, the actual killer must've been known and welcome to the victims, or else he would never have made it past the animal alive. Now, seeing the power of these dogs, I found myself inclined to agree.

I wiped a glove across my face, fighting the urge to race back to the car. First, I wanted photographs. With a bit of luck, I could use them not only to win Reid's appeal, but to close down this particular branch of a sick trade for good.

I dropped the pipe and rummaged through my coat for my phone. Ignoring the text onscreen, I enabled the flash and photographed the cages from a distance, then the secateurs and the other makeshift apparatus of this cruel animal gymnasium: in one corner a home-made treadmill, its running platform fixed at an uphill angle; across the room, hanging ropes designed to strengthen bites. It was about this time, while I was distracted and deafened by the cacophony of barking, that the tenth dog in the room managed to get near enough to lock its teeth around my right ankle.

The impact sent me to the floor with a strangled cry. It was shock more than pain. Sprawled and frantic, I aimed the light down and braced myself for freshets of blood pouring out from my trousers. But there was no wound. My attacker, a black Staffordshire bull terrier, was strapped by collar and chain to a water pipe in the corner. She was already cowering, and when she opened her mouth to whimper, I saw that her teeth had been manually filed down to blunt stumps.

'For Christ's sake,' I said, getting carefully back onto my feet then crouching at her level. 'What've they done to you, girl?'

What remained of her left ear was tattered. There were myriad white scars criss-crossed through her dark fur and a portion of her lower lip was missing altogether. She was a bait dog, I realised: more apparatus for the trainee fighters. She backed up to the pipe, quivering, and when her eyes flickered off to one side, revealing their whites in the glare of my torch, I followed her gaze and saw yellow light had appeared under the crack of a closed interior door.

'Shit.' I crammed the torch and phone into my coat pockets. 'Here we go.'

Instead of heading back the way I'd come, I just managed to get into position behind the opening door before a scrawny hand reached through and powered up the stark industrial lamps overhead with the flick of a switch.

The newcomer roared a single word into the room: '*Obey!*'

The caged dogs fell instantly silent, and sat up straight in their pens.

'What's got into you lot?' the man grunted from the other side of the open door. 'I could hear you all the w—'

His voice went out like a flame in a wind tunnel. He'd spotted the open fire escape, the pipe dropped in the middle of the room. I shouldered my weight into my side of the door, crunching it into his body. By the time he'd hit the concrete I was over him, glaring down at his greasy hair and pallid face as if it were something unpleasant smeared beneath my shoe. From one of his hands, a plastic bag of cheap steaks oozed pink fluid onto the ground.

'Jacob Werner.'

He blinked in disbelief. '*Rook?*'

'This can't be right,' I noted, still towering above him. 'You were in court last week on a charge contrary to the Dangerous Dogs Act, and yet here you are now in a supposedly abandoned building, surrounded by illegal animals.'

He grumbled, struggling to get himself upright in the raw, fetid juices. 'What the hell are you doing here?'

I wanted to know who he'd been breeding for, but Jacob Werner had a mouth the size of Greater London; pressing him to roll on his customers would be dangerous for the both of us. 'You think I don't look into my clients before we go to trial? It's your cousin who owns this building, isn't it? Last week I had you acquitted for breeding dangerous dogs. Two days later I hear about a girl finding a mutilated pit bull on Wandle Park, five minutes away from here. Christ, Werner, even a dog knows not to shit where it eats.'

He finally steadied himself on two feet, sweeping dust from his backside, picked up the bag and shrugged. 'You were paid enough to defend me. I assume you haven't come here to give me the money back now you've seen how it was made?' He rubbed his shoulder where the door had smashed into it, and shook his head. 'You're a criminal lawyer. You tell lies for money. What's the issue?'

From the cages beside me, one of the dogs began to whine. 'Let's just say I've been struggling to abide certain cruelties lately.'

'*Cruelties?*' He giggled nervously, running a hand through his lank, thinning hair. 'You're getting on your high horse about some dead mutt?'

'I convinced those magistrates to let you walk. I thought –'

'Whatever you thought, Rook, that doesn't give you the right to break in here.' His eyes glittered towards the cages and the animals salivating there. 'What if I opened these crates? What do you reckon would happen to you then?'

I swallowed, ignoring the dull throb in my ankle. 'Nothing good for either of us, I'd imagine. You know how it ended for Ramsay Bolton, don't you?'

I could tell from the downward roll of his mouth that he didn't, but the implication was clear enough. He scratched his stomach, a strange pot on his otherwise scrawny frame, and sniffed. 'So, instead of leaving me to earn a living, you've come to get me nicked and have my dogs destroyed, have you? Very noble.'

'That'll be for the courts to decide,' I told him, and all those watchful eyes, so rabid only moments ago, seemed to lean on me with physical weight.

Werner laughed. 'Maximum sentence is, what? Six months? I'd be out in three, but *you* …' Now his flat eyes moved pointedly between the broken doorway, the pipe on the floor, the gloves on my hands. 'Queen's Counsel breaking and entering. You'd be struck off, at least.'

At least, I agreed, but Werner clearly hadn't realised that my intentions had never been so rational as to involve the police.

'I won't be the one to put these dogs to death,' I told him, 'but you're going to put an end to this once and for all. If you don't, I will be coming back for you.' I patted the outline of the phone through my pocket. 'I've got proof now, should you decide to keep this sadistic little business of yours afloat.'

'If these dogs are put to death, Rook, then we'll both be joining them soon enough. You don't know what you're getting involved in. These aren't just mongrel status dogs. These are quality animals. They're ordered and paid for before birth. You have them taken away, and you're nicking from the sorts of people you don't want to be nicking from.'

'Like who?' I gestured to the Argentinos drooling behind bars. 'Who would want one of these things around?'

'People with big investments to guard. People like –' For a second, I believed his big mouth was going to work in my favour; it flapped open wide, ready to boast, and then stopped. 'Wait. Is *that* why you came here? You expect me to shop my own customers?'

'Of course not,' I lied. 'As I said, perhaps it's time you started looking for better ways to make a living, that's all.'

He licked his lips, catching beads of sweat, and lifted his chin defiantly. 'We'll see which one of us keeps earning once this gets out. How much work do you think it'll cost you after every player in the city hears Elliot Rook's gone soft? Once it gets around that you can't be trusted to keep a client's affairs to yourself no more, and all because you're crying over some lousy animals?' His gaze danced over my face, evaluating the impact of this gambit, and whatever he saw there satisfied him enough for a bloated smirk. 'If ever the day comes when you *do* feel like showing up again, Counsel, then I suggest you stop and think about that first.'

The bulbs overhead made him look even pastier than he had last week in court. The dogs were panting now, desperate for the flesh in his shopping bag, and their collective sound was monstrous.

'Well,' I said, trying to sound regretful, 'if that's the case, then it appears we're stuck at this status quo. Pity. I thought I might be able to talk some sense into you.'

I turned for the exit. The rush of adrenaline pulled at my knees, giving me all the good grace of a drunkard as

I retrieved the pipe I'd found in the skip outside. Werner followed, cagey enough to maintain a constant distance of six feet or so now that I was armed.

I was almost out when my attention turned back to the quivering little bait dog with the tattered ear and missing lip. I stopped. I couldn't bring myself to go any further.

'Ah, fuck it,' I sighed, and with one huge turn I launched the lead pipe double-handed like a hammer throw into Werner's gut. He was airborne for about three feet before he went down hard, clutching his vitals and gasping for wind.

I stepped over him, freed the trembling terrier from the pipe as gently as I could, wrapped her into the woollen folds of my overcoat and carried her out in both arms.

Dusk had dropped to full dark outside. I paused in the opening of the broken fire escape and spoke without looking back over my shoulder. 'Might I suggest that, in future, you seek alternative representation for your defence? I think this puts an end to our business relationship, Mr Werner.'

He managed nothing better than a long, strained groan.

By the time I'd made it back to my car, I could hear the rest of the dogs baying again, but the sound travelled no further than the factories that slumped and crumbled all around this forgotten pocket of the capital.

And that was the last time I saw Jacob Werner alive.

2

The following morning, I was still feeling strangely exhilarated. I decided on a whim to forgo the usual options of Tube or car and instead chose to walk the two miles into work.

The pavement was hardly any quieter than the Underground or roads might've been – this was Monday in central London, after all – but there was an upbeat ambience noticeable from the very moment I stepped out of my front door onto Gloucester Place, as tangible as the first valiant daffodil to push up from dirt into sunlight. Last week had ended below freezing point, the tabloids relishing headlines like KILLER FREEZE, THE BEAST FROM THE EAST and ICE AGE BRITAIN, but this morning the mercury was already up to double figures. The date was 5 March, and spring was finally returning to our great city.

It took me ten minutes to walk the length of my road, then a left turn at the bottom took me onto Oxford Street. All I had to do from there was amble eastward through that straight commercial pantheon for another thirty minutes. I got myself a warm pain au chocolat for the journey, my diet forsaken at the first hurdle for yet another week, and then wended my way between the hundreds of workers dressed in suits or various retail uniforms. The gigantic window displays were already flaunting red-and-white bunting, despite the World Cup being three months away, and I was momentarily overcome with nostalgia for Spain 1982: the simplicity of being seventeen years old and caped in a St George's cross, all gathered around the colour screen in the Miners' Welfare for every match. Simple times.

It wasn't until I glanced down to brush the flakes of pastry from my coat that I saw the dog hairs caught up like wires in the black wool there, and all at once it made me feel giddy and arrogant, like a teenager carrying the dirty, thrilling secret of losing his virginity the night before.

I wanted to feel bad for demeaning the legal system I'd upheld for so many years, but the guilt wouldn't surface. Somewhere over the course of this long, dark winter a part of me had changed, and I couldn't tell if it was ever going to change back. Compulsions, such as the one that had sent me out to that launderette last night, had been coming upon me like coughing fits in a silent courtroom. The more I'd tried to suppress them, the more suffocating they'd become. I hadn't found exactly what I needed to appeal against Isaac Reid's conviction, but it was obvious that the Dogo Argentinos were being bred for some seriously unpleasant people.

I'd driven the Staffy to an emergency vet, who had agreed to take her on to the Blue Cross in Victoria once it opened this morning. I gave the vet cash for his troubles and hoped that the dog would be all right. There was nothing more I could do. I swept the hairs away and they disappeared like dandelion seeds into the sluggish rush-hour swell of black cabs and crowded double-deckers.

Soon, a short, dumpy figure dressed in a shabby deer-stalker and red sleeveless jacket shuffled into my path. '*Big*

Issue?' she called indifferently, and then looked over the stack of laminated magazines and into the shadow beneath the brim of my hat. 'Oh, hey, Rook.'

'Morning, Margaret. Hope you kept out of the snow last week.'

'Who, me?' She beamed proudly, showing brown teeth, and lifted a copy to show me the headline: UNDEFEATED: OUR VENDORS WHO WRESTLED THE BEAST AND WON! There were photos of half a dozen vendors standing diligently in powdered white. One was dressed in a recognisable deerstalker.

'Impressive,' I said, fumbling through my pocket for change.

'I'll be on the cover of *Vogue* next,' she winked. I paid her double for the copy and she managed a stiff curtsy, keenly eyeing the shirt collar and tie peeking through my coat. 'Say, did you ever get yourself a wife?'

'Once.'

'You're not looking for another?'

I shook my head and smiled. 'Once bitten.' I rolled the magazine under my arm, tipped my hat and carried on.

It took two cigarettes to walk the whole repetitive sprawl of Oxford Street – another Next store, another River Island, the third or fourth McDonald's – and then I was back in law-land, the place that still made the most sense to me, passing the open green of Lincoln's Inn Fields where I used to spend my nights.

I cut straight through the grounds of Lincoln's Inn itself, winding between the ancient stone buildings that had housed the chambers of various legal firms for generations, then crossed Chancery Lane and continued into the cobbled

Took's Court, coming to rest at the bronze sign for Miller & Stubbs Criminal Barristers. I paused there for a minute, savouring silence. Then I opened the heavy red door and stepped up into the town house.

Immediately they swarmed me.

'Morning, Mr Rook!'

'Good morning, sir!

'Can I get you something to drink? Tea? Coffee? Water?'

'Need a hand with that briefcase, Mr Rook?'

Pupils. They were everywhere. I moved like a great white through an undertow, aiming for the staircase at the other side of the lobby. I caught the eye of Bronwyn, our receptionist, standing at her desk. She gave me the familiar pitiful smile, the sort that most in the building had adopted since reading about my divorce in any one of the intrusive articles printed over the course of winter: *Rook made the chilling discovery after dropping his wedding ring, the final memento of ex-wife Jennifer, into the snow ...* God save our country's right to journalistic freedom. Thankfully, the reporters hadn't bothered stretching too far into my past. I wasn't quite a household name, but the national coverage *had* brought work flooding into chambers from all over the country. To the horde of new pupils enlisted to deal with the surge I was practically a celebrity.

Fortunately, my room was up on the third floor, away from all the chaos.

For two decades I'd been crammed into shared rooms, elbow-to-elbow with my fellow junior barristers, but now I enjoyed the benefits of being one of only four silks in our set. I had myself a spacious, private nest in which to retreat.

Or, at least, I should have.

I was still grousing to myself when I walked into my room and shut the door behind me – 'Can't get a moment's peace … let me get into the building, why don't you? Bloody pupils …' From the rear corner of the room, which should have been empty, came a familiar voice.

'Oh? And what's your problem with pupils?'

I stopped, and made a show of rattling the door handle behind me. 'This must be broken,' I said, 'because I'm almost certain I locked it before leaving for the weekend.'

'No, you did. I got Ernie to let me in. You don't mind, do you?'

'Mind?' I tossed my hat, briefcase and *Big Issue* onto my desk, and took a seat, or rather a slouch. Zara Barnes was sitting with her back to me, bent over her iPad and a spread of documents on the old writing bureau across the room where she so often squatted. 'Why would I mind? There's nothing in here except for a few dusty books, a tatty old wig and boxfuls of confidential papers that might be priceless to any number of criminals across the city. Who am I to question the authority of Ernie, our revered caretaker, when he decides which locks shall be undone?'

'He guessed you'd say something like that.'

'Did he now?'

She turned to face me, scrunching her eyes up behind her heavy glasses and adopting a dreadful impersonation of a cockney accent. '*Whale, Miss Bornes, ol' Rook ain't gonna begrudge you no space to work, consid'rin' 'ow you saved his life a few months ago. Withart your quick thinkin', ee'd be good as brown bread!*'

I staved off a smile and started arranging last week's paperwork from my briefcase into the plastic in-tray on my desk. 'You're sure this was Ernie you spoke to? It wasn't Bert the chimney sweep?'

'Undoubtedly.'

I shook my head. 'Whatever happened to that aspiring young go-getter we used to have around here who would always have the coffees waiting?'

'She emptied her overdraft and maxed out all her credit cards. As soon as she can afford one, the round's on her. I've got a meeting with the bank later this afternoon, so you never know …'

She hadn't said it with any kind of resentment, but it made me feel acutely selfish all the same. Zara's assistance had proven invaluable in the fraud case that had occupied most of my last two months, but as a pupil she hadn't been paid for her time, and she was left scraping together a living out of the scant fees brought from her cases in the magistrates'. I'd twice suggested that she take some of my own payment and her reaction had taught me well enough to drop the subject. I probably would've acted the same way at twenty-four. In fact, at fifty-two, the fraud case had only just put my own finances back into the black.

In short, I should've bought the coffees.

'You've been working a lot of cases lately,' I said. 'Haven't they fetched you any decent fees yet?'

'Sure, another few hundred shoplifters and I might be able to afford this month's rent.' She leaned back into a straight slice of pale light that crossed the room from the window and fell serious. 'Not that I mean to sound ungrateful, you know I love what I do here.'

'It's fine. I know how frustrating it is living from hand to mouth.'

'Especially when everything comes with a London price tag. I ordered two pints last night and gave the barman a tenner. I thought I'd misheard him when he asked for fourteen quid. Honestly, there has *got* to be an easier way to make a living.'

'Easier?' I nodded. 'Certainly, but everything comes at a cost. Don't forget that this is only temporary. You won't be a pupil forever.'

'No,' she said, 'I won't,' and went back to her tablet in silence.

Since I'd first invited her into chambers last September, Zara had grown from a nervous stranger into a near permanent fixture in my room, as much a part of the decor as the towering, overcrowded bookshelves or the faded Tabriz rug. She'd even taken it upon herself to fill the compartments of the bureau with her own personal touches: a blue-and-white ceramic pot from her mother's side of the family in Multan, Pakistan; novelty erasers shaped like pieces of sushi and whole wedges of rainbow-coloured Post-it notes for her to stick all over the place; the emergency charger for her iPad and phone; and a mug declaring her to be the *No. 1 Barrister in London*, which matched the *No. 2* version she'd concurrently gifted me for Christmas.

I knew what she was doing. Like any casual partner leaving a toothbrush in the bathroom, she was staking out her ground. I didn't mind, though I couldn't help but worry about the weeks to come. Zara had been accepted into chambers on a six-month pupillage, the final stretch of unpaid learning necessary to become a qualified barrister, and those six months would end in three weeks' time.

By all rights she should have been offered a permanent tenancy, not least because she had saved my own life and quite possibly the lives of others with her bravery not so long ago, but that wasn't something that could be quantified on paper. There seemed to remain a deep-rooted, unspoken attitude among a great many of my fellow barristers – not so much a direct prejudice but most definitely an outdated typecast – for what was considered a *suitable* candidate in chambers, and I still feared that a gay woman of mixed race with a council-estate background and thick Nottinghamshire accent might prove a step too far for such limited sensibilities. She suspected it too. I could tell by the dimming of her mood each time another public-schooled pupil was drafted in to manage the increasing workload.

There would be only one permanent position available in chambers, and in twenty-one days its allocation would come down to a vote.

We didn't talk about it much, just as we didn't talk about what had happened up in Nottinghamshire all that often. Occasionally, Zara would joke about the events of that winter, as she had done this morning, but more often than not the safeguard of humour wouldn't come, and I'd catch her plummeting into deep reveries beyond which the slightest disturbance would put her on edge.

We both had our own ways of dealing with the horror of it all, I supposed.

'So,' she said, talking down into her iPad, 'what's happening?'

'With what?'

'Good weekend?'

I hesitated, focusing on the brief in my hands: *Regina* v. *Jacob Werner*. I quietly filed it as finished and moved on. 'Nothing to report.'

'Oh.' It was the kind of response that comes with an audible full stop. I looked back up. She flicked a twist of lint from her trousers onto the floor. 'Thought you might've had something going on, since you didn't reply to my text last night ...'

'Your text?' I rummaged for my phone and opened the message that had come through while I'd been searching Werner's launderette. 'Must've fallen asleep before looking at it ...' For a moment I felt like telling her the story of Jacob Werner and his tortured animals. What stopped me was not the fear of her disapproval, but rather the inkling that she would have wanted to come along. 'You were asking for help with your case?' I said apologetically, reading the message. 'Did you try asking Stein? You are his pupil, I'd say it's the least he could do after dumping more work on you.'

'He didn't *dump* this on me,' she said tetchily. 'It's a massive case for me. Besides, have you been down to see Stein? The second floor is a madhouse. They've got six juniors in every room and that's without these new pupils. I'm not getting help from there.'

'I avoid the lower floors like the plague,' I remarked. 'Percy hasn't been up with my papers?'

'Not since I've been here. You know Mondays.'

I checked the time: twenty to ten. My impromptu walk had cost me an extra half an hour, but I couldn't start work on my new case until our senior clerk had printed off my papers. The legal world was rapidly turning digital, and cases were often distributed via email, but I still preferred papers I could hold, mark and tab. I liked to think of myself as a traditionalist; Zara called me stubborn.

21

'All right,' I said. 'I'm yours until my new brief arrives, and then you're on your own.'

The change in her mood was instant and electric. 'You're the best, Mr Rook.'

'I've told you a hundred times to stop calling me *mister*. The correct way to address another barrister is by surname.'

She bundled her paperwork up into her arms along with the iPad and dragged her chair towards me, stomping Doc Martens and grinning.

'What's the charge?'

'Drugs,' she said proudly, wasting no time in filling what little space I'd cleared on my desk. 'Possession with intent to supply.'

'Class?'

'A.'

'Really? That is a big case for a –' I faltered.

'A pupil?'

'Yes,' I admitted, looking down at the papers. 'What's the catch?'

'I guess you might call getting nicked red-handed a catch.' With both hands she parted the falling strands among her tangled black hair, which had grown long over the last couple of months. 'The magistrates' declined jurisdiction and sent it to Crown court. I've explained to the client that if he pleads guilty he'll get the standard third off, and if we plead on a limited basis it could be much more than that, but he's insisting on a trial. He says he's not guilty.'

'Lose at trial for intent to supply Class As and his sentence might be approaching double figures,' I said. 'He was really caught red-handed?'

'By the police, but there's more to it than that.'

'There always is.'

'I've got a meeting with the client after lunch. I put your name down when I booked in case you wanted to, you know, tag along.'

'Tag along?' I frowned. 'You know I have my own work-load, don't you? My new case goes to trial in a week and I know next to nothing about it.'

'Yes,' she said guiltily, 'but it's easier for me to turn up at the prison without you than it is for me to add you at the last minute if you *did* want to come. The client's asked me to submit a second application for bail, but that requires a change in circumstances.'

'And you're not sure if his circumstances have changed?'

'Pretty much. That's where I could use a little bit of that *silk magic*.'

I thumbed through the top pages of her case papers. 'When do you go to trial?'

'Next Monday.'

'Your client can't tough it out on the inside for one more week?'

'I think he's been assaulted in prison. Beaten up. He's a really interesting guy, actually, and you have such a good intuition for these sorts of things. I've been to see him a few times down at Wormwood Scrubs, and –'

'The Scrubs?' I glanced up, and then hesitated. Something quiet and almost glacial shifted between us. 'He's on remand at the Scrubs?'

She didn't answer. Just a nod, pseudo-casual.

'How many times *have* you been to see him?'

'Well, not *that* many ...'

She went quiet. Uncomfortable silences were rare between us, but this one stretched a while. Before I opened my mouth to carry on, there was a sharp knock at the door. Our senior clerk, Percy, entered with a buoyant stride.

'Rook!' He looked almost ready to clack his heels together. Financially, it had been a very good month for chambers, and as Percy was on a percentage of the turnover, it had been a very good month for him too. He was the image of debonair, with straight teeth and classically handsome features, but he drank and consequently tended to surf through his mornings on suave perkiness instead of allowing any hangover to bring him down. When he approached my desk, he practically yelled. 'A fine morning to you, my learned friend!'

This was followed by a noticeably stiff yet amicable nod to Zara, garnished with a bemused half-smile. Percy had made no secret of his initial distaste for her, but now he tolerated her as if she was some bizarre pet roaming the rooms of a shared house; he was clearly grateful for the cash our combined efforts had brought into chambers, but no doubt comforted by the belief that her presence was finally drawing to an end.

He produced a clutch of papers from behind his back like a skinny amateur magician. 'Your instructions in the case of the Crown versus Charli Meadows. Smuggling drugs into prison. Private payer,' he added cheerily, and laid the papers down directly over Zara's. 'You're scheduled for a conference with the client at ten thirty this morning.'

'Cutting it fine,' I said. 'Where?'

'Right here.' He gestured to the space occupied by Zara, and without a word she started gathering up her work.

'Anything I should know?' I asked, peering over the cover sheet of instructions, which were bound together with unbroken pink ribbon like an early Easter present.

'Only that there is plenty more where that came from, so work your magic and aim for a swift conclusion.'

I didn't have to see Zara's unimpressed expression; I felt it like a draught over the desk. Percy must've sensed whatever silent charge passed between us because he hooked his thumbs under his fine leather belt, hung his head like a sulky adolescent and pushed out his lower lip.

'Christ almighty!' he said, forcing an exaggerated sigh. 'I've never seen such disappointment at the prospect of paid work. Lighten up, the pair of you!' He leaned lower, coming between us in a blond cloud of rich cologne and last night's vino, and shared with us a sly, devilish smirk. 'Haven't you read the papers? Our dear London is once again in the midst of a *crime spree*! So smile! It's reaping time for the lawyers.'

3

My client arrived twenty minutes earlier than scheduled, which left me no real opportunity to study the case papers once I'd hurried Zara out of the room, and I went on to blunder our introduction from the start.

'Mr Meadows?' I offered my hand to the stocky black fellow waiting alongside two women in the reception area downstairs. 'Elliot Rook.'

The man returned a firm grip, sealing it into a clasp with his second hand. 'Delroy Meadows, Meadows Motors, Hackney Wick. Pleased to meet you.'

'Delroy …' I glanced down at his hands and noticed oil in the cracks. 'I thought … You're not Charlie?'

Behind him, one of the accompanying women cleared her throat. 'Mr Rook, Delroy is Charli's brother. I'm Lydia Roth, solicitor for the case. *This* is Charli …'

With one hand the solicitor gestured to the third in their trio, and I felt heat prickling my features. 'Of course,' I said, abruptly switching the aim of my hand like a clumsy cannon. 'Charli? Is that short for Charlotte?'

'No.' She nervously wiped her palm dry on her denim jacket before offering it in return, but it was clammy again by the time she took my hand. 'Just Charli.'

'That's all right,' her brother assured me, 'she's used to it by now, aren't you, Charli?'

She neither agreed nor disagreed.

I led the three of them up in single file through the tight staircase that seemed built for people half my size, and I didn't get a good look at the client until I was back in my room with the door shut behind us.

It would be ignorant to say that Charli Meadows didn't look like the *ordinary criminal* – I had dealt with lawbreakers of all shapes and sizes during my decades at the Bar – but, in appearance at least, she certainly challenged the misconception of an average. Like her brother, she was early thirties, black; they shared the same curved outlines to their features and spoke with comparable east London accents, but the physical similarities between the siblings seemed to end there.

Charli Meadows looked used up. Many defendants do, with the seriousness of charges often measurable by the radius of shadow around the eyes. Some look positively proud of themselves, and others don't even bother to hide their dumb, smug smirks, but Charli Meadows was not one of those. She'd put effort into her outfit, enough to look presentable even in a simple denim jacket and clean white shirt, but nothing that spoke of spare cash hidden in the secret places of her home. The rings she wore were costume-grade, the stones in her ears too dull to be diamonds. There were no whites left along her fingernails, and her mascara was uneven. The lines around her mouth looked as if they'd been loaned from a woman twice her age. Here was a picture of despondency.

By comparison, her solicitor Lydia Roth moved with the sweeping confidence of a high-class professional. She was more than comfortable in her own fair, almost ashen, skin, and wore her strawberry-blonde hair in a short, stylish cut that looked as expensive as her designer glasses. As she took a seat, I found myself checking with what I hoped was discretion: no wedding ring.

She, Charli and I sat down around my desk, but the brother, Delroy Meadows, paced the room with a heavy tread. He selected books at random from my shelves, turned them in his hands and then clunked them down again. He seemed restless. Unsettled. I wondered if he was nervous, though he didn't strike me as an easily unnerved figure.

I flicked through the case papers, imitating familiarity. 'Miss Meadows,' I said, 'while I'm sure you're well aware of the charges against you by now, perhaps we ought to start from the top to avoid any confusion going forward. I'll be representing you in your upcoming trial. Now, you've –'

'You been doing this long?' It was her brother, who was off to the left weighing my battered copy of *Crime and Punishment* in his open palm. 'We saw you in the news back at Christmas. That's why we wanted you, but they told us you were booked up, didn't they, Charli?'

I waited to see if she'd respond – she glanced to her solicitor as if for a cue, but Roth didn't say a word – before I replied. 'I've been doing this quite long enough to be of use to your sister, I think.' Turning back to her. 'You are being indicted for bringing prohibited List A items into prison, contrary to Section 40B of the Prison Act 1952.'

'Drugs,' her brother remarked, shaking his head as he plonked the novel back onto the wrong shelf, face down, without looking at me. 'Let's tell it like it is, Mr Rook. They're calling her a smuggler. Honestly, does my sister look like a drug dealer to you? Does she?'

I caught a rolling glance from Lydia Roth, sneaking out over the frame of her glasses, which suggested that she'd already had her own fair share of these interruptions.

'Honestly?' I replied. 'Some years ago, I had a client in her late eighties who had been selling cocaine from her Tuesday-evening bridge club. An otherwise charming old lady, I assure you. She carried a flathead screwdriver in her stocking for protection. I'm not quite sure *what* a drug dealer is supposed to look like.'

'It's crazy,' Delroy went on, rapping a knuckle against my wig tin, apparently capable of dismissing any anecdote that failed to support his opinion. 'This whole thing, ridiculous. She doesn't look like a drug dealer to me.'

By now Charli's eyes were moving around the office, disconnected, as if this was all a film to which she was nothing more than a passive observer. I leaned into her sight, fighting for attention, avoiding the urge to rudely snap my fingers in her face. 'First, I'd like to discuss your role as prison officer at ...'

'HMP Wormwood Scrubs,' she said, monotonal.

'Really?' There must've been surprise in my voice, but nobody seemed to notice.

'Not an officer,' her brother added, swiping his hands together as if he was checking for dust. 'Operational Support Grade. They call it Band 2, one level below officer, which is Band 3.'

'Operational Support.' I reached for a pencil and then scribbled the words onto my legal jotter. 'What does that consist of?'

'General staff work,' Charli said. 'Portal duties like gates and doors, anything with locks ... Working the control room … Processing and escorting visitors … Wall patrols … Driving duties … Censoring correspondence and checking prisoners' possessions … Food deliveries …' She took a slow breath. 'All sorts.'

'Four years she's kept that place running,' her brother said, 'haven't you, Charli?'

Charli blinked.

'The Scrubs was your first prison?' I asked.

'Yes.'

'You worked there full-time?'

A nod.

'Good salary?'

'Excuse me?'

'The money. How are your earnings?'

She hesitated and glanced again to Lydia Roth, who said patiently, 'It's one of the first things the prosecution will look at.'

Relenting, Charli rubbed her hands together; the cheap jewellery made a hollow, rattling sound. 'Twenty-three thousand before tax.'

I noted it down, which she regarded with some disapproval. 'You're the only earner in the house?'

'Yes.'

'And whereabouts do you live?'

'Walthamstow.' Her brother answered for her, burying his hands into his overalls and rocking on his heels behind her. 'That's an hour to and from the prison every day.'

'You live with her?' I asked sceptically.

'Me? No. Just her and three kids. Single mum, different dads.' He didn't say it cruelly, but there was a sharp enough edge behind it. Once again, his sister didn't seem to notice.

'No partner?' I asked. 'No boyfriend?'

'No,' she said. 'Just me.'

'Do you rent or own your home?'

'On twenty-three grand a year? What do you think?'

'If you could just answer the questions, please.'

'Rent.'

'And how old are your children?'

'Twelve, eight and two.'

I jotted the numbers down. 'You pay for childcare?'

'No.' She watched me work on the notepad. 'What are you doing?'

'Calculations. The prosecution is going to perform a very public autopsy of your finances, and the first move will be to weigh the cost of keeping three children and a rented property in the Waltham Forest borough against your annual income. If there are discrepancies to be found, Miss Meadows, then they will do their utmost to find them and use those to speculate over alternative means of income. I'm just trying to ease you into how that might feel in a court full of strangers.'

Her brother snorted. 'They'll argue that she earns an impossible wage, but they're part of the same system that pays her a peanuts salary to begin with. Then they're going to accuse her of being a crook because she's somehow managed to make ends meet. Everybody knows that drugs are rife in that place. They're everywhere. Charli's being scapegoated because a few junkies kicked the bucket the other month. I know it, you know it, and the prosecution know it for sure.'

Patiently, I placed the pencil down on my jotter. 'Mr Meadows, while I appreciate you coming here to support your sister, unless you plan on climbing into the witness box and speaking for her in the courtroom then I suggest that she gets into the habit of answering for herself.' He rolled his eyes and went back to pacing. I continued. 'Being staff, you'll know that prohibited articles within Her Majesty's prisons are graded according to their seriousness and classified as List A, B or C articles. List C covers the likes of food, drink, tobacco and clothing, and carries a maximum penalty of a fine after summary trial. List B is more along the lines of alcohol and mobile phones, can be tried either way, and the penalty on indictment is imprisonment not exceeding two years or a fine. Offences regarding List A articles, however, which include weapons, firearms, explosives and *drugs*, are triable on indictment only and carry a sentence of up to ten years' imprisonment.'

I couldn't tell if she'd nodded or just trembled. She must've known the outcome by now, but hearing such things aloud always lent them serious weight.

'They found the drugs in your car, correct?'

'Allegedly,' her solicitor said, cutting in and raising her hand to object. It reminded me of characters in those stylish American legal thrillers, and I briefly wondered if she was deliberately trying to emulate them. She certainly looked the part. 'The prosecution claim that our client had been smuggling the contraband into the grounds from her vehicle outside. A search was conducted using dogs, and the illicit material was apparently discovered concealed beneath the spare tyre in the boot of her car. Synthetic cannabinoids. Spice, a Class B substance.'

'Spice. Now, I may be wrong,' I said, 'but I was under the impression that one of the main reasons for this Spice's popularity in prisons was that it couldn't be detected by canines.'

The solicitor nodded. 'That used to be the case, and it's still early days, but they've recently managed to train a handful of dogs across the country to identify it.'

'And who says you can't teach an old dog new tricks?' I said. Nobody smiled.

'It used to be a legal high,' Delroy Meadows said bitterly, coming to rest and wrapping his hands over the back of his sister's chair. 'Spice! Used to sell it in the shops up in Camden, for God's sake.'

'Alcohol is still perfectly legal,' I said, 'but I wouldn't recommend trying to carry a bottle of Jack into prison.' I flicked through the case papers until I found the printed photographs of the evidence: a blue Vauxhall Corsa, 2000 model, sitting in the staff car park of the prison; a close-up of the open boot, contraband packed tightly underneath the spare tyre; the contraband itself, laid out on a table with a ruler alongside it, and then again on a set of scales; the images went on. 'I'm confused – it looks like rolling tobacco.' The pouches were standard Golden Virginia, their contents brown, leafy, recognisable in texture to any smoker. 'It *is* rolling tobacco, isn't it?'

'Synthetic cannabinoids are typically designed to look like cannabis,' the solicitor explained, 'but they are actually just liquid chemicals spayed onto existing products. If it looks like cannabis, more often than not it's actually a weed called marshmallow or another similar herb. Oregano, even. The ten pouches you see in those pictures are supposedly worth a total of up to ten thousand pounds on the prison market. The prosecution claims that it is tobacco, but drenched in the chemical and is, therefore, classified as synthetic cannabinoids.'

'That's interesting,' I said slowly, a defence already forming in my mind. 'I assume you went through some sort of professional training course prior to being hired, Miss Meadows?'

'Yes,' she replied quietly. 'A two-week entry-level course at the Prison Service College in Rugby.'

I nodded, mostly to myself. 'Which immediately contradicts a lack of *mens rea* on the whole, but I just wonder ...'

'Men's what?' she asked, straightening slightly.

'*Mens rea*,' I repeated. 'The knowledge that you are, in fact, committing a crime. The Crown only has to prove that you knew you were conveying *something* prohibited into the prison, but it does not have to prove that you knew exactly what that item was in order to make a charge. In other words, whether you believed that this Spice was still a legal high or not would be irrelevant. You've done enough training by now to know what is and what isn't allowed beyond those walls ... *But*, if we could convince the jury that you genuinely believed you were smuggling *regular tobacco* onto the premises, which is only a List C article, then I think we may just have enough –'

'But I didn't,' she interrupted. 'I didn't try to smuggle *anything*, I have no idea how it ended up there. I drive my children around in that car, Mr Rook. I pick up their friends. Why in God's name would I ... Why would I risk ...' She lost whatever stride she was finally beginning to gather and faded out to miserable silence.

'I understand that this isn't easy,' I said, 'but it's going to be a lot more difficult in the courtroom. The prosecution will consider every possible scenario that might have put those drugs into that car, and they're going to ensure that the answer always leads back to you. Who else uses your car? Anybody? Ever?' She shook her head. 'You have the only keys?' A nod. 'What about you, Mr Meadows? Didn't you say you were a mechanic?'

He did a double take, startled by the query. 'I make a damn reasonable living out of my own business, thank you very much. Who do you think is paying your fees?'

'I didn't mean to cause offence, Mr –' I started, but he was off.

'I haven't touched that damn car since its MOT in December. You think it's *my* fault she's got herself into another one of life's little messes? You want to see *my* annual turnover while you're at it? Do my tax return, maybe?'

'Not in the slightest.' I raised my palms non-judgementally. 'I'm just making the enquiries that those empanelled twelve will want to hear explained. It comes down to a simple enough question. How *did* ten thousand pounds' worth of Spice end up in the boot of that car?'

Of course, nobody had the answer.

'This is making me sick,' Charli whispered. 'Physically sick.' When she buried one hand into the pocket of her jacket, I heard cigarettes rattling against cardboard, shaken by the tremor in her palm.

'Perhaps now would be a good time for a short break?' I suggested. 'Some fresh air, and then we can go over this defence in more detail?'

'Yeah,' her brother added, moving one of his hands onto her shoulder, talking mostly to himself. 'Come on, Charli. You've got to keep it together. Man's just doing his job, you know what I mean? Just doing his job. Let's go for a fag. Sort your head out. He's only doing his job.'

She nodded, momentarily placing her own hand over his, and then followed his lead out of the room.

The solicitor stayed behind. She waited until the sound of the creaking staircase had completely faded beyond the door and then blew a mouthful of air.

'Brothers,' she said, pushing back into her chair until her spine cracked loudly. She crossed her legs and looked me up and down as if I'd only just materialised before her. 'Elliot Rook. Corny, I know, but your reputation does precede you.'

'Whereas yours doesn't,' I said. 'I'm surprised we haven't met before. I thought I knew everyone in the small world of London serious crime.'

'I don't do a lot of fraud. Nothing of the calibre you're used to, anyway. Mostly drugs. A few murders here and there.'

'Who do you work for?'

'I'm independent.' She tilted her head. 'Entirely independent, in case you were wondering.'

I cleared my throat. 'What are we looking at here … Miss … Ms …'

'Call me Lydia,' she insisted politely, inclining off to one side to stare straight past me and check her reflection in the window. Whatever she saw there gave her a smile. 'Do you spend much time down at the Scrubs, Elliot?'

'Not lately,' I replied, feeling strangely naked and disarmed; few people called me by my first name any more.

'I work with a lot of clients there. Dozens. The place is a cesspit. Infested with cockroaches and rats, and I'm not talking about the convicts. Enough drugs to put Glastonbury to shame. You heard about the inmates who died there in January?'

'Of course.'

'Overdosed on a tainted batch of this Spice crap,' she said. 'The CPS actually considered manslaughter charges for Meadows, what with the drugs being found in her car the following week, but everybody knew damn well that there was no evidence to say she'd been in any way responsible for past supply, even if –'

'It was that soon?' I asked abruptly.

She blinked, adjusting her glasses. 'Hmm?'

'The date …' I quickly rifled through my case papers until I found it. 'Monday the fifteenth,' I read. 'They found the drugs in the vehicle on the fifteenth, and you say the deaths occurred a week before?'

'Tuesday or Wednesday, I think. I'd have to double-check.'

'Doesn't that seem a touch expedient to you? Thirteen inmates die, causing a national scandal, and the Prison Service, which has famously struggled against the influx of drugs for years, somehow manages to put a stop to one of its suppliers within the week?'

'Seems cogent enough to me.' She shrugged. 'Scandals mean searches. Increased security. If they were ever going to find anything, it makes sense that it would be then.'

'Perhaps,' I said, tapping the date on the paper with the end of my pencil. 'Just strikes me as rather extraordinary that one of the staff members involved in security procedures, who has no doubt been briefed on such crackdowns, still chances smuggling more potentially lethal product through the gates within the week.' I clicked my tongue, considering the client who was almost certainly chain-smoking below my window.

'You believe her?' She sounded surprised. 'You think that she really didn't know anything about the drugs?'

'No. No, I suspect that she probably did, though that doesn't matter. What I find most jarring is the risk involved. I'm interested in *why* she might have done it. Whether or not she had a choice at all.'

The solicitor cocked her head, causing her neck to stretch elegantly on one side. 'You think she was coerced?'

'I'd say there's a strong possibility – either from outside the prison or within.'

'It *was* suggested throughout the arrest interviews, but she'd never admit to it.'

'Not many do.'

'Plus, duress is a difficult defence without proof of an immediate threat. An *extremely* difficult defence.'

'Yes, and still difficult even if we *could* prove the threat …'

I gazed into the empty chair beside the solicitor and took a moment more to deliberate our client. There really was no archetype, no *ordinary* criminal. We all built excuses to vindicate behaviour. I'd done it myself, during my own time in prison.

I was a convicted fraudster, but not because my hand had been forced at eighteen years old. Stealing had quite simply been easier than working – easy, that is, until I got caught.

But if Charli Meadows *had* been smuggling – and the supporting evidence seemed sound enough – then she was just a single link in a long chain. The fact that she hadn't

offered information on her suppliers in exchange for lenience suggested fear.

'What are you thinking about?' Lydia asked after I'd sat
mutely for a while. She sounded genuinely interested. Her
eyes burned green through the lenses of her glasses.

'I was just thinking that it *has* been too long since I've
been down to the Scrubs,' I said. 'I should probably start
there. Get a feel for the place.'

'Excellent.' She opened her laptop, adjusted her glasses
and began hitting keys. 'I've got several clients on remand
there at the minute, I could arrange for the two of us to go
down on, well, let's see –'

'Ah, you needn't worry about that,' I told her quickly,
waving a hand.

'No?' She looked up over her glasses. 'Why's that, Elliot?'

For another millisecond, I was disarmed again. 'I'd prefer
to make my own arrangements.'

'Oh.' The second audible full stop of the morning.

I didn't want to tell her about Zara, or my chance of
visiting the jail this afternoon.

I wasn't even sure why.

The Meadows siblings returned a moment later, flooding
the room with the smell of smoke, and when I looked into
our client's eyes, searching through her exhaustion for hints
of truth, I was reminded of that sorry little bait dog. It was
all I could do to refrain from getting up and going downstairs for a cigarette myself.

4

HMP Wormwood Scrubs was built by convicts.

Designed by Edmund Du Cane as a monument to prison reform after the abolition of overseas penal transportation, it was erected on a patch of west London that was, as the name suggests, nothing more than open scrubland. Construction began in 1874, with trusted convicts working out of a small prison of corrugated iron alongside a simple shed for the warders. Bricks were manufactured on site, and the permanent prison was finished almost two decades later in 1891.

Du Cane's vision was a triumph and the Scrubs became a pioneering model for jails across the world. Its initial success, however, did not stand the test of time.

'Did you know that Ian Brady and Peter Sutcliffe played chess here?' Zara asked as I fed change into a meter down the road outside the prison.

'The Moors Murderer versus the Yorkshire Ripper?' I shook my head. 'No, I've never heard about that.'

'Sutcliffe found Brady chilling, or so the story goes. Can you believe that?'

I returned to my beaten old Jaguar with the ticket and placed it face up in the windscreen. 'I wonder who won.'

Because of my impromptu walk to work, we'd been forced to take the Tube back to mine to pick up the car before coming west across the city. There was no public parking within the prison grounds, and when we walked through the outer gates we were momentarily held up at a booth where a rather old man was watching over the entrance and exit barriers. I hadn't visited the Scrubs in a couple of years, but approaching the prison still reminded me of its cameo scene in *The Italian Job*. Nothing much had changed since Michael Caine famously walked out of those gates at the beginning of the movie. At the far end of a short driveway, symmetrical octagonal towers of red brick and Portland stone flanked the arched gateway, complete with moulded plinths, bands, arcades and cornices. It maintained the impression of a medieval castle, a fortress: a power to be reckoned with. Each tower boasted a huge bust of a celebrated prison reformer in a stone rondel – Elizabeth Fry to the left and John Howard to the right – to further emphasise the prison's original dedication to changing a broken system.

Before the Scrubs, those convicts that hadn't been hanged, flogged or sent to the colonies for their crimes were typically reformed using the silent treatment. As its social namesake still suggests, the silent treatment was based around depersonalisation through the allocation of a number and being forced to do physical labour in absolute silence. Du Cane believed that faith in God was a more practical route to rehabilitation. He had a chapel large enough to hold every inmate constructed within the grounds, and designed the wings to run parallel in rows from north to south so that each cell would see sunlight. These days there were cameras everywhere, perched soundlessly like monstrous crows.

'Keith Richards was imprisoned here in 1967,' I told Zara as we made our way through a series of gates. 'The guitarist from the Rolling Stones.'

'I know who Keith Richards is,' she bit. 'Pete Doherty was sent here as well.'

'Doherty …' I stroked my chin. 'He's one of those Antarctic Monkeys, right?'

She gave me a look; it was the sort I'd received more and more since slipping into the hopeless age of uncle jokes. 'The worst thing is I don't even know if you're messing.'

I was deliberately trying to ease the tension that I could sense gathering around her like bad weather. I didn't know how to bring the subject up, but she did it herself shortly after we'd been checked into the prison's electronic system.

'You can mention him, you know. Hazeem.'

We were sitting in an empty holding room awaiting a guard to lead us further into the building. There weren't enough staff members to go around, it seemed, especially now that one had found her way onto my schedule. We'd dumped all of our belongings into lockers except for the standard: Zara's loose case papers, plain paper for writing and two pens. Above us, there were two more cameras. Only one still had its lens.

Zara had mentioned her cousin Hazeem to me only once before, not long after we'd met, but I remembered the details well enough. An argument between teenagers had turned into a fight, and the fight had ended in a fatal stabbing. A case of mistaken identity led to Zara's cousin being picked up for conspiracy to murder. His counsel talked him into entering a plea for a reduced sentence. It was a poor, idle defence and Hazeem ended up in the Scrubs.

'Your cousin,' I said. 'He was sent here, but didn't he live in … where was it again? Birmingham?'

'He was studying medicine at UCL.'

'Ah. How long was he in here …?'

'Before he killed himself?' She was staring blankly at the locked door ahead. 'Five months. He pleaded guilty to a crime he didn't commit on his shitty counsel's shittier advice and died a drug addict in this shithole five months later.'

I looked down at my shoes. I didn't want to be sitting here any more. I felt guilty for coming in the first place. Zara believed I was here to help, as if I possessed some mystical talent for gauging strangers that might earn her client bail or provide a winning defence by the end of our meeting. I hadn't told her about the smuggling case because I hadn't wanted her to feel used when I'd abruptly agreed to join her this afternoon. After a long pause, I spoke. 'This client of yours … I trust you didn't go out of your way to represent him as a way of, I don't know, perhaps –'

'He deserves the best defence I can give,' she replied tightly, 'same as anybody else. That's all there is to it.'

Her voice was neither reproachful nor hurt. Just oddly flat, in a way I'd rarely heard in her before.

'Good, because that's all you can do, remember? Your best.'

I dropped a hand briefly onto her shoulder. It was supposed to be something warm and paternal, but without having had much experience of such things it landed heavier than I would have hoped, like a slab of meat dropped onto hard bone. Still, I saw a murmur of gratitude lighten her features, and that was about all I could've hoped for.

It was another ten minutes before we were led deeper into the prison. That's where the cracks began to show. What was originally built to be the best prison in the world was now widely considered the worst in the country. We passed walls engraved with graffiti ranging from coarse doodles and slapdash gang signs to outright death threats. The floors felt grimy beneath my shoes and many of the lamps were dead in their fittings. Shattered windows were held together by wire-mesh innards, with broken shards available for exploiting.

Zara's client wasn't faring much better by the time we found him hunched over a table in one of the prison's small conference rooms.

His face was buried in his arms and it took me a moment to realise that he was, in fact, fast asleep when we entered. Only when the door was shut behind us did he jump to attention, snapping upright in a kind of cautious terror.

'Miss ...' He sighed, easing at the sight of her. 'Wasn't sure you was still coming.' His face revealed the colourful leftovers of a fairly recent hiding. His left eye was swollen to a blackened slit and his dark skin blushed in nuances of yellow, green and purple across his cheekbones.

'Andre!' Zara gasped. 'What happened now?'

'What, this?' The young man shrugged it off coolly as if he'd hardly noticed taking a good kicking. 'Nothing. You know how it is.'

Zara dropped the papers to clasp a hand over her mouth, and leaned closer across the table to inspect the damage. 'Tell me you've reported this!'

'Oh, yeah.' He managed a pained smile. 'They've got some crack team coming down tomorrow. Bringing Sky

News, cameramen, newspapers and shit … What do you think?'

'Was it because of the case? Those other men who were –'

'No,' he interrupted sharply. His gaze turned onto me.

I was standing silently in front of the closed door with my arms folded, watching their repartee closely. He was obviously very happy to see her, and I couldn't blame him for that. There is value in a familiar face that you don't realise until you're deprived of them completely. That was something I learned during my own time locked up.

Where Charli Meadows might have challenged society's archetype of the inner-city drug dealer, Andre Israel had the unfortunate look – as far as any jury might be concerned – of a young man who had been rolled right out of a statistician's paperwork: he was black, twenty-one years old, born and raised in Newham, east London, with a gold canine tooth in the left side of his mouth, a patchy, juvenile goatee and hair that might once have been stylishly faded, which had now grown out to a standard jailhouse fuzz. His plain T-shirt hung off his chest and shoulders as if he'd recently embarked on a crash diet or fallen gravely ill. His knuckles were clean; he'd had no chance to fight back.

'Oh, sorry.' Zara twisted round in her chair. 'Andre Israel, this is Elliot Rook.'

He started a little but held on to whatever nonchalance was his standard setting. 'The silk man from that serial killer madness?'

I arched my eyebrows disapprovingly at Zara. She'd already looked away, but I could see a flush warming her ears.

'You working my case?' he asked hopefully.

I cleared my throat as I took the empty seat opposite him, alongside Zara. 'Officially: no. Miss Barnes is an excellent barrister. You're in superb hands, I assure you. I'm here today as more of an adviser regarding any second chance you might have in applying for bail.'

'Mr Rook is sort of like my informal mentor,' Zara added. 'He has a great mind for this and I was hoping, Andre, that you might be able to go through the night of your arrest once more with him. See if anything jumps out this time.'

He leaned forward, dumping his chin onto his fist, looking disappointed and exhausted. 'So, you're not here to get me out of this? I'm not going home?'

'Not today,' I said regretfully. 'Let's hear what happened to you first.'

'I'm only here cos of a bad resolution.'

I blinked between him and Zara. 'A what?'

'New Year, man,' he explained. 'All I wanted was to shift some timber.' He patted one hand across his shrunken, boyish gut. 'Careful what you wish for, innit?' He laughed hollowly at that, flashing the gold tooth, but winced when the ripple effect of movement came to his swollen eye. 'New Year's Day I started running. Couldn't last ten minutes at first, but a couple of days in I was pushing it to, like, half an hour every morning and night. I ain't no Mo Farah, but it was all right. Headphones in, beats on. Started round Upton Park, few blocks either way, then down to Central Park after that. Four days it lasted. Some resolution.'

'Beats any of mine,' I said, weighing my gut with both hands.

He half grinned. 'Thursday night I was thinking of going up West Ham Park, but when I stepped outside there was *bare* fog coming in. Couldn't see shit for shit by seven o'clock. I should've gone back inside, stuck to the PlayStation, but man don't quit like that. So, I went down Barking Road way, sticking to the lights on the pavement, taking it slow towards Canning Town. But the cold, all that damp in the air, it … does something to me, you get me?'

'I'm not entirely sure that I do.'

He hesitated, glancing towards Zara. 'I had to take a piss, man.'

'Ah.' I swallowed back an inappropriate smile. 'Well, when you've got to go.'

'Straight up,' he muttered. 'So, I was on, like, the last stretch of Barking where it's all takeaways, Turkish barbers and shit, looking for somewhere to stop. Alleyway or something … That's when I noticed something *booky* coming at me through the fog.'

'*Booky?*'

'Yeah,' he said, 'like, suspect, you know?'

'Suspicious,' Zara clarified. 'A car.'

'That's it!' He snapped his fingers at her appreciatively. 'Feds creeping at me, eyes locked all the way. Then another car, this one full of undies. Undercovers, I mean. They was moving like one of them convoys or something. Lurking. Couldn't have been going more than five, maybe ten miles an hour. That got me nervous.'

'Why?' I asked. 'What did you have to be anxious about?'

He frowned as if I'd just asked the most ridiculous question in history. 'Black youth like me, running streets in the dark with his hood up. What d'you think?'

'They stopped you?'

'Nah, man. They just doubled back and passed me by again.' With one sweeping hand, he mimed the slow, almost leisurely passing of the cars to his right. 'By then I was busting, but there was no way I was stopping to slash with them around. That's when I saw this pub at the traffic lights ahead, sign all lit up through the fog. Princess Alexandria. The Alex. Just stuck there on the corner, nothing special about it, but all bars got to have facilities, right?' He stopped for a moment, closed his eyes and shook his head introspectively, contemplating his own misfortune. 'Swear down,' he said, 'it sounds like bullshit, I know, but that is *all* I went in there for.'

'What happened at the pub?' But I could already guess.

He sighed, tipping his head back, illuminating the colourful blotches in his flesh. 'Straight away, I knew something was *badly* wrong in there. It was just, like …' He fumbled for the word, rapping his fingers across his half of the table.

'Booky?' I said.

Another half-smile. 'No doubt. That place was *quiet*, man. I ain't never seen no roomful of n— uhh, *people* so silent. There was these boys in there. Cold-looking, edgy, heads down. But as soon as I walked in they looked about ready to bounce up out of them seats. I'm telling you, they were waiting for *something*.'

'What did you do?'

'*Do?* I was about to piss into my Nikes, man. I just sprinted for the toilet. Soon as I was done, that's when it happened. I was standing there at the sink, thinking I'd wait more than a minute for them feds to move on, when the door goes *blam!*' He thrust his palm forward to demonstrate the impact. 'Truthfully, I thought this was it. You hear about it every day. Man walks into the wrong place and gets himself merked. It was this moment of, like, *clarity*. This is it, I thought. You try to lose a couple of pounds and get yourself cheffed up in a shithouse. They came in, these boys, all of them, only instead of clocking me they just started piling into them cubicles.'

'What were they doing?'

'Turning pockets out. Flushing. I couldn't see much, but the ones at the back of the line were pulling out *bricks* of dope, man. Serious shit. Only problem was, they weren't too wise. They kept yanking that fucking chain till the system backed up and the armed feds stormed in and cut us down, yours truly included.'

'Sounds like you had quite the night,' I said. 'Enough to suggest that jogging is bad for your health, anyway. You're being indicted on a conspiracy charge, then?'

'No,' Zara replied, turning to the loose case papers she'd brought. 'They're aiming for substantive counts instead of conspiracy. Possession with intent to supply heroin, and they're adding intentional obstruction of a police constable, concealment of items, on account of the drugs going into the toilet.'

'I ain't no trapper, man,' Andre grumbled. 'Truly, only thing *obstructed* was some dickhead's cosh by this.' He tapped his skull.

'Getting away without a conspiracy charge is one good thing,' I said. 'At least you'll only have to account for what were allegedly your own drugs. How many were arrested altogether?'

'Six,' Zara said, 'including Andre.'

'Any particular reason why you've been held on remand for the past two months?'

Andre looked to Zara. She answered for him. 'Andre has a previous conviction for failing to appear, which prevented him from getting bail.'

'After what charge was that conviction?' I asked.

'Being an artist,' he said petulantly. 'Trying to have, like, an *outlet* for creativity when you come from ends.'

Bemused, I turned to Zara. 'Is that a crime?'

'It was incitement to commit violent disorder.' She sighed. 'Andre is a musician with a fairly big following on YouTube. Last summer his music got him into trouble.'

'Look –' Andre leaned forward, clasping his hands together as if in prayer – 'I'm not even gonna lie to you. I dropped a couple of beats without thinking and shit got *riled up*, but it was supposed to be a joke. Like now, looking back on it, I know it was stupid.'

'Andre's lyrics were blamed for instigating an argument that ended in a violent confrontation,' Zara explained. 'It's called drill music, a type of rap. Andre made a comparison between two opposing gangs and, well, I guess both parties felt like they had something to prove because of it. They faced each other off with weapons in a shopping centre, somebody got burned with a corrosive substance, Andre was charged with conspiracy and he failed to turn up to the magistrates'.'

'I had a gig the night before court. I warned them about it. That didn't finish until five in the morning, then this fit girl asked me back to hers. It was either that or court and, you know ...'

'Yes,' I replied drily, 'and here you are remanded in custody because of your record of failing to appear. I hope it was worth it.'

A slight grin broke his sulky expression. 'You should've seen her.'

'What about that charge for violence?' I asked. 'Did they claim that you were a member of one of those gangs?'

'No, it was just the music,' he said, his good eye turning glassy again. 'Just words. I don't have no gang affiliations. Just cos I talk a bit street, it doesn't make me no delinquent. Not all rappers are criminals. Yeah, I've smoked a bit of green here and there, who hasn't? I don't use hard shit and I don't sling hard shit neither.'

I nodded, neatening one shirt cuff. At that time, I had no reason to believe or disbelieve a single word he was saying. 'What about drugs here at the prison? Have you seen anything of the sort?'

'Here?' He studied me questioningly. For a moment, I thought he was going to clam up, but he answered slowly, a little more carefully, lowering his voice. 'Two months I've been here. By the end of week one I'd been offered charlie, brown, rock, you name it. Day and night, them wings are *smoky* with weed.'

'What about Spice?'

'Everywhere. Some of the boys call it Cloud Nine. Turns men into zombie-lunatics like *The Walking Dead*, for real. There's three or four ambulances coming out here every day. Whenever one does, another screw has to go with it, meaning nobody's watching the wing, meaning another eight hours banged up in pads. What else is man supposed to do? It's easier to get loaded in here than it is back in ends and everyone is playing the game. Only thing is, you're gonna find yourself in somebody's pocket *fast.*'

'Whose pocket? The officers? Other inmates?'

He turned to Zara, who offered no assistance, and then glanced up to the camera in the corner of the ceiling, almost flinching. 'I ain't no snitch, all right?'

'Of course,' I said, 'but a second application for bail requires a change in circumstances, and you look like you've had a rough week.'

He hesitated again, straining against pride. 'You think it might get me out of here?'

'I'm just exploring angles,' I told him. 'When you say that people are in one another's pockets, how so exactly?'

'Easy maths, innit? What costs you a fiver outside moves for a hundred in here, maybe two, but it's all on tick. There's no cash. Everyone's got mobile phones to sort their money but even the phones are on credit for a grand apiece. Cons are ringing their mums and dads asking for cash transfers into the trappers' accounts. Got junkies crawling from cell to cell begging for tea bags like tramps in the gutter. Grown men giving blowies for gear.'

'And you know this how?'

'*Everybody* knows this.'

'What about members of staff who might have found themselves in the dealers' pockets?' I asked. 'Have you seen any—'

'Look,' he whispered abruptly, pressing his hands flat onto the table in an exquisite gesture of finality, 'I want out of this place. Couple of these fuckers they locked me up with are *madmen*. The ones taking Cloud Nine are even worse. Last week, one of them snatches a rat up off the floor at breakfast, right? This thing's the size of a dog, I'm not even lying to you, just running around for crumbs.

Man catches it by the tail, yeah? Lifts it up over his head and takes a bite out of it! Blood and fur and shit all over his face. Then the thing starts to bite him back, and these boys, they're all just *laughing*, man. They're laughing like it's the funniest fucking thing they've ever seen. But I wasn't laughing. Apparently, man who don't laugh got something to hide, so …' He pointed to his bruises, a movement that required no great accuracy.

'You need to report this,' Zara said.

'What I *need* is bail! They'll kill me in here. I was there in custody with them, don't you get it? I heard it all. I know too much about them.'

'*Them?*' I grimaced and looked to Zara. Her expression grimaced straight back. 'Who?'

'The ones who were sitting in the pub that night!' he whispered impatiently. 'Don't you hear what I've been saying? Call themselves the "E10 Cutthroats". *They're* the ones that done this to my face. They're the ones running things in here now. Drugs, blades, you name it. That raid, it wasn't no win for the police. It was played, man.'

'Cutthroats? Who on earth are –'

'Not now. You get me bail, then maybe we'll talk. I can tell you *stories*, straight up. I can tell you about the one that got away. The one nobody's seen since. Way I hear it, he's gone ghost. On the run or something. Maybe dead.'

'Another dealer?' Zara asked. 'I didn't think any of them got away.'

'One did,' he said. 'He was the only one I recognised in the bar that night. He never needed to make bail cos he was never arrested. Feds parted like water for Moses and let him walk.'

'Why would they do that?'

'Obvious, innit?' he said. 'Got to be a snitch, on their books or something. Word is he's been playing both sides. One of them double agents you hear about. KGB shit.'

'Interesting,' I muttered. 'You're saying that the Met have got themselves a Kim Philby?'

He shrugged. 'Don't know who that is.'

'This dealer,' Zara said, 'does he have a name?'

Andre nodded. 'Wouldn't be much of a person without one.'

'But you won't give it to us?'

He glanced up to the camera again, chewing his lip, so I interjected once more.

'Look,' I said, 'if this lad really was carrying drugs that night, and you truly weren't, then one could argue that you're sitting here in his place. So, have the last two months been so enjoyable that you don't mind serving a few more years on his behalf?'

Before he even opened his mouth, I knew from the strain on his face that we had him.

'Omar Pickett. That's who I recognised. The one that walked away. Omar Pickett.'

'Where is he now?' Zara asked.

'On his toes or dead. These Cutthroats aren't into prisoners.'

I nodded. 'It's a dangerous world you live in, Mr Israel. No doubt more dangerous since you landed in here, especially with inmates dropping like they did back in January.'

'January?' Zara frowned, glancing between us, missing something. 'What happened in January?'

A brief silence. Andre sniffed, weighing me up. 'You think you know about that? You don't know nothing.'

I managed a dry smile. 'Thirteen deaths. Misadventure. Bad drugs, right?'

'Wrong, Mr Rook. Dead wrong. Thirteen bodies. Not one of them was accidental.'

5

'I thought you were quitting,' Zara said as I lowered my
window and blew smoke out of the moving car. We were
over the Westway, returning east along the elevated dual
carriageway.

'I did for a couple of days. They say stopping smoking
is good for your health, so why deprive your body of the
benefit by never smoking in the first place?'

'Must be hard.' She was scrolling through her phone.
Instagram, I guessed from an absent glance. The usual. Next
thing I knew she seemed to be staring straight through me.
I followed her gaze to the right and saw the gutted ruins of
Grenfell Tower standing like a charred monolith over the
west of the city. Seventy-two people had lost their lives in
the enormous block of flats the previous summer. 'Do you
think that would've been allowed to happen if ...'

'If what?'

'If the residents had been on the other side of the poverty
line, maybe. It's the same for most of the inmates back there.
People like Andre.'

'You think social hierarchy would've made a difference
in that fire?'

'No. I don't know. Maybe. I can see what you're thinking, by the way.'

'What am I thinking?'

At her lap, she locked the screen and pocketed her phone. 'You think I'm fond of him or something. Andre. Like I'm taking a shine to him because of what happened to my family. That's not the case.'

I didn't answer immediately. I didn't want to lie, so what I told her was the truth. 'I trust your intelligence. I know your head is in the right place … but it's common for barristers in the early stages of their careers to want to throw everything they have into their first big cases. Not because it is the correct thing to do, which it is, but because they truly wish to see their client freed. You believe him, don't you?'

She hesitated, seemingly considering the ramifications of admitting this aloud. 'Yes.'

I smoked, changed lanes and twice knocked ash out of my window. I wanted to tell her how dangerous that could be, but I had to remind myself of my own recent doings, which took most of the wind out of my desire to tell her off. 'The more of yourself that you invest into a case, the more you're opening yourself up for potential disappointment. I just want you to be cautious, that's all.'

'You think he's lying, then?'

'I think he's full of excuses. Then again, he really might just be the unluckiest young man in London. It's whether the *jury* believes him or not. Have you asked your solicitor to speak to the staff of this pub? You might be able to fish some witnesses out of there.'

'Tried and failed. The bar staff don't want anything to do with this. In fact, I think the woman who was working that night has actually quit just to distance herself from it all. The solicitor requested copies of their CCTV, which should have at least shown evidence of Andre's separate arrival, but all the footage covered was the bar and the till. Nothing useful. We've tried getting images from the surrounding roads as well. All they show is fog.'

'He might well be telling the truth about jogging, but that doesn't necessarily mean he wasn't also trying to flush his own wares when the police stormed the building.'

'True,' she replied, 'but there's also a chance he's being fitted up.'

'I'm not sure why they would bother. What's the use in framing one defendant when they have five more bang to rights?'

'Well, considering we haven't been working together for half a year yet and we've already proven *two* coppers to be lying headcases, you really reckon it's so far-fetched that a few more might've planted drugs on some black lad from Newham?'

'Far-fetched?' I shook my head. 'No, but not entirely likely either. We did have quite the case last year, but it won't do you any good to maintain this idea that the police are villains. That was something I saw a lot of growing up, and it didn't make for a healthy culture. This idea of the working class versus the police. ACAB. You ever heard that?'

'All coppers are bastards,' she said. 'It was scrawled all over the parks when I was a kid.'

'Yes, you used to see it tattooed across knuckles, mostly in the seventies and eighties. We all hated the police until we needed the police, then it was a case of dial 999 and all is momentarily forgiven. The truth is that there are far more decent coppers than bad. The vast majority are just ordinary people trying to do a little good between paydays.'

She grunted non-committally. The vacuum from my open window was whipping her hair into a frenzy behind her head. 'All right,' she said, 'so where would *you* start with this?'

I took a measured, thoughtful drag. 'I'd pay more attention to the raid itself. Were the police prowling the area in anticipation? Did they have a warrant, or did they simply follow Andre Israel on a hunch and end up striking gold? And what did he mean when he said it wasn't a win for the police?'

'I've no idea. He's not mentioned anything like that before.'

I looked to my hand; the filter was now cold between my fingers. I tossed it. A mental wave was sweeping all of the disparate details up inside my head and then dropping them back into chronological order like sediment beneath the tide. It was a while before I spoke, and when I did, I was contemplating dates. 'Even if Andre wasn't carrying that night ... the raid must have placed five verified dealers into Wormwood Scrubs only days before thirteen inmates died, supposedly as a result of tainted drugs.'

I closed my window, quietening the inside of the car. From the corner of my eye, I saw Zara's hair fall flat with the change in pressure. '*That's* why you came this afternoon! Your new case has something to do with those deaths from the news, doesn't it? You sat there implying that any information he gave you could improve his chance of getting bail, but it was just to help with your case?'

'I don't believe that my case *does* have anything to do with those deaths,' I replied truthfully. 'Not directly, anyway. But yes, I am defending an employee accused of smuggling drugs into that prison.'

'Bastard!' Her fierceness caught me by surprise. 'Oh, not *you*. This guard. He's supposed to be responsible for keeping those inmates safe.'

'The accused is a woman.'

She groaned. 'Well, you could've told me earlier. You should have. I don't like being used.'

'I wasn't using you. I was worried that my case might prove a little too close to home, all things considered.'

'Still, it wouldn't have hurt you to keep me in the loop.'

A moment's silence followed, and I was relieved when my phone started vibrating in the cup holder between us. 'Could you check who that is for me?' I asked.

She did. 'Landline. London number.'

'Answer it, won't you? See what they want.'

She straightened up, cleared her throat rather aggressively, and answered.

'Hello, this is Elliot Rook's phone, he's driving at the moment. Can I take a message?' She listened in silence while I negotiated the lanes on the carriageway. 'No,' she said. 'I'm sorry, but I think you have the wrong number … That's right, this *is* Mr Rook's phone, but … No. No. No, he definitely doesn't have a dog.'

My hands clenched around the steering wheel. I glanced across and caught her frowning. Heat spread through my face.

'Oh,' she said, her voice flattening out. 'Oh, I see … Last night, was it? OK, well, I think it might be best if he rings you back, he doesn't bother to share these things with me, apparently. Is this the number to call ...? Victoria Blue Cross. OK, and when you say she'll be *euthanised*, what exactly does that –'

'Wait!' I blurted. 'Tell them we can be there in ten minutes.'

We made it in nine.

Zara stared down at the dog for quite some time before speaking.

'I don't get it,' she said. 'I just ... I don't get it.'

'It's a blood sport,' I told her quietly. 'Werner had been breeding some to fight to the death, and others to sell on as guard dogs.'

'No, I understand *that*,' she muttered. 'But why did *you* have to get involved?'

'It comes back to something a drug dealer called Isaac Reid told me. He's been convicted of assassinating rivals in Margate, and he wants me to conduct his appeal. His defence was that the place he allegedly burst into was protected by a Dogo Argentino, an extremely rare breed of fighting dog originally from South America. He suggested – and fairly, I thought – that if he'd turned up at a rival's front door with a knife, as it appears the killer or killers did, he wouldn't have been welcomed into the property, and he certainly wouldn't have made it out again without at least a few bite wounds. Last week, Jacob Werner was accused of running fights with similar breeds, so I thought it was worth a look.'

I stuffed my hands into my coat pockets like a wayward schoolboy and watched the dog sleep soundly on its blanket in the cage.

'Isaac Reid?' Zara said. 'When did you meet him?'

'I haven't yet. The information came from paper instructions. We'll be meeting him in Belmarsh for a conference later this week.'

'We?'

'Well, if you want – I need a junior, and you've got to admit that we make a great team.'

'Hmm.' My attempts at flattery did nothing to lighten her mood. 'So,' she said, 'because of paper instructions from a prospective client that you've never met, you decided to break into private premises. Premises that you suspected were being guarded by rare, vicious fighting dogs.'

'Well, yes. It sounds a lot dafter when you put it like that.'

'Daft?' She clicked her tongue. 'You could've been disbarred.'

'I know.'

'You could've been arrested.'

'Yes.'

'You could've been killed. Did you ring the police?'

'No. There'd be too many questions. The animals would've been put down. I couldn't do it.'

She leaned her face closer to the bars, studying the pattern of scars, watching the dog's back quiver slightly as it rose and fell, rose and fell.

'Did you hurt him?' she asked. I didn't answer. When she eventually turned to face me, her expression was as cold and hard as a stone on a riverbed. 'I hope you did.'

Footsteps approached from behind. We'd been standing alone in a room lined with cages along one wall, not entirely unlike that place in which I'd found the dog last night, except that this one smelled of antiseptic and the patients were all heavily sedated. The cages were stacked on two levels with the smaller animals on top. Most of the animals wore bandages and cones around their heads.

'Dogfighting,' the vet said as we both turned to face her. She wore an intense shade of red dye in her neatly tied hair, but otherwise looked very formal in her scrubs and stethoscope, flicking through the file she'd left us to go and retrieve. 'They call the fights *urban rolls* when they're at amateur level like this. Gangs host them in parks, warehouses, fields. This one here is the bait dog, most likely the runt of a separate litter bred for sport. Tied up like a punchbag for the other dogs to cut their teeth on. Somebody's been at her mouth with a rasp file, blunting her teeth to stop her fighting back. You say you found her running stray?'

'Yes. I was the one who dropped her off with the emergency vet last night.'

'She's had a lucky escape then. Trainers usually prefer to get every last bit of value out of their bait dogs, right up until they're in pieces. She's about two years old, we think, which makes her ancient for the world of dogfighting.'

'What will happen to her now?' Zara asked.

'She's suffered a lot of puncture wounds in her life, as you can tell, and from the scar across her neck I suspect that her jugular has been lacerated at some point. She's completely deaf in her damaged ear, and the missing lip can never grow back. Severely dehydrated, undernourished, exhausted … That's just the physical damage. As for the *psychological* … a dog like this will always be difficult to rehome. She's wary of people, terrified of other dogs, and almost certainly going to pose a risk to any other animal, possibly even children. You did the right thing getting her here, and we'll re-evaluate her progress overnight, but I'm sorry to say that the most likely result will, as I said on the phone, be euthanasia.'

'I see,' I replied limply. I hadn't been sure that my interfering with Werner could've done much good, but I'd at least felt justified since saving this animal's life. Now, knowing it would likely be for nothing, the feelings that had bolstered my walk to work seemed vacuous.

'I think I know a place,' Zara said. 'A place she could go.'

I turned to Zara and shook my head. 'Not with you. It's too much to put on yourself, and I don't think that a shared house would be the right place for her.'

'No,' she agreed. 'I was thinking of somewhere quieter, where she isn't likely to be disturbed by friends or excitement. Somewhere boring.'

'Boring?' I replied. 'Where do you think is – oh …'

I sighed. Frankly, I should've seen it coming.

6

I managed to nab a parking space only a few yards down from my door, which was a fortunate rarity. Zara took the carrier bags from the boot while I negotiated the long, cumbersome flatpack box out of the back seat and up under one armpit.

'Do you think we left the windows wide enough?' she fretted, peering back towards the passenger seat. 'Because you know what they say about dogs in cars ...'

'You're thinking of hot cars,' I said, glancing up at the cool blue sky. 'I'm more worried about what's going to happen to that leather if we don't get a move on. Let's just hope those blankets hold out.'

Zara bent forward, resting the carrier bags on the toes of her Doc Martens, and swept the thick layer of fine hairs the dog had spent the drive shedding onto her lap. 'I didn't realise you lived at this end, so close to Regent's Park! *La-di-da!*'

It only occurred to me then that, in the eighteen months of living here on Gloucester Place, I'd never had a visitor. That made me uncomfortable. Apart from collecting my car from further up the road this morning, even Zara had never come close.

'Perhaps you ought to wait out here,' I said.

'How come?' She stared up at the faces of the identical, immaculate town houses. 'Worried what the neighbours might say?'

'Oh, no. I'm just not used to entertaining guests.'

'Ah, come off it. You've picked me up and dropped me off at my place loads of times, and I think we can agree that I live in a proper shit-tip. You're seriously going to stand there and get all humble about some swanky town house in Marylebone?'

'Swanky?' Hanging the keys from one finger, I overshot the building's main entrance and began to lumber the box down the narrow steps that descended to basement level. 'Come on then. Prepare yourself for the opulence of a silk's abode.'

Inside, with box and bags dumped onto the carpet, Zara took a moment to fully appreciate the entire 140 square feet of space: the clothes dumped over the free-standing rack, the slump in the middle of the folded futon, the faded records above the stereo. 'I bet the letting agents described it as *cosy*, didn't they?'

'You know something?' I said. 'I believe they did.'

I opened the box and unfolded the metal dog crate into the corner by the door to the bathroom. Zara emptied shopping bags onto the short worktop in the kitchenette. A tweed collar and lead, tins of the softest food we could find, scented plastic bags.

With the room as prepared as it was ever likely to be, Zara followed me back up onto the pavement outside. It was kickout time at the girls' school round the nearest corner, and the street was swarming with pupils in pink shirts and burgundy sweaters. When I lifted the dog out of the passenger seat, a cluster of the girls gawked with big doe eyes.

'Aww!' one of them cried. 'Look at the cute doggy!' Then the dog glanced towards them and I heard subdued shrieks as they bolted off down the road.

With one hand, I patted the dog's ragged ear. 'Happens to the best of us, girl.'

She accepted the flat slowly, looking frantically from corner to corner with her hackles raised. Then she began to sniff around in tight circles. I might never have showed it, but all my former misgivings were instantly overcome when the remains of her tail started to bounce from side to side.

'See!' Zara cried, jumping on the spot and clapping her hands. 'She loves it!'

'I think you might be r—' I began, until the dog trotted into the middle of the room, lowered the back portion of her body and urinated onto the carpet. 'For Christ's sake.'

'Ah, yeah,' Zara said, 'you're probably going to want to buy some kitchen roll for that.'

As I blustered for the bathroom, my phone began to vibrate in my pocket. I checked the screen and didn't recognise the number. I thought it might be the animal hospital.

'Hello?' I answered, tossing a loo roll out from the bathroom into Zara's waiting hands.

'Elliot?' Straight away, I knew it was her. 'This is Lydia Roth.'

'Oh?' This caught me off guard, and I quickly cleared my throat, perhaps a little louder than I'd meant to.

'I just wanted to tell you what a thrill it was to finally meet you this morning.'

'A thrill?'

'Absolutely,' Lydia replied softly. 'It looks like we have quite the case on our hands, doesn't it? I was thinking we could discuss it further. Perhaps one evening this week?'

I could see Zara craning her neck to eavesdrop from where she was blotting the wet patch out of the carpet, which made me stumble through the rest of the short conversation.

'Who was that?' Zara asked after I'd hung up a minute later.

'Solicitor in my smuggling case.'

'Work then?' Even from behind, as I watched her carry the bunched-up paper through to the loo to flush it, I could tell that she was smirking. 'Didn't *sound* like work.'

'I think …' I paused, trying to work out exactly what I thought. 'I think she just asked me out for a drink … Only to discuss the case, I'm sure.'

'Really?' Zara turned round, grinning. 'Is she hot?'

Before I had chance to think of a reply, I heard a drizzle of liquid and turned to see the dog marking another area close to my stereo. 'Oh, for fuck's sake.'

At least Zara found it amusing.

Zara rushed off to make her meeting at the bank – she was trying to extend her overdraft, again – and I was left alone with the dog and some leaflets on pet ownership I absently flicked through. After several minutes I discarded the brochures onto my joint bedside/coffee table and opened the drawer underneath. It was here, close to where I slept, that I kept my wedding ring. At least I didn't carry it around any more, a habit that had almost got me killed not so long back.

Things were undeniably better than they had been even six months ago. *I* was better. Looking over that lost time now was like reflecting on a long drive, the sort where you sporadically tune in to find you've been paying no attention whatsoever for the last thirty miles or so – you've been on autopilot, and if that autopilot had failed you'd have crashed ... but you didn't, somehow, and now you're closer to your destination for it. There was a common diagnosis for the blackness that had engulfed those eighteen months, but it was a word that men of my age and background were still not in the habit of using.

Instead of just sitting around, overthinking Lydia Roth's brief phone call, I managed – after some time – to get the collar around the dog's neck and take her out for a walk. It was slow going along the pavement, with the dog cowering at every passing motor and distant siren, but Regent's Park was only a corner away. We stepped out of urban bedlam into tranquil greenery and walked a while in agreeable silence. It made a fine change, being out in the fresh evening air, until the dog left a royal mess on the royal lawn and I remembered that I'd left the plastic bags at home.

I needed to get my head into my case. Unfortunately, it wasn't only *my* case on my mind. There was Andre Israel, and what he'd told me about the flow of drugs in and out of Wormwood Scrubs. These so-called E10 Cutthroats.

I got back from the walk before the sun went down and waited for the last of the rush-hour traffic to thin out before deciding to drive back to chambers. I had to collect the case papers I'd left there after rushing off to the Scrubs with Zara. Exhausted from her first real walk, the dog had collapsed inside her crate, but I still apologised as I bolted her inside. 'Sorry, but we can't have you trashing the place, can we, girl?' I realised that I didn't have a name by which to call her. I doubted Werner had ever thought to give her one. 'I'll have to think about that,' I said, but she wasn't really listening.

Miller & Stubbs Criminal Barristers was closed for the evening when I unlocked the front door and stepped into the empty reception. I knew there'd be a handful of juniors still scattered around the rooms of the building, working hard and late into the night as I'd so often done while Jenny Rook ate supper alone. Upstairs, in my room, I turned on the lamp and began to pile up the papers from where I'd left them strewn over my desk.

All cases require meticulous preparation before they ever go near a courtroom. The actual case papers themselves are novellas of witness statements, exhibits and interviews, but the typical working day also covers the organisation of interview edits, agreed facts and admissions, the preparation of the PCMH – plea and case management hearing – form, the drafting of the defence statement, activating secondary disclosure of any relevant material raised in said defence statement, and the planning of any legal arguments over issues such as bad character. In this case, there'd be no lenience from the jury for having been thrown in with only a week to prepare. I needed to submit the defence statement with whichever defence we were going to go with, but my mind was restive.

Charli Meadows. Andre Israel. Wormwood Scrubs connecting the two. I could feel the start of a headache coming on. I crossed my room, poked my head out to glance up and down the vacant corridor outside, and then closed the door and locked it. There were no blinds or curtains at my only window, so I turned off the lamp, shoved the window open and sat on the ledge to light a Marlboro from my coat pocket.

As I blew smoke out of the building, I dialled Zara.

'What's up?' she blurted after a single ring. 'Is it the dog?'

'No, she's sleeping. At least I hope she is. I'm back in chambers. Any luck at the bank?'

A bitter laugh. Behind the laugh, I could hear the rise and fall of passing engines, the bleeping of a pedestrian crossing: the sounds of central London. 'Not really.'

'You know, I do still have some cash left over from the Kessler fraud case. You were a big help there, and ... that is, if you're seriously in the shit, I could al—'

'No. We don't know what's going to happen after this month and ... No, I'd just rather not.'

'That's fair enough.' I didn't push it.

'Thought of a name?' she asked.

I held the cigarette between my teeth, and with my empty hand patted my stomach loud enough for her to hear it down the line. 'I'm still waiting for the next scan to find out if it's a boy or a girl.' I left a pause for laughter. 'Honestly, I wouldn't know where to start.'

'How about naming her after your ex-wife?' she chuckled. 'I'm sure that'd really stick it to her!'

I winced. Instinctively, my eyes moved through the shadows to the shelf where I kept my first-edition copy of *To Kill a Mockingbird*, which Jenny had gifted me on the morning I passed the Bar. 'How about Harper?' I suggested.

'Not since every wannabe Beckham named their kid it.'

'Boo Radley then? She looks almost scary enough for a Boo.'

'God no. Boo is like a pet name between Insta-couples these days.'

'*Insta-couples?*' I laughed. 'In my day, we called those blow-up dolls.'

'I bet *you* did. If you're going *Mockingbird*, why not Scout?'

'Scout …' I turned to the window and gazed at the parallel building across the narrow passageway, the long shadows pushed up its stone face by the lamp post far below. 'I like it.'

'You're welcome. So, how come you're back in chambers at this time?'

'Rushed out earlier without my work. Say, you have digital copies of Israel's case papers, don't you?' I knew she did; Zara was digital in all the ways I was still analogue. 'Any chance you could forward me copies?'

'Absolutely!' She sounded brightened and surprised. 'I'm still central. If you hang on in chambers another fifteen minutes or so I could come meet you and print out the hard copies …' She coughed guiltily. 'Then, if you're feeling charitable, I wouldn't say no to a lift back down to Brixton to save me the Tube fare …'

'Deal.'

'Nice. You're following the drugs then?'

'Yes. Whether your client really does know anything of value or not remains to be seen, but I think it's worth a punt.'

'You're probably right …'

A big, blatant gap. 'But?'

'Well, I'm not going to lie, the thought of using my client like this makes me feel a bit weird. It's a shame you don't know anyone else.'

'Anybody else?'

'Yeah. I mean, you've worked with enough clients over the years, I thought maybe you'd know someone else with an inside perspective of the Scrubs. Maybe someone who could give us a different opinion on this gang.'

I paused, stumped, only just seeing the obvious answer. 'Barnes, you are a genius.'

'You reckon?'

'Yes. Meadows lives in Walthamstow. As it happens, I know just the place where we could –' I stopped abruptly. Distancing the phone, I strained my ear towards the landing. There were soft footsteps approaching, footsteps accompanied by the rumbling of small wheels and the jangling of keys. 'Ah, great ...' Back to the phone. 'Meet me at chambers.' I hung up and sent the fag spinning out of the window.

No sooner had I shut the window than the door was unlocked, and our caretaker came tottering into the room carrying his shopping basket of cleaning products and dragging his Henry vacuum behind him with the wheels squeaking. He hit the light switch, squinting indifferently across the room, and then dropped his basket when he saw me perched on the windowsill.

'Jesus Christ!' he cried, almost spitting his dentures as spray bottles went rolling over his wide, orthopaedic shoes. 'You trying to finish me off, Rook?'

'Sorry, Ernie,' I said, pocketing the phone.

'What the hell are you thinking, sitting up here in the dark like ...' He scrunched his nose, sniffed somewhat distastefully, and then started gathering his spilled wares from the rug. 'You know, Stubbs would have your guts for garters if he caught you doing that up here.'

'I'm quite sure Rupert will be off sharing his excellent company with a Scotch of some fine vintage by now. What concerns me more is whoever else you might let into my room while I'm not around.'

'What's *that* supposed to mean?' He straightened at once, frowning indignantly until he figured out where I was going and conceded a dry, bashful smile. 'Barnes.'

I nodded. 'Barnes.'

He shuffled over to my wastepaper basket, readying a black bag from the pocket of his overalls, and tipped the papers from inside. 'Won't happen again, if it's a problem.'

'It's not really. I was thinking of letting her have her own key.'

Ernie had been working weekday mornings and nights in chambers for more than thirty years, changing light bulbs, cleaning lavatories and replacing screws in those curious places where screws tended to unwind. During that time, he had made only one demand: for the first months of my solo residency on the third floor, he had refused to clean my room. I didn't blame him, considering the mountains of clutter I'd built during my former nosedive into neglect.

We were quiet for a moment; old colleagues of a sort, old friends of another.

'Well.' I got to my feet. 'I'll get out of your hair …'

'What's left of it.'

I clipped the papers into my briefcase and paused on the way out. 'Hey, Ernie, what would you recommend for cleaning carpets?'

'Carpets? Depends what you got on 'em.' He looked me up and down. 'Red wine, knowing you lot.'

74

'Urine, actually.'

'Ah!' He nodded, lowering to a whisper. 'Nothing to be ashamed of, Mr Rook. Whiskey does the exact same thing to me ...'

I could only shake my head.

7

We were walking south along St James Street in Walthamstow, passing through the yellow glow of lamp posts, when Zara asked me about my time in prison.

'Whatton Detention Centre,' I told her. 'Wouldn't recommend it.'

'Whatton?' She coughed nervously. 'Isn't that a …?'

'Prison for male sex offenders? It wasn't back in 1983.'

'Thank God. How come they remanded you in custody? Seems extreme for a man who emptied fruit machines.'

'Doesn't matter if it's fruit machines or bank vaults, once you're a few grand up they tend to notice. Remember me telling you that I'd let a few other blokes in on my method?'

'And they did the same, right? That's why it was conspiracy to defraud?'

'Correct. The problem was that the police still hadn't nicked them at the time of my arrest. They applied to the court for a remand in custody to make sure I couldn't tip any of the others off, and the magistrates didn't need much persuading.'

'And how was it?'

'Prison?' As we walked through the wonders of Walthamstow's high street – chicken shops, bookmakers, a pharmacy with a mattress dumped outside – I did my best to recall a time I'd tried hard to forget. 'Lousy food. A lot of concrete. It's a peculiar feeling, losing control. In life, you often think you can't walk out of a situation. A job or a relationship, an awkward moment – but you can. All you have to do is put one foot in front of the other. In prison, for the first time in your life, you actually can't.'

'Sounds grim.'

'It was enough to scare me straight. That's why I understand your client's frustration. Being held on remand is so maddening because you have no countdown. You see, a convicted inmate is *always* counting down. Another decade, another six months, another week. But being remanded in custody until trial, I had no idea how long it would go on for. The thought of being convicted was terrifying. The hope for acquittal was perhaps even worse.' Hearing that realisation leap unguarded from my throat made me feel extraordinarily stupid for taking so many chances of late.

'I guess you don't blame Andre for offering information then?'

'No. Pride goes before destruction, but so does being labelled a snitch. We have to be very careful in choosing who we speak to about this.'

'And who exactly are we going to speak to now?'

'Mark Patchett. He was my room-mate in 1987, if you could call a couple of sleeping bags lined with cardboard any sort of a room. We both used to hunker down with the homeless crowd at the Bullring near Waterloo Station. He's not the sort of person you'd keep on a Christmas card list, mostly because he rarely kept a postal address back then, but throughout the nineties I'd often come here to meet him for a drink. Charli Meadows lives five minutes away from here. A mile further south is Leyton, the E10 area. If these Cutthroats are genuine, this man is likely to know of them.'

'And he was in the Scrubs,' she said, wary. 'Is he violent?'

'Violent? No, but I'd keep a tight grip on that bag of yours.'

'And for some reason you think he'll be sitting here in this pub, even though you haven't spoken to him in how long? I don't see why we couldn't have just messaged him on Facebook.'

'It's a generation thing. Men like Patch are defiant to change. That's why he's been caught so many times. It's eight o'clock on a Monday. That means he's either in the pub on this corner ahead, or in a cell somewhere.'

'All right,' she said, 'but I can see at least one flaw in this master plan.'

'Which is?'

She pointed ahead. 'There *isn't* a pub on this corner.'

Like an ocean liner beached, I came to a slow, deflating halt.

On the corner was the same Victorian brewery I'd first known as the Tap, which had boasted new ownership almost every time I'd sought Patch out here over the years. Now, though, the windows were lined with sweaty clients straddling treadmills and cross-trainers. A gym.

Zara sighed an I-told-you-so sort of sigh and took out her phone. 'Facebook then?'

I was turning in useless circles, as embarrassed as I was annoyed. How long *had* it been since I'd last drunk with him here? Five years? Ten? Habitual character or not, this was *London*, one of the ficklest cities in the world. On the opposite side of St James Street was the NHS Health Centre.

Two doors back we'd passed a small family business for horse-drawn funerals. And beside the pub that was now a gym was a small, pale, nondescript building with no sign other than a discreet green poster tacked to the exterior: Cue Club Snooker and Pool.

'Hang on a minute.' I said. 'I know where he'll be.'

I paid a couple of pounds to a surly attendant to get us each into the building, which consisted of one long, gloomy room filled with green tables under trios of low-hanging lamps.

There were as many as thirty men scattered around the place in pairs or quartets, half of them bent over felt, the others standing off in the side-shadows waiting for a turn. Almost every table had coins amassed on one of its mahogany rails. The only noises were clacking sounds of various strengths; the place smelled chalk-dry with a history of stale cigarette smoke.

I found Mark Patchett bent almost parallel to the surface of a pool table in the back corner, staring down the length of a custom-made cue with lamplight glaring off his balding head. He was a huge man, corpulence now smothering a body that had once been a formidable weapon. He was dressed in a black Thin Lizzy T-shirt that had washed to watery grey. A rabbit's foot hung from the zip of his shapeless cream coat, which had many pockets – pockets being infinitely useful to a man like Patch.

His right eyeball was a dull prosthetic made of acrylic. His left flicked up briefly, dropped back to the ball at the end of the cue, then did a double take in my direction. He was in his fifties, but those strangely dilated years behind bars had been enormously cruel.

'Rook.' He gave the white a neat click, sinking a red. 'No representation needed today, thank you very much. Been on my best behaviour.'

His bearded opponent and those on the nearest tables glanced up, slightly interested. The room was altogether too quiet for my liking.

'I haven't represented you in years,' I replied, coming to a stop in the warm glow of his table. 'I'd never make that mistake again.'

Patch guffawed and struck the white again. While his challenger was still focused on me, I spotted Patch's hand move swiftly and almost imperceptibly over the very edge of the felt, nudging another red into the corner pocket, leaving only a scatter of yellows and the black on the table.

'Hey, fellas!' Patch called out to nobody and everybody at once, expertly twirling his cue. 'I ever tell you about the barrister that got me off after I was filmed pasting that copper when I was working the doors in Brixton? I was going to plead guilty until this ugly bastard argued that the pig had no right to enter the nightclub, whereas I had the right to batter him if he tried!'

'The copper at the door,' Zara marvelled, remembering the riddle I'd set every pupil I'd ever interviewed. She was still the only one who'd got it right. 'That was a real case?'

I nodded.

Patch's opponent had turned back to the game and was scratching a fine powder of dandruff from his beard, counting the balls with a muddled expression.

'You got a couple of minutes to talk, Patch?' I asked, keeping my voice low. 'After your game, of course.'

'What, *this* game?' He lined up carefully and made his final strike.

The bearded man stormed off without even waiting to see the black ball finish its inevitable course into the side pocket. '*Cheap hustler ...*'

'Lucky for you that I am cheap, John!' Patch chuckled, shovelling the coins into one of his many pockets. 'What do you want to talk about?'

'Old times,' I said, and then quieter still, 'time served.'

Once more, this briefly caught the attention of the closest tables.

'One of those talks, is it?' Patch said, indifferently potting the remaining yellows for target practice. 'Tell you what, I'll play you for it. Might as well be earning something for my time.' With the table clear he stuck a hand into his coat and produced not the coins he'd won, but a grubby, scrunched-up twenty and waggled it like bait on a hook.

I sighed, taking my wallet out and checking the folds. I laid my own twenty onto the side rail and flicked a fifty-pence piece across the green. 'All right,' I said. 'You never know, I might actually beat you one of these days.'

He laughed hard. 'That's the spirit,' he said and tossed me the diamond. 'You break.'

Zara moved silently to the thinning plush beside the cues on the wall and took a seat in the shadows that bordered our table's radiance, watching closely. She didn't seem uncomfortable, despite being the only young woman in the room, although she was holding on to her bag with both hands.

I set up, broke and potted nothing.

'Tough break,' Patch tutted, twirling his cue once more as he advanced on the white.

'Well, you must've had a lot of time on your hands to practise,' I remarked, 'what with you spending most of your life on remand.'

Zara, who Patch only now seemed to notice, spoke up, a little more sheepishly than usual. 'They have pool tables in prison?'

Patch blinked at her, one lid falling fast over his sharp green eye, the other going slowly over the milky prosthetic. 'What else is a bloke meant to do? Apart from, you know …' He made a crude gesture with his right hand.

She rolled her eyes, then considered it for a second, still holding her bag to her gut. 'Read?'

This got Patch guffawing again, so hard that he doubled over and had to wait to calm down before attempting his move. 'Who's this, Rook? Your daughter?'

'No. This is Zara, one of our pupil barristers at Miller & Stubbs.'

'Another lawyer, eh?' He easily potted two yellows in a row and turned his eye back on her. 'Honestly, you've got to love the balls on this bloke. One week he's kipping out in the Bullring with me and the boys. The next he tells us he's leaving to be a barrister. Funniest thing we've heard all year. Few months later the Great Storm hits London and I figure he's been swept off to the land of Oz.' Another neat pot. 'Years later, nineties now, I'm living up here in Walthamstow and some lad's sitting in the pub next door telling me he's been dossing out on Lincoln's Inn Fields with this tramp who's claiming to be a trainee barrister. I go there and who do I find? Older, fatter, dressed in robes, the one and only Elliot Rook.'

'She knows the story,' I said sharply.

Patch caught my eye and, despite his size, turned away. 'I'm only winding you up, mate. I know you wouldn't have brought her along if she wasn't in the know. Rook here spent the first few weeks of his pupillage living with me, and in return I got myself a resident barrister. How many trials did you win on the bounce for me again? Six?'

'Seven. You did a fair bit of time on remand though.'

'Occupational hazard.' He shrugged, turning back to Zara. 'People often ask me about a life of crime. I tell them the pay is good, the hours are great, but you get fucking long holidays and not in the places you want them.'

'Like the Scrubs,' I added.

'Yeah. Like the Scrubs.' He potted another yellow but this time the white quickly followed. 'Shite. Two shots to you.'

I placed the white back onto the playing field and leaned over the felt. I could smell the chalk on my fingertips. 'When were you last up in the Scrubs, Patch?'

'Late nineties, I reckon. Sometime around then.'

From the corner of my eye, I saw Zara frown. 'You don't remember?'

'Missy, I've been banged up in places I didn't even bother to learn the names of. Course, when I was there it was *really* the Scrubs, you know? Nasty place. They had an onsite bar for the screws back then. What an idea *that* was.'

He pressed his hand out flat on the felt, my shot narrowly avoiding his beefy wrist. I missed again; it had been a while.

'See that?' He was obviously referring to the two fingers that were unnaturally crooked. 'Screw did that with his boot cos he thought I'd looked at him funny. As I remember

83

it, I'd been facing the opposite direction. Hell of a place back then.'

Zara cocked her head to read the faded green ink across his knuckles: ACAB.

I hit another useless rebound off the cushion and backed up from the table. Patch grinned, chalking his cue, and cracked his shoulders loudly before leaning forward again.

'Say, Patch, you still keep your ear to the ground, don't you?'

'Always.' Clack. The fifth ball rolled into the nearside pocket. 'Why?'

'Don't suppose you've heard much about a few scrappy gangsters going by the name of Cutthroats, have you? E10 Cutthroats, I believe.'

There was a dull thud. The cue's nose had slammed into felt and the white ball went shooting from the table and hit the wall beside Zara's head. Patch did one of his slow, nauseating blinks around the room.

All around us, heads lifted.

Patch picked up the two remaining yellows, one by one, and dropped them into the nearest pocket, followed by the black.

'That's my game,' he said hoarsely. He scooped up both twenties and shoved them into his pocket. He dismantled his cue quietly, methodically, and cased it. The men around us were still watching intently.

Patch nodded towards the exit. 'Got any fags?' And we quietly followed him out of the building.

8

A man called Roy Macey had been running things in the back in the day.

That's what Patch told us in the empty darkness of the smoking area behind the club, which was just a bucketful of sand surrounded by poorly aimed filters like so many pale, flattened cockroaches.

Roy Macey had been the sort of career criminal that late-night, low-budget movies were still being made about. He controlled half the docks and owned property all over the capital. He dealt cocaine from his sleazy lap-dancing club in Soho and carried enough of the Metropolitan Police in his back pocket to never concern himself with the dreaded boot at the door. He didn't hide. He dressed in fine suits, shook hands with esteemed Members of Parliament and donated considerable amounts to London-based charities. He was just another philanthropist whose disparagers had a knack for sleeping in burning buildings, tumbling off bridges and tripping onto the tracks of the London Overground.

'Macey didn't need to get banged up to control the gear going into the Scrubs back when I was first there in '86,' Patch said, repeatedly turning his good eye back over his left shoulder as if he expected to see the aged crook lurking in the dark. 'Prisons were built to keep people from getting out.

They weren't designed to stop things coming in. I remember when dead birds were fashionable.'

'Dead birds?' Zara grimaced.

'Oh yeah! You'd be sitting out in the yard, minding your own business when *bonk*, pigeon lands at your feet, like something out of *Monty Python*. Seconds later a con would walk up, cool as you like, and stuff it down his knickers. The birds were hollowed out, crammed full of gear, sewn up and given the old fast-bowl over the wall. Course, now there are drones that can do the same thing. The Smack Spitters, now *they* had a good system. These blokes would get loaded on heroin right before getting sent down so that it'd show up in their bloodwork and they'd get put on a rehab course inside. They'd queue up for their cup of methadone every morning, hold it in their gobs and then spit it back out in their cell. Save up a week's worth of that and you've got a powerful dose to sell on to the junkies.'

'And people actually wanted to buy that?' Zara said distastefully.

Patch shrugged. 'I've heard it all, me. There was this old biddy visiting her grandson up in Strangeways. When she got searched they found half a kilo of charlie stuffed right up her –'

'All right, Patch,' I said, settling him down. 'Surely Macey can't still be controlling the drugs in the Scrubs. People in his career don't tend to last too long.'

Patch shook his head, smoking hard. 'Roy's been out on the Costa del Crime for twenty years now. There's a Nando's where his nightclub used to be, and all his bent coppers are either retired or dead. Whatever empire he'd built up the old way was dismantled and taken over by these smaller gangs dealing in local areas, every man ruthlessly defending his own corner. But word has it that Roy's running out of money, and he's spotted an opportunity back in London.'

'Which is?'

He scratched the topmost of his chins and lowered his voice. 'You ever seen that film *The Warriors*?'

'Long time ago,' I said. 'Some dystopian New York City divided into dozens of street gangs?'

'Exactly. Love that film. There's this one bloke in it, Cyrus, who does the maths one day and realises that unifying all these separate gangs would create an army *three times* the size of the city's police force. He figures that you don't need to be wasting time squabbling for turf if you all join together instead. That way it's *all* your turf, you know? So, this Cyrus calls a truce and offers the olive branch or what have you to all these different gangs. That's the plan, anyway. One gang. One business. One army.'

I cleared my throat and tried not to sound too condescending. 'You believe that Roy Macey, some old forgotten lag, has come back across the Channel after twenty years and asked these lifelong rivals to simply forget their differences, hold hands and work together?'

'I didn't say that,' he hissed. 'For a start, this is the twenty-first century, Rook. Roy will be running things from the comfort of his yacht in Puerto Banus. He'll never step foot on English soil again.'

'Then how would he maintain day-to-day control?' Zara asked, apparently more impressed than I was. 'Surely he'd need to be here on the street to keep discipline.'

'The Macey name still carries a lot of weight around these parts,' he said, his voice low. 'Enough to get people listening. But could be scare stories.'

'Scare stories?' she asked.

'Right.' He leaned closer. 'They say it's his kids. Real chips off the old block. Twins. Personally, I don't buy it. I know *everybody*, and I haven't met a man who's actually seen them. These twins, they're myth, a couple of ghosts to make the Kray twins look like Girl Guides. But that's how it works in this game. The Krays only ever killed two low-level gangsters fifty years back and they're still legends. The Macey twins don't even have to exist to incite terror.'

'Urban folklore,' Zara said.

'Couldn't have put it better myself. As for these gangs holding hands and putting differences aside, well, it never works like that. These Cutthroats you're on about, they're just kids. Disorganised before Macey's offer came along, but game. Last year, the Yardies made a move on their turf. Now we're talking about serious Jamaican gangsters here.'

'Oh, I know the Yardies,' I said ruefully.

'As did they. These Cutthroats knew the danger. A few of these Yardie lieutenants were sitting in their M3 one night when two kids, and I do mean *children*, put so many bullets in their car that the fire brigade had to saw the roof off like one of them motorway pile-ups. These kids are fearless. Walk a mile down the road into E10, start asking your questions, and you'll find that out soon enough.'

'So, they *are* from E10?'

There were footsteps passing on the pavement beyond the building. Patch waited, statuesque, until they'd faded before continuing.

'Started out there in the towers in Leyton,' he said. 'Each group alone is madder than a box of frogs, but *unified* ... Used to be a risky little business, dealing, not that I ever indulged. You'd move a bit of gear and use the profits to buy more. Rinse and repeat. Eventually, you'd either get killed or get caught and do a bit of bird, and someone would take your place. Then it got so anyone could be a gangster, and all you needed was a phone line and a ready supply of drugs. The old boy Macey is changing that. Things are going back to how they used to be. Organised. Controlled from the top.'

'Controlling the whole of east London, you mean, and using these Cutthroats as a front?' Zara asked.

'East London?' Patch shook his head. 'Think bigger. This is the age of instant communication. We're talking about a system with the potential to swallow the *country*.'

'Oh, like county lines offending?' Zara said. 'There was a National Crime Agency report I read last year. "County Lines Violence, Exploitation and Drug Supply".'

'I read that too,' I added. 'Inner-city gangs exploiting vulnerable people to branch out and sell drugs in small towns beyond the Home Counties.'

'In a nutshell,' Patch said. 'After Macey left, the war went back to being about which ends you come from.' He paused. 'You know what *ends* are, don't you?'

'Territory,' Zara answered. 'Home turf. Estates. My end would be St Ann's, Nottingham.'

'Smart lady. Every end had its own gang fighting postcode against postcode, spraying bullets into playgrounds just to hit one target. It was all about bling, fast cars and guns, and members had a limited shelf life. Then along comes

Macey's truce, and now these bastards are growing. Soon they'll have enough to take over the country, one town at a time, with east London as the distribution hub.'

'What about existing drug trades?' Zara asked. 'Surely those towns will already have established set-ups.'

'Same way Britain built an empire,' he said, 'and that wasn't with cups of tea and scones. They'll dispatch workers and spread into any place they can.'

'Including the Scrubs,' I said quietly, checking around; in the shadows, Patch's paranoia was infectious.

'You know me, Rook. It serves a man of my talents to keep up to speed with these sorts of things. I'm telling you this because we go back, but I don't want to be any sort of witness in whatever you're into. You two aren't Starsky and Hutch, and I'm not Huggy Bear. I don't want my name coming up in or out of the courtroom.'

'Never. All we're looking for is a nudge in the right direction.'

He nodded, spinning the last of his cigarette into the bucket; it glowed brightly for a second or two before suffocating. 'What's the best way to start a burger business on a street full of McDonald's? How do you make an impact when there's already a business that customers are loyal to?'

'By offering a better burger?' I suggested.

'Maybe. A quicker way would be to put a dozen of your employees on that street and tell them to stick pubes in every sodding Big Mac they can get their hands on.'

'A hostile takeover,' Zara whispered. 'You're saying these Cutthroats sent a group of their dealers into prison on purpose?'

'It wasn't no win for the police ...' I muttered, echoing Andre's words.

Zara shook her head. 'I don't believe that anybody would *choose* to go to prison.'

'Some people aren't built for civvy life,' Patch replied. 'For some, prison is like a Friday night out. They know everybody in there and get to shoot the shit with mates they haven't seen in a while. The maths, well, that's a no-brainer. You can work your knackers off in a lousy chicken shop for the next two years and earn thirty grand, minus tax, or you can go inside, forget about where next month's rent is coming from, eat three square meals a day and earn two hundred grand tax-free, which'll be waiting for you on the outside. These people wouldn't see that sort of money in a lifetime working straight. As for walls, there've always been walls holding them back. Least they can see these ones. Accept them.'

'What about officers?' I asked.

'Screws? Same thing. They're mopping up suicides and stabbings, getting spat on every night. Somebody offers them a few grand to bring something in. Just once. That's a quarter of their salary in one morning for putting some-thing in their back pocket. They do it. Take their kids on that Disney holiday they've been promising them for years. Clear a couple of credit cards. Only, once they've started on that road, the cons have got something to hold over them.'

'And you end up in somebody's pocket,' I said.

'Deeper and deeper.' He looked around and sighed. 'I should be getting back inside. People talk. It was good seeing you, Rook, but let's keep it social next time, yeah?'

'Sure, Patch.' I shook his hand; it was incredibly large and rough as bark.

'Before you go ...' Zara said slowly. 'I might've missed something from your burger analogy. You said that getting your employees into the restaurants was only the first part of the takeover. Then you'd corrupt the existing product?'

'Smart.' He smiled thinly. 'Didn't I say she was smart, Rook? Pays more attention than you do.'

'Yes,' I said. 'You're saying they chose to go to prison so they could corrupt the supply and win customers away from the existing product?'

'Maybe. What happened could've been coincidence. Smoking chemicals *is* risky.'

'Holy shit!' Zara gasped, and it echoed loudly off the bricks around us. She lowered her voice. 'They didn't just want to attract new customers to their product.' She turned to me and her eyes were bright. 'They tainted the existing product to kill any customer who remained loyal to the old dealers. The killed them. They killed them all.'

9

I was glad to get home to the dog.

After a quick growl she seemed pleased to see me too.

'Hello, Scout.' I let her out of the cage and took her down to Dorset Square at the south end of my block before she had chance to further stain the carpet. Then, after returning home, I unfolded the futon and turned on the television for background noise; she settled down to watch it, while I opened my laptop and got to work.

First, I googled Roy Macey. A few stories from the seventies and eighties. Very little of interest. Wanted by Interpol on a number of inquiries. A mugshot in a *Crimestoppers* appeal for fugitives hiding out on the Continent. Just another stone-faced white man glaring into the camera. It all fitted with Patch's description of the man's formative years.

After that, I began to refresh my memory on the finer points of HMP Wormwood Scrubs.

Glancing over the Prison Service's website, it almost read like the brochure for a self-catering Swiss chalet: in-cell power and cooking facilities, television for a pound a week, and an *enhanced package* including personal bedding and a PlayStation. A full-size gymnasium with sports including badminton, basketball, weight training and volleyball.

It was only in the digitalised archives of national newspapers that the uglier side of the prison was revealed. Ever since Russian spy George Blake managed to scale the outer walls to freedom in 1966, the Scrubs had remained a tabloid favourite. There was the infamous IRA rooftop protest of '79, repeated riots, and so-called *dirty protests* during which inmates smeared themselves and their surroundings in excrement. One former governor penned a letter to *The Times* before resigning in 1981, calling the prison a 'penal dustbin'. Inspectors consistently complained of poor hygiene and vermin infestations.

The situation was aggravated in the early nineties after Michael Howard, then Home Secretary for the Conservative government, conceived his famed 'prison works' sound bite, and the subsequent bipartisan efforts almost doubled the national prison population without bothering to provide the resources needed to support it. By the end of that decade, the Scrubs was revealed to have been the setting for the worst case of staff brutality in modern British penal history. The Prison Service had no choice but to publicly admit that its officers had subjected inmates to beatings, racial abuse, physical torture and even mock executions.

Almost twenty years later, things hadn't improved much. Just a month before the almost concurrent capture of Andre Israel and suspension of Charli Meadows, a whistle-blower from the Prison Officer Association published a damning report on the jail, citing forty to fifty violent incidents every month along with the resignation of fifty-seven officers in the last year alone.

The biggest problem now was drugs, and Spice reigned supreme. By 2012, rumour of its inability to show up in blood or urine tests had given it a foothold in most UK prisons. It was made illegal under the Psychoactive Substances

Act four years later, but by then almost half of all prisoners across England and Wales were suspected of using it.

I was sitting under the duvet with the laptop open beside me, making basic notes on the drug, when Zara texted asking if I was still awake and free to talk. This was another of those disparities between generations. Where I would usually call, she would almost always text. As a case in point, I responded by ringing her back.

'Ten o'clock news is cheerful tonight,' she said on answering. 'More stabbings. Another shooting. London has overtaken New York City in killings for the year so far.'

'I'm sure our senior clerk will be thrilled. Percy would make a fine ambulance chaser if he wasn't too busy watching out for hearses.'

I could almost hear her smile. 'What're you watching?'

'Watching?' I blinked indifferently at the television. '*Gladiator*, apparently. Channel Five.'

'That's one way to rile the dog's PTSD.' I could hear leaves of paper turning. Then, nearer to the phone, the clicking of a retractable ballpoint pen; from that distance it sounded like a stapler against my head.

I asked what she was working on.

'Just going over the raid on the pub,' she said. 'Don't know if you've had time to look yet, but there really isn't much about it in Andre's case papers. It does say that the police had a misuse of drugs warrant to search the licensed premises, but it doesn't say how or why they got the warrant. As far as I can tell, the pub is clean.'

'The magistrates most likely issued the warrant because of Omar Pickett, our supposed informant.'

'That does make more sense, but if that's the case then Pickett should be available to stand up in court, so he can tell the jury Andre wasn't involved.'

'Assuming he wasn't.'

'Well, yeah,' she responded crankily. 'If, on the other hand, the police had already been gathering surveillance on the suspects, and *that* led to the warrant, and their inform-ant just happened to be there, then I want to know about that too.'

'Your best bet is to ask via a disclosure request called a Section 8 application, which will demand that the Met provide an answer in court.'

'Section 8 application,' I heard her mutter, pen scratching paper. 'Of course. I should've known that. My head is all over with this. I'm sitting here trying to work out exactly how your case connects into mine, but there are still so many pieces missing ...'

'That's because we don't know that the cases *are* connected,' I reminded her. 'Yes, my client worked there, but Wormwood Scrubs is a huge prison. Any correlation could be coincidental. You mustn't forget that *your* client will most likely tell you anything you want to hear if it might help him walk, and *my* client has denied knowing anything about the drugs in her car to begin with. Your raid involved Class A drugs, while mine was Spice. As for Patch, well, I've always found it best to take his insights with a pinch of salt.'

'But it sounds so plausible ... in an implausible, far-fetched, mental sort of way. Luckily, we're in one of the few professions that actually works on argument's sake.'

'That's one way to put it.'

'So, for argument's sake, I was thinking we ought to go through the facts of both cases. Chronologically and geographically, I mean. Get things in order.'

'I'm assuming that you don't mean to do this tomorrow?'

She paused. 'Well, if you're watching your film …'

'No.' I yawned. 'I wasn't.'

'Cool. I'm getting a map of the city up on the iPad in front of me, but my bearings outside the centre still aren't that hot.'

'All right, hold on while I do the same …' Turning back to the laptop, I opened Google Maps and positioned the screen broadly over Greater London with Westminster in the centre. 'Stick Big Ben in the middle,' I told her, 'that should make this easier.'

I waited a moment. 'Done,' she said brightly. 'First, since this seems to be happening around the place, Wormwood Scrubs. That's up and to the left, right?'

'*West*, yes. It's just above Shepherd's Bush in Hammersmith and Fulham, about a half-hour drive out from the centre. If you're looking at London as a clock face, with Big Ben there in the centre, the Scrubs should be at around the ten o'clock mark. Charli Meadows has worked there for four years, though she lives in Walthamstow, a corner away from where we were tonight.'

'And that's where these E10 Cutthroats are supposed to have come from?'

'A mile down the road in Leyton, according to Patch. E10 is its postcode district, E for east London, so that would make sense. Walthamstow and Leyton are in the north-east of the city. On your map, that'll be to the right of Hackney and above Stratford. About … half past one on our clock face.'

'Half past one?'

'More or less, if the Scrubs is over there at ten. It's a good hour's drive from the prison, anyway. Newham, where your client lives and where the raid took place, is around five miles south of Leyton, close to the north bank of the Thames and London City Airport.'

'Got it.' She was quiet for a while, her presence marked only by the scratch of ink on paper. 'That brings us to where this begins, four days into the new year when Andre manages to jog his way into an armed police operation being carried out on some mystery warrant.'

'Correct.'

'For some reason, a bunch of dealers from this E10 crew are just sitting around in a bar five miles south of their own area, twiddling their thumbs and waiting for the cops.'

'It's worth noting at this point that they did try to *flush* their drugs,' I countered. 'Despite the recent theories, these men weren't so eager to be jailed that they cuffed themselves and marched in two-by-two. Plus, that's a hell of a big risk. Even if their plan *was* to wind up inside, who's to say that they'd be remanded at the Scrubs?'

'They were bound to be remanded in the same prison,' she said. 'Maybe they didn't care which they went to. Maybe that's why they had Class A drugs, to throw the scent off the Spice. I don't know. What I *do* know, though, is that five men were taken –'

'Six,' I interjected. '*Six* young men were arrested for possession with intent to supply and banged up in the Scrubs.'

'Right,' she replied. 'Six, including Andre. They were all charged at the station that night, refused bail the following

98

morning and banged up in the Scrubs en masse by the weekend.'

'What comes next?'

'The following Wednesday morning, when thirteen men were found dead in their cells.'

'Spice,' I said.

'According to the newspapers from the time, though, the official conclusion was death by misadventure. Spice is synthetic, man-made crap, it doesn't come out of any FDA-approved lab.'

'The FDA is in the USA,' I told her. 'Ours is the MHRA.'

'Same difference. What I'm saying is it doesn't exactly come with a list of ingredients or allergens.'

'No. I've just been reading up on it actually …' With my one free hand I swapped the laptop for my notebook and looked back over my scrawl. 'Spice was initially a brand name that has come to be used generically for any synthetic substitute for cannabis. In the past, it was marketed as a legal high.'

'I remember it. There used to be a stall selling it at Leeds Fest, right there alongside the bar. Thankfully, I stuck to overpriced cider.'

'Good. These synthetic cannabinoids can be made from any one of about seven hundred research chemicals, apparently, which are thought to come from China via Eastern Europe. Their effects vary depending which compounds have been used, though we're seeing so many *zombies* because the chemicals reduce respiration, causing the body to suffocate as the heart rate soars.'

'And that's appealing to these users?' she asked in disbelief.

'Well, that's not all it does. On a good day – when it doesn't suffocate you to death – Spice can create feelings of euphoria and altered perception. It has also been known to give its users impossible strength, an inability to recognise pain and delusional, animal aggression.'

'Like the Hulk?'

'More or less. The Internet is full of reports from all over the world about Spice addicts who have gone on gruesome rampages. Biting faces off. Strangling animals. Being tasered, stabbed and even shot repeatedly, only to keep on coming.'

'God, and that's how those thirteen men died?'

'Yes, at some point between their cells being locked on Tuesday night and then opening again on Wednesday morning. The following Monday, ten thousand pounds' worth of Spice disguised as regular rolling tobacco was found hidden inside a vehicle in the staff car park. The car belonged to Charli Meadows, which would have travelled from her home, a mile outside of the E10 area.'

'How'd they find it? Was it a tip-off? Did *they* have a warrant?'

'It doesn't appear so. As part of their contracts, staff consent to searches at any time while on the premises. Spice is notoriously difficult to identify, most canine units can't even detect it, but it sounds as though the Prison Service had brought in some new, specially trained super-dogs to search the vehicles after those deaths.'

'And yet she still risked smuggling it in ... Surely she must've known there'd be an increase in searches.'

'I was of the same opinion.'

'You think she was being forced into it?'

'I think there's a strong possibility. Either that, or we challenge *mens rea* and convince the jury that she believed it to be regular tobacco.'

'But if Macey and his gang are genuinely trying to control the flow of drugs already in the Scrubs, then which side was Meadows working for? The old dealers or the new? Must have been the new, right? Being so close on the map.'

'Therein lies our mystery,' I said. 'There's a chance she was doing it for some time before getting caught. Then again, these so-called Cutthroats would've been brought into the building just the week before. Meadows did mention that she was often responsible for searching and processing new inmates. They might've propositioned her then.'

'I can ask Andre. Find out if Meadows was the one working the inductions when he arrived at the prison. What about the night the inmates died? Was she on duty?'

'I don't believe so.'

'She didn't say?'

'She barely answered a question for herself.'

'We need to clarify,' she said. 'When are you next seeing her?'

'Not until the start of the trial a week today. I don't have anything arranged before then.'

'What do you have on tomorrow? We should talk to her.'

'*We?*'

'Of course *we*,' she said. 'Why not?'

'I don't know. I'm not sure how comfortable I am with you rocking the boat this near to the end of your pupillage. Not to mention the fact that these dealers are no doubt nasty people. I wouldn't want to drag you into any sort of danger. Not again.'

Which, in hindsight, was a funny thing to say, because it wasn't just Zara I ended up dragging into danger.

10

'You think she'll be happy to talk with the two of us
ambushing her like this?'

We were sitting in my car late the following afternoon,
back in Walthamstow, kerbed while I checked the address
on my paperwork.

'It's a gamble,' I confessed, 'but I don't want to give her
time to work herself up again.'

That was a half-truth. What I really wanted was to
speak to Charli Meadows and without her brother and her
solicitor.

I studied myself in the mirror. I hadn't slept well, and I
feared it showed. At worst, I'd expected the dog's presence
to amount to a low, steady breathing sound. Something
peaceful. Instead, she'd walked in tight, unsettled circles as
soon as the lamp was out, rattling off the walls of her cage
and crying softly, every noise amplified by darkness. For the
first hour, I wouldn't get out of bed to open her crate. In
my exhaustion, I worried that she might claim her revenge
on mankind by taking those blunted teeth to my throat as
soon as I was unconscious. But I let her out, eventually, and
after a few more pointless laps of the room she flopped like
a warm, rolled-up carpet onto my lower legs.

In the dark, I hadn't been able to keep my mind from
Lydia Roth. I'd faced gangland killers without breaking

a sweat, but the thought of a woman – *any* woman after my marriage – made me anxious. It brought about images I wasn't ready for, and I had decided not to ring Lydia back even to arrange this meeting. I resolved to see Charli Meadows without her.

After yesterday's traipsing back and forth across the city, and today's paperwork, I was feeling quite drained. I sensed a migraine on the horizon. If Meadows had just been straight with me from the beginning, I suspected, it would've saved me a great deal of time.

She lived on Low Hall Lane, an incredibly narrow, curved, almost-rural road with houses lining only the south side. All these houses faced a vast greenery of allotments that stretched off behind wire fencing on the opposite side of the road. I left the car under a canopy of the allotments' over-hanging trees and we walked the curvature of the lane on foot while I looked for the correct address. The houses were small, terraced, squashed up together like drunks in a crowd.

'It's this one?' Zara said as I stepped through a front gate onto gravel that was more dandelion than stone. 'She's no Tony Montana.'

I got to the front door and lifted a knuckle to knock politely, but I didn't manage to make a sound before a massive, snarling dog threw its entire weight into the glass from the other side. I jumped, catching my footing before falling backwards onto the gravel, and Zara burst into laughter.

'Jesus Christ!' I fumed. 'If I haven't had enough of damn *dogs* for one week!'

Even through the door's frosted pane, it was obvious that the dog was a huge white beast of postman-eating proportions.

'Who're you?' somebody called out from behind us.

We turned. Directly across the thin road, standing in a patch of grass that looked particularly wild among the tended allotments, was a boy of around eleven or twelve years old. In his concern, it wasn't difficult to spot the family resemblance.

'I'm looking for Charli Meadows,' I said loudly over the dog's baying through the closed door behind us. 'Your mother?'

The boy's face tightened. 'School send you?'

'School?' We came back out through the front gate and stepped into the empty road. Dusk was coming softly, and the allotments smelled sweeter for it. 'No, the school didn't send us.'

His eyes darted between us, knees twitching under what appeared to be an almighty fight-or-flight struggle. 'That bitch Miss Rotenberg put you on to me? I've been sick.'

'I don't know Miss Rotenberg. We're not education welfare officers, if that's what you're worried about.'

He scowled. 'What are you then? Pigs?'

'Do I look like a pig?' I asked. 'Actually, no, don't answer that. We're helping your mother out with a problem at work.'

'Lawyers?'

'Barristers,' Zara answered, 'but close enough.'

He eyed us for a moment more, still resentful, then turned away to yell: '*Mum!*'

Some distance off, from a tiny potting shed: '*What?*'

'Someone's here for you!'

'*What?*'

'*Here!*'

We waited, separated by the fence. I looked at the nearby sign: Honeybone Allotments. To the boy, I jabbed a thumb over my shoulder and smiled. 'Dogs, eh? I just got one myself. Yesterday, actually, and they really are –'

'You going to get my mum off?'

No messing with this boy. I discarded the smile. 'We're going to do our best.'

From the potting shed behind him, Charli Meadows appeared, trailed by two little girls. She was wearing a pair of gardening gloves, hair tied up in a bandana, soil stains on the knees of her jogging pants. She looked worried. 'Mr Rook? What's going on? Is everything all right?'

'Quite all right,' I said, looking past the boy's unbreakable glower.

'Where's Lydia?'

'Quite busy preparing for the trial,' I told her. I had no clue. 'This is Zara Barnes, one of our brightest young stars at Miller & Stubbs. We were in the area and I thought I ought to swing by and see how you were getting on.'

'You were in Walthamstow?' she asked doubtfully.

'At the court,' I lied, lighting up a cigarette; Snaresbrook was only fifteen minutes away. 'We pass through here on the way back to chambers.'

'Oh, of course.' She was wringing her gloves together as she led us to the nearby gate in the mesh – her on the grassy side, us in the road – and then she opened the gate and invited us through. There'd been a lock on the gate, but it was broken off. She noticed me noticing. 'Kids were trying to grow weed out here earlier this year, I think. Can you believe it? They cut the lock off to get in.'

'Not really the climate for it, I'd imagine.'

She shrugged.

'So, how have you been?' I asked.

'I'm getting on all right. Keeping busy. Not much else I can do with myself, now I'm out of work.'

'For now,' I noted, stepping over a terracotta plant pot. 'Keeping busy is the best way to handle this situation. You actually have an allotment here?'

'I do!' For a moment, she did something quite remarkable. She smiled, and beckoned us to follow between rectangles marked into the earth and a forest of bamboo stakes. 'I know they're for pensioners but, whatever, I like it. After spending every day moving between locks and bars, stuck behind concrete, you've got to get some space wherever you can find it in this bloody city ...' She paused, a shadow crossing her face, then shook it away. 'Been renting it for two years now. We don't have much of a back garden, so I thought it would give Roland and his sisters a nice place to come and get a little sunlight. You still help me out, don't you, Ro? Whenever I can get you off the PlayStation.'

The boy didn't answer; he was still standing close to the fence, watching us negotiate the crowded terrain towards his mother's shed at the back of the land with something very like jealousy.

'This patch here will be peppers,' she said, showing us a strip of overturned dirt with an enthusiasm I would never have imagined possible back in chambers, 'and this will be tomatoes, as long as I can figure out how to keep clear of the damn aphids this time. Over here by the shed I have these paving slabs, you see they're actually different shades? Been wanting to get them down as a sort of border ever since I saw something similar on Pinterest, but I haven't had time since …' All at once, she sobered up, lost to the thought. Silence fell, and I was sorry to hear it.

'It's very nice,' I said. 'Peaceful.'

She gave a perfunctory nod. The brief gleam in her eyes had been snuffed out to leave something remarkably sad.

I cleared my throat. 'Might we come inside the house for a brief chat? There are a couple of things I'd like to discuss before we get to court on Monday. Things we didn't get around to yesterday.'

'I don't think that's such a great idea,' she said quietly. 'Coming inside, I mean. The dog – he's a bit of a handful.'

'Yes, I saw.'

'I just wanted a dog because I've been having a bit of trouble in the area.'

'What kind of trouble?'

'People disliking the fact that I work at the prison, I guess. To them it's as bad as being police, and there are plenty of people with family on the wrong side of the law. Come sit down, though.' She gestured to a stack of wooden planks that had been arranged as walls around her intended tomato patch. There was netting over the soil, but beneath that I could see soft, vulnerable green shoots peering through. 'Roland, go inside and take your sisters with you.'

'Uh-uh.' He stood defiantly at the fence, some fifteen feet away, eyes moving between the three of us.

'Roland!'

'Why should I?' he spat, rattling the fence behind him with a backwards kick and stretching as tall as the last of his stubborn childhood would allow. 'I'm the man of the house!'

It was an odd statement, almost Dickensian, coming from this skinny boy who probably weighed eight stone wet and was still a year away from puberty. The tantrum might've been laugh-out-loud funny, if it hadn't been such a poignant reflection of the state of the Meadows household. Charli didn't even argue. She sighed and left him standing there. 'What do you want to know?'

I felt awkward getting into it in front of her children, but she wasn't giving me much of an option. 'The Tuesday before your vehicle was searched, the night those thirteen men died in their cells. Were you at work?'

I watched closely for any change in her expression. Thinking towards this bombshell through the small hours, I'd expected a telltale widening of the eyes or a nervous twitch, if not a full-on wail of guilty horror, but there was no alteration whatsoever. Perhaps because her nerves were so permanently frayed. 'I wasn't on shift until the next morning. The ambulances were lined up outside when I got there.'

'Must've been shocking,' I said, 'pulling into work and seeing that.'

'Only a little. The ambulances are often called out several times a day.'

'Because of the drugs,' Zara added; it wasn't soft, and it wasn't a question.

A few seconds of dead air followed. I had this awful, sweeping feeling that I'd made a crucial mistake in bringing Zara here. That she might have planned this whole encounter just to get face-to-face with precisely the sort of smuggler responsible for her cousin's death in the Scrubs all

109

those years ago. Thankfully, neither one of them bit, and my concern was only fleeting.

'Because of prison,' Charli replied simply. 'Convicts or not, though, deaths on the wings seem to hit officers and staff harder than they do the other inmates. I've always thought so, anyway. To some cons, we're just the faceless screws trying to keep them inside, but the reality is that we're there to keep them safe. Nobody wants to have a man end his life on their watch. Nobody. Losing so many in one night, that hurt the whole prison from the governor down to admin.'

'Did you know any of the deceased?' I asked.

'Barely. Band 3 staff – officers – they would've known them well enough, but they're each responsible for up to a hundred inmates. The prison holds an average of thirteen hundred at any time with over two thousand moved in and out each month. I'd usually process anywhere from, Jesus, fifty to a hundred newcomers a day.'

'Were you blamed?' Zara asked in a tone I didn't like, one that was entirely opposite to the one she'd adopted with Andre. 'After your car was searched, did your colleagues turn on you?'

'Some. The ones who found the bodies.' She turned her face to the potting shed, an adjustment of only a couple of inches that somehow took her miles away. 'I don't resent them for that. We're supposed to be on the same team. Nobody wants to find a cheat on their team, do they? But they're wrong. I didn't have anything to do with what happened. I feel for their families, of course. Their parents …' She turned back to us; more accurately, to Zara. 'But nobody forced them to smoke that crap.'

I could actually see the strain on Zara's face, her sharp, occasionally brilliant mind working overtime to veto whatever her mouth wanted to say.

'Who searched your vehicle again?' I intervened. 'It wasn't colleagues of yours?'

'No, they were independents from the Prison Investigation Unit.'

'And you don't have any grudges with anybody at work, or outside of work for that matter?'

'Not that I know of,' she said. 'And the neighbours wouldn't go that far.'

'What about the fathers of your children?' I asked.

'God no. They're long out of the picture.'

I nodded, eyes trailing to the back of the land; there was a fence there, and behind it the flowers grew wild and purple. They looked almost exotic. 'And there *definitely* wasn't anybody else that might've had access to your car?' The subject had been well traversed, but I was looking for a fresh response now that we were out of the blanket of her brother's presence. 'There was nobody who – I don't know – might've slipped the contraband in there to *encourage* you to take it into the prison grounds?'

A hint of a frown knitted her eyebrows below the edge of her bandana. 'Nobody has access to my car except for me.'

'I appreciate that, but with all due respect, as I said yesterday, if you truly *were* the only person capable of getting into your vehicle, and the drugs really *were* found inside your vehicle, which by all accounts they were, then it doesn't present the jury with a whole lot of reasonable doubt, does it?'

She didn't answer. Whatever frown had been forming crumbled back to that familiar melancholic gaze.

'However,' I went on, 'as I also mentioned before, if we submit that you were acting under the assumption that you were carrying plain tobacco onto the premises, then I think we have a serious shot at challenging the prosecution's ability to prove your *mens rea*. The punishments for smuggling List C articles are considerably more lenient than those involving List A drugs.'

Still no answer. A mumble perhaps, almost inaudible.

I decided to get serious. 'We're running out of time to update our defence statement. If we delay it much longer, and *then* you decide to change your story, it may result in the jury drawing an adverse inference against you before we've even begun. The prosecution will jump on that. A trial is only fair if both sides, prosecution *and* defence, disclose their full plans of attack to one another in advance, to grant the opposing side a reasonable chance to prepare a counter-argument. If, on the other hand, you *knew* what was in your car all along, and somebody else did put you up to it, if you were pressured into smug—'

'If my mum says she didn't know,' Roland interjected hatefully from the fence, 'then she didn't know.'

In our ludicrous quartet we were quiet then, as if this twelve-year-old boy's really was the ultimate word.

Then, before we could continue, music started blaring from somewhere nearby. I wouldn't have paid it any mind if not for Charli's face, which visibly blanched at the sound.

The music circled the perimeter of Honeybone Allotments, drawing nearer; a high-performance engine growled through twin exhausts, and the combined racket reverberated from the perfect horseshoe of buildings across the road until it sounded like something out of *Apocalypse Now*, except that 'Ride of the Valkyries' had been replaced by Wagner's lesser known foray into thumping jungle beats.

Whatever change I had been looking for in Charli Meadows finally occurred. Her brown eyes swelled. She yanked off her gardening gloves and bandana. That same fight-or-flight tension that had marred her son's reception of us now stiffened her into a fragile, scarecrow paralysis. Zara and I followed her gaze back to the road and we all sat as erect as a trio of meerkats assessing the Kalahari.

The car, an immaculate white Audi RS8, came to a smooth stop, leaving a foot between the kerb and its custom gold alloys. The music followed its engine into deathly silence as the driver stepped out.

During this arrival, it was something altogether subtler that stole my attention. It was the downstairs window of the house next door to Charli's on the right. At the sound of the car, the netting had twitched aside, and a tiny old lady had appeared, shaking her head. By the time the driver had opened his door, the netting had fallen back into place.

For all his former attitude, Charli's son Roland now looked like a much smaller boy, eyes popping as if Father Christmas had just parked up his sleigh and brought his bottomless sack to Low Hall Lane. '*Deacon!*' he cried, not bothering to accuse this much cooler customer of being a spy sent here from the school.

It wasn't a bottomless sack that Deacon was carrying. It was a shopping bag in the distinguishable shade of Harrods green. I placed him as being six or seven years younger than

Charli, late twenties, a white lad with stylish jeans and a tight Stone Island jumper that spoke of a body he'd earned in the gym. His inquisitive eyes glinted out at us like broken diamonds from beneath his baseball cap as he sauntered straight for the allotments' gate.

Roland, looking as if he was about to wet himself with excitement, ran to meet him there.

'Wagwan, little man?' Deacon asked, and they clasped hands as he stepped through onto the grass.

'You know how it is, D!' Roland said, aiming for cool while his treacherous, boyish voice cracked and wavered. 'Just chillin. What you got in the bag? What is it?'

'What, this?' Deacon shrugged one shoulder. 'Ah, it's nothing …'

'Don't play with me!' Roland jumped between the allotments and booted the flowerpot I'd previously stepped over. 'What is it? What *is* it?'

Deacon held on to the bag a while longer, watching the kid bounce around like a firework in a tin box – he flashed a wink across the gardens to Charli, somehow failing to notice that the mother was a sculpture of mortification – and then yielded and tossed the bag to Roland. 'Now, if I hear about that damn dog getting anywhere near these …'

The kid screamed. *Screamed.* He tossed the bag onto the vegetation behind him and what was left in his hands was a black shoebox. I had to blink. It really said Gucci. 'Sick! Sick! *Siiiiick!*' He took the lid off and aimed the contents at us all, showing off a pair of white trainers with green-red-green striping on the sides and a distinctive bee embroidered in gold. 'D, you're the man! Wait until my boys see these! Just fucking wait!'

'Language!' Deacon said, aiming a playful slap at the boy's head, but Roland was already sprinting across the road towards the house. He opened the front door, moving quick enough to catch the dog inside, and slammed the door behind him. I caught only a glimpse of the animal before Charli recaptured my attention.

'*Deacon!*' she managed through gritted teeth. If a hole had appeared in the overturned soil right then, I would've put money on her climbing into it. 'I thought you weren't coming tonight.'

'I'm only popping on the way from the gym, babe.' Deacon grinned with sly, childlike defiance as he strolled through the bamboo maze towards us. 'What? I can't treat the boy for helping his mum out? Kid's going through enough shit lately.'

Nobody answered until my mouth did it for me. 'Gucci for skiving off school? Wish you'd been around when I was a boy.'

Those eyes, once playful jewels in the shadow of his cap, dulled. He looked me up and down, measuring my black coat, white shirt, black tie, hat. 'Who're you? Messengers of the Watchtower? You look like you've come to bless the ground.'

'Deacon,' Charli coughed, 'this is Elliot Rook, my barrister.'

'Barrister?' That caught his attention. 'What happened? They cancel the trial?'

'Not that I know of,' I told him. 'I had some things to discuss with my client.'

'*Your* client?' He passed us for Charli's side, leaving a draught of syrupy cologne between us, smells of a post-work-out shower. 'I thought she was Lydia's client. You some new sort of barristers that make house calls?' He slipped an arm around her waist. She allowed it but didn't appear to like it. In fact, she looked very much like most liars do when their deception is unexpectedly revealed to the court. She was smart enough to know what I must be thinking: if she had lied about having a boyfriend …

'They were in the area,' she answered for us, trying to stay onside.

'Where?' he asked. 'Snaresbrook?'

'That's right,' I said. 'You know it?'

He smirked. 'Shithole.'

'You have much experience in Crown courts?'

The following silence spoke loudly, and what it said was 'almost certainly'. Charli's face pulled back from regular humiliation into a bewildered grin of disbelief. The sun was going down now; Deacon adjusted the brim of his cap a degree to the right and sniffed.

'Still,' he said, 'I don't get what was so important that you couldn't arrange a proper meeting.'

'Dead men,' I told him flatly. 'Thirteen of them.'

I was glad to see the wind momentarily knocked out of his sails. He looked between us. 'They're adding those dead druggies to her charge?'

I didn't respond. I'd already had my fill of answering to the men in Charli's life and I didn't appreciate being lied to by my own clients. 'We should be going. Anything further we can discuss on Monday morning.' I was already on my feet when I motioned to Zara. 'Let's go.'

We were passing back through the gate into the road when Deacon shouted us, arm still wrapped around his woman's waist. 'Rook, is it?'

'Yes?'

'Maybe don't come around here again. You want to talk, you can sort out a meeting and make sure her solicitor is involved, all right?'

I looked at Charli for confirmation. She looked away.

I tipped my hat. 'Whatever you say, D. Whatever you say.' And left.

Zara and I didn't speak until we'd circled the curve in the lane and made it back to my car, which was parked well out of sight of Charli's plot.

'What was that all about?' she asked, settling into the passenger seat. 'I'm guessing by the look on her face that she didn't mention her flashy fella before today?'

'No,' I said. 'In fact, she outright denied having a partner.'

'That's interesting.' She met my eye knowingly. '*Very* interesting.'

'Not as interesting as the dog,' I said. 'That was a Dogo Argentino.'

11

'Feels like we're on a stakeout,' Zara said, lifting her Doc Martens up onto the dashboard. 'Got any binoculars?'

'No. Now get those bloody boots off the walnut.'

She rolled her eyes as she lowered her feet and went back to her phone.

I'd turned the car round so that it was facing in the same general direction as Deacon's, to save us staring straight at him when he came round the corner.

Five minutes passed. Ten. It got darker.

At first, I'd been genuinely concerned for the safety of the Meadows brood – there was something about Deacon that had rubbed me up the wrong way as soon as I'd heard him coming – but, on reflection, Charli's son's excitement wasn't much cause for concern. Still, my hunch remained.

I was watching the rear-view mirror, in which I could see both the bend in the road and my own eyes. 'Do we really look like Jehovah's Witnesses?' I asked.

'Probably. You do, anyway.'

'I should buy some new clothes.'

'Probably,' Zara said again. 'At least we know who put those drugs in the car.'

I turned to face her; she didn't look up from her phone.

'Might as well say what we're both thinking,' she continued. 'I have to admit, I did think our Keyser Söze would look a bit more impressive than Slim Shady on steroids, but there you go.'

'We don't know anything for sure.'

'No? Growing up on my estate, I saw a lot of drug wagons. Now *that*, my learned friend, was a drug dealer's car. He rocks up with his gold alloys, dressed in a few hundred quid's worth of clothes, gives his girlfriend's kid a pair of £500 trainers and just so happens to be familiar with the local courts. He put the drugs in the car. Next case, Your Honour.'

I clicked my tongue. 'You know, you wouldn't make a very good spy, staring at your phone like that. It's lighting up the whole car.'

'Research.'

'How's that?'

'I'm rereading that National Crime Agency piece from last year: "County Lines Violence, Exploitation and Drug Supply".'

'I can save you the time,' I said, eyes back on the mirror. 'It's a simple enough tactic. A group of dealers establishes an untraceable, disposable mobile phone line between their urban base and a distant county location. Orders are placed on that one phone line, and the group will typically exploit vulnerable persons, usually children, to travel out to whichever county whenever there's stock to be replenished and cash to be collected. Seaside towns are a popular choice. If a child is nicked it's no big loss to the dealers. A young offender can only receive a limited punishment and, as far as their bosses are concerned, they're expendable.'

'I know that, but there's something in particular I wanted to check over ... Ah, here it is. *Cuckooing*. Basically, it's when a gang operates from the home of a susceptible person, typically a drug addict or sex worker, although this report also includes the elderly and people with mental or physical health impairments. Often, it says, cuckooing involves a drug dealer who forms a relationship with a single mother, essentially tricking her into feeling loved while using the house for storage of their product. Sound familiar, considering what we've just seen?'

'It's certainly persuasive,' I had to admit.

'I'd bet my tenancy on it. Then there's the fighting dog. Didn't you tell me those are rare?'

'Very. Werner, the breeder I defended, told me they were being bred for specific people. It sounded as if he was talking about a gang.'

'A gang like the Cutthroats?'

'Quite possibly,' I admitted.

'And they're used for guarding the homes of dealers?'

'Often.'

'Then she's probably guilty,' she said.

'Remember not to confuse guilty with whether or not she has done it,' I replied. 'Guilty is a jury verdict, and that's a long way away. We trust in the system. That's justice.'

'I know,' she said, 'but you've been doing this long enough. Surely there've been a couple of cases you've wanted to lose.'

'Never. I want to win them all, and I try my best to do so.'

She inhaled deeply. 'Because that's what the client deserves, right?'

'That's right.'

Our wait continued. Another couple of minutes passed before Zara started to speak, hesitated, then started again. 'I ... I messaged Omar Pickett.'

I turned to face her. 'You did *what*?'

'Only through Facebook,' she replied quickly. 'And Instagram. Twitter ... Oh, and Snapchat.'

'Zara!' I groaned.

'Uh-oh. You only ever call me by my first name when I'm in trouble.'

'You bloody well might be! That was a thoroughly unprofessional, dangerous, *stupid* thing to do.'

'But this could be the solution to my whole case! This guy Omar is supposedly on the run from his own gang, so he's got nowhere else to go. My client, Andre, was arrested in *his* place. All I said was that I wanted him to talk to me. If he does that, then maybe I could get him into witness protection in exchange for any information he has on –'

'What about your *own* safety?' I snapped. 'Did you stop for one moment to consider the possible ramifications? You've personally messaged a drug dealer, a fugitive for Christ's sake. It is totally irresponsible.'

'Really?' She looked me dead in the eyes. 'How's your dog?'

I opened my mouth. A few seconds later, I closed it again and turned my shoulder on her. After another minute of silence, music started playing from her phone. A hard, thumping, electronic beat with dark, slow, almost sludgy rapping over it. At first, I thought it was in a different language altogether, but there were definitely parts from the *Oxford English Dictionary*. Something about gutting somebody's infant sister and burning down a hospital, as far as I could make out.

'What the hell is this?' I grumbled.

'This,' she said, 'is Omar Pickett.'

It was enough to snag my curiosity. Reluctantly, I looked at her screen. A YouTube video. In it, a figure in a tracksuit was gesticulating in the half-pipe of an otherwise empty, graffiti-covered skatepark. He appeared to be a very young man, and he also appeared to be rapping along to the dubbed track, though both were hard to confirm as he was wearing a mask that completely concealed his identity. The mask was fabric and painted with a sinister red skull.

Unimpressed, I huffed. 'How can you even tell who that is?'

'He doesn't try to hide it on social media. The mask seems to be for effect. His rapping alias is Post Mortem but, sure enough, that is Omar Pickett. Eighteen-year-old drill musician, former student of Leyton Sixth Form College, and the final, elusive dealer from my drug bust.'

'A drill musician ...' I could hear my own annoyance succumbing to interest. 'That would explain how Andre Israel recognised him in the pub.'

'Oh, there's more. A lot more. Listen to this ...'

She played a twenty-second clip of the song. Rewound it and played it again, looking at me attentively.

I shrugged. 'What am I supposed to be listening for?'

'Can't you hear it? Though to be fair it took me a few listens to pick it up myself.'

She played it once more. I shook my head. 'I'm not getting anything,' I said.

'He says: "Cutthroats pulling them strings / Unlucky number's feeling the wrath / Gaza Strip caught up in things / Sorry, Palestine–Israel's off!"' She tapped the screen excitedly. 'This was uploaded a month ago!'

I frowned, working it out. 'He's rapping about the bust?'

'Yes! Think about it! Unlucky number – that's *thirteen* – feeling the wrath. And the Gaza Strip caught up in things –'

'Andre Israel.'

'Exactly.' She silenced the music, exhaling deeply, a day's pent-up secret finally off her chest.

'In that case,' I said, 'Omar Pickett might as well paint a great big target onto that mask of his. He uploaded it himself?'

'That one, yes, though his older material all seems to have come through Banged Up Records, a YouTube channel based in the East End, which also happened to post music by ...'

'Andre Israel?'

'Yep.'

'Jesus. I don't suppose Israel spent any time rapping about being either a drug dealer or an innocent jogger, did he?'

'Never. In fact, as far as drill music goes, his material was pretty tame. Seemed to be social commentary as opposed to direct threats, from what I've heard.'

'That's good for his trial at least. The last thing you need is for the prosecution to pull out a lyrical confession. Post Mortem, on the other hand ... he's hardly Bob Dylan.'

She shrugged. 'You don't like hip hop?'

'No, I like hip hop just fine. Public Enemy. Grandmaster Flash and the Furious Five. Run DMC. This sounds like a whole different genre to me.'

'Hey, I'm not saying drill is my own personal cup of tea, but I do think it's getting unfairly condemned in the media. If the papers are anything to go by, this music is partly responsible for nearly every violent crime in the city, which just isn't true. I think it's another case of art imitating life, not the other way around.'

'I don't know,' I said doubtfully. 'I'm not surprised it's under fire with lyrics like those. It sounds to me like nothing but inflammatory instigation.'

She tapped her boots; the car was getting chilly. 'You were big into punk music, weren't you? Didn't that cause a similar – I don't know – moral panic?'

'That was different,' I said. 'Punk was anti-establishment, it wasn't anti-individuals.'

'No? I bet there were plenty of individuals who would disagree.'

'Perhaps you're right, but this drill is –'

'Wait!' Zara said abruptly. 'Look!'

Slick headlights were coming round the bend behind us; they blazed through my rear window, illuminating the inside of the car, and in unison we pushed back against our seats, Zara crouching slightly, to hide ourselves. The Audi passed. There was a speed bump at the end of the lane; it slowed there, indicating right to turn onto Markhouse Road. I noted the registration number in case we lost the car. It wasn't hard to memorise: DM1.

'Well,' Zara said, 'looks like he was only popping in after all. Now what?'

'He's turning south,' I said. 'That's towards Leyton ...'

Zara met my eye. Ahead, Deacon turned the corner, disappearing from view. 'What shall we do?' she asked.

'In the films, what usually happens after a stakeout?'

She shrugged. 'They'd put a tail on him?'

'That's right.' I turned the key in the ignition. 'They would.'

He was easy enough to follow, bright white between street lights, music blaring, carefully obeying every speed limit. He followed the same road south for a little more than a mile until it entered Leyton and turned into Church Road, at which time he indicated left past St Mary's Parish Church.

'Shit,' I muttered. 'He's turning onto the Grange estate.'

'So?' Zara asked. 'Have you got a problem with estates?'

'No problem.' I flicked my own indicator. 'Don't forget that you're talking to a man who was raised on a slum.'

'Glad to hear it.' She didn't sound glad; her voice had turned an octave sharper. She must've known, as I did, that we were entering the stronghold of the so-called E10 Cutthroats.

The Grange was a housing complex of ten prefabricated four-storey courts built around the bottom of a lofty block of flats called Slade Tower; it was well known as one of the most deprived areas in Waltham Forest. Shadowing the Audi had been simple enough on the straight, clear route down into Leyton, but now we were following it into a cramped maze of single lanes, tight corners and stunted roads. It didn't help that there was nobody else around, making the presence of our headlights extremely conspicuous. Most of the flats in the courts had balconies with clothing hanging from makeshift washing lines. Some had hung sheets of cotton or hessian up there for privacy. Several of the parked cars I negotiated between had tarpaulin over broken windows.

'Reminds me of home,' Zara said.

Each court had caging around its outer doors and a blue sign illuminated by an overhanging lamp. I clocked them as we passed: Fitzgerald Court, Underwood Court, a sharp right to Clewer Court and a left past Cochrane, another left past Allanson and Eton Manor, then it was another two quick corners to Fitzgerald and Underwood, a sharp right to Clewer Court …

'Hold on.' I slowed down to double-check the last sign. 'Bollocks.'

'What?' Zara sounded alarmed.

'He's on to us.'

'What makes you say that?'

'He's leading us in circles.'

'He must be lost,' she said. 'I'll bet that's why he's on his phone.'

'His phone?' As we came up behind him on the next short stretch, I could see the dim glow of a phone against his ear. 'Maybe you're right.'

This time he took a different turn and I let him gain a few seconds before following through the car park of Slade Tower; the ten-storey block had warm lights behind closed curtains and red steel balconies at every level, but I still couldn't see anybody around. A moment later, even the Audi was gone.

'Where'd he go?' Zara was craning her neck in all directions.

'I don't know.' I turned back out onto another slender one-lane road, then another. Somehow, they seemed to be getting narrower.

Then Zara shrieked, making me jump out of my skin. 'Watch out!'

I slammed my foot onto the brake and we were both shunted forwards into the hard grasps of our seat belts.

Something metal – two things, in fact – had come rolling out of the darkness on either side, directly into our path. They were bicycles, one rolling from the pavement to the left and another from the right. Without passengers they wobbled unsteadily, as if the owners had simply vanished, then crashed into one another with almost expert precision and clattered to the tarmac, blocking the road.

'What the ...?' I looked around for the riders.

Something was wrong with the picture outside. It took me another moment to realise what it was. Every street light on this particular stretch was out. The nearest lights were those in the highest windows of the flats on either side.

I looked at Zara and her face was stiff. With one elbow, she slammed the lock down on her door. 'Lock your door,' she breathed.

'Excuse me?'

'The door!'

I was turning to do it when my attention was stolen by a child in front of my car. Ten, maybe eleven years old at a push, dressed entirely in black with his hood up. I assumed he was going to pick up the bikes and be on his merry way. Instead, he came to a standstill in front of my bonnet as if we were playing some stationary game of chicken. I blasted the full beams to move him along; from that distance, the light turned his skin the colour of spoiled milk with freckles, making his green eyes burn while casting an enormous shadow up the road behind him.

Instinct brought my hand to the horn.

'Don't!' Zara started, but the hand was already down, and I held it there for a hearty five or six seconds. Even with the horn close enough to blow him backwards, the kid didn't even blink.

Then I saw the rest of them. Five. Ten. Twenty. More.

They were everywhere, not a single one of them old enough to shave. Boys and girls, black, white, Asian, it didn't matter, almost all with their hood up or hat pulled low. They were standing on the pavement and the grassy verge behind it; there were even some watching silently from the balconies, faces no more distinguishable than those of smooth plastic dolls in the shadows. They'd appeared as if from nowhere, like the birds in Hitchcock's eerie film. A sickness started to rise up from my stomach.

There were two dull thumps behind us before I'd even shifted into reverse, and when I checked the mirrors I saw two heavy wheelie bins dumped on their sides there, blocking me in. Back at the front, the boy had now turned his attention to the chrome jaguar emblem leaping from the bonnet, and he was wrapping both hands around it.

'Oi!' I yelled, slamming the horn again. 'Get your hands off my –'

I didn't even notice my door opening until the interior light flared above our heads. Here was another boy, this one older with severe acne across both cheeks, holding a knife that looked bigger than his forearm and pulling on the door with all his might.

'Get out of the fucking car!' is what I think he said, though I couldn't hear much above Zara's own yelling. I managed to catch the door just in time and yanked it back with both hands. The boy might've been armed, but I weighed twice what he did; his knife-arm got caught in the first slam, causing it to bend horribly, and on the second attempt I got it closed and locked.

I revved the car, inching forwards until I touched the first boy's waist. Instead of moving aside he simply clambered up onto the bonnet and balanced there, brightly coloured trainers on steel, bending down to pull at the jaguar as if it was a stubborn weed in the garden.

By now the rest of the children had come closer. They surrounded the car, pressing their faces up against the glass, howling with laughter.

'Nice car, fat man!' one of the girls jeered.

Zara held her phone up for them all to see, took a deep breath that sounded shaky with adrenaline and yelled: 'Fuck off, you little pricks! I'm ringing the police! You're all in for –'

She was interrupted by a dense clunk as the first boy went flying backwards off the bonnet. He landed among the fallen bicycles and held the jaguar emblem up high like a trophy.

'You little fucker!' I roared. The rest of the children began to cheer.

What came next sounded like a hailstorm of biblical proportions; rocks, shoes and makeshift weapons of all denominations began slamming off steel and glass. Two whacks and both wing mirrors went spinning off into the dark. I heard air escaping the tyres as something sickeningly heavy bounced across the roof. A chunk of concrete fell straight through the rear window with a loud crunch.

I reversed several feet, shunting the bins backwards until I had enough room for a decent run-up, then I hit the accelerator. For a split second, it looked as if the boy with the bicycles wasn't going to move. He soon realised that I had no intention of stopping and rolled aside.

The bicycles screamed beneath the wheels, and the car veered from side to side as the children gave chase with their bricks and knives. At the end of the road we bounced up over a grass verge and came down hard, and I looked into the rear-view mirror in time to see the first bicycle fall away in a shower of sparks, taking what looked like my exhaust pipe with it.

The boy with the jaguar was fast. He followed for two roads before giving up and waving us off with two fingers high in the air. I kept my eyes on him through the empty frame of the rear window until we turned the next corner and made it back onto Church Road.

The entire ordeal had lasted no more than a minute and a half.

Zara was still trying to control her panicky breathing, but my mind remained on the boy from the bonnet.

'That little bastard's trainers ...' I growled.

'Wh-what about them?'

'Did they look like Gucci to you, too?'

PART TWO

OLD FLAMES

12

I wasn't just livid. I was devastated.

Shallow as it might have seemed, rusted though it certainly was, that car had been the driving force behind my aspirations ever since I'd been homeless, when I'd first come across an identical, brand-new model owned by a barrister back in 1987. To me, it was more than a vehicle. It was a turning point in my youth, a physical reward in my thirties, a trusted companion in later life and the only thing I'd kept from the divorce.

Now it was ruined.

The furious hooligan of my past wanted revenge; it seemed obvious to me that Deacon had lured us into a trap and then called for backup. The seasoned barrister of my present insisted that Deacon might not have been to blame.

Wrong time. Wrong place. Wrong decision to follow him at all.

I was out of my flat half an hour before sunrise on Wednesday morning, sometime around six, hoping to get the car moved before the roads started to fill. Already there were a couple of early starters dressed in suits hovering on the pavement beside the Jag, muttering between themselves. I couldn't blame them. Despite dumping it as far away from the nearest street light as I could manage, it didn't look any better than when I'd left it there last night.

The rear window was shattered over the back seats. Deep white cracks rippled across the windows and quarter glass of both rear doors. The driver's door was dented, the passenger side scratched. A headlight was broken. There were no wing mirrors to speak of and only a hole from where the jaguar itself had once leapt.

'Morning,' I said politely, stepping between the onlookers to unlock the door.

'M-morning?' one of them said.

'Supposed to be another warm one today,' I noted, climbing in behind the wheel.

The man cleared his throat. 'That's … That's great.'

I nodded. 'Well, have a good one,' I said and shut the door.

The car started, which was a blessing, though without an exhaust it sounded like heavy artillery fire and the bystanders recoiled a couple of feet. The chassis shook so furiously that one of the cracked panes collapsed inwards from the door directly behind me. I flared the one headlight as if I hadn't noticed, waved a casual farewell, then chuntered slowly up the road.

I'd been searching online for a reliable mechanic when the idea had come to me. It wasn't the most sensible thing to do, driving east across the centre of the city, but it seemed to have at least a little poetic value, so I rattled all the way to Hackney Wick.

It was a peculiar spot for a garage, I thought, inexplicably tucked away on Rothbury Road between a few discount furniture warehouses and an enormous building site advertising a complex of unfinished spacious apartments for sale. The entire length of the building site was hidden behind panelling that was, in turn, smothered in vibrant graffiti. Right alongside that, camouflaged in the same palette of spray paint, was a garage with a small, almost imperceptible sign: Meadows Motors.

The place didn't open until eight – it was a couple of minutes past seven – but I'd only just managed to get the car up against the kerb when the garage door lifted, and Charli's brother came out like a hungry man to the sound of a dinner bell. He was dressed in a beanie hat and overalls and his face widened into something between a horrified gape and a grin when he saw the mess I was driving; the pound signs were practically visible in his eyes. From behind him, another mechanic appeared, this one remarkably handsome with long red hair, a Norse deity of a man who was apparently apathetic to the cacophony.

'Elliot Rook!' Delroy Meadows said as I got out of the car. 'What'd you do, enter into one of those demolition derbies?'

'Kids,' I replied. 'Think you can work some magic on her?'

He drew air between his teeth in a pained hiss and circled the car, admiring the mob's handiwork with a stern, appraising look. 'Well, she's never going to dance again.'

'A write-off?' The air caught in my throat.

'Hard to say for sure without getting underneath her for a look.'

'Whatever it takes.'

He turned to his employee and gesticulated with both hands, signing. The employee did the same back. They conversed silently like that. For a moment, I had the funny idea that this was a neat trick, something they'd learned

135

between themselves to privately discuss how badly they could fleece their customers. But mechanics would never need to go to such lengths to have a customer's pants down.

Delroy caught my eye. 'Danny here's a deaf-mute. Like that pinball song.'

'I think that's a rather outdated way of putting it,' I told him.

He shrugged. 'Who's he going to tell?'

Danny, who had been watching our lips closely, pointed a finger at Delroy and then began to beat his own chest with both fists like a gorilla. They both laughed, Danny silently, and shadow-boxed one another. I felt acutely out of place.

Delroy checked his watch. 'We've got a couple of MOTs in this morning but, as my sister's future rests squarely on your shoulders … Come inside and I'll get you a coffee. Leave your keys with the Pinball Wizard over here.'

I removed the car key from the ring and Danny caught it one-handed.

Inside a back office, Delroy poured us coffees from a twenty-year-old machine that sounded like a circular saw. There was a simple desk on a carpet that was blackened and greasy with boot prints, and a shelf of motoring manuals. The place smelled of oil, iron and leather, the perfumes of hard graft. There was an interior window overlooking the garage floor. I watched Danny, who was down on one knee peering up at the bottom of my raised car. He was shaking his head. His face was almost ageless; he could've been anywhere between twenty and fifty.

'Here,' Delroy said, handing me the coffee.

'Appreciate it.' The cup was thin white plastic; I used my cuff to shield my palm from the heat.

'Hope this has got nothing to do with your job?'

'Mindless vandalism, that's all.'

'Huh.' He cocked his head. 'You take it to the police yet?'

'No. The police and I have a turbulent relationship at the best of times.'

Delroy sipped his own drink, oblivious to the scald, and watched Danny work. 'We have a bit of banter, me and him, but he's a good lad. Came here a couple of years ago, recommendation from one of them communication charities, and never left. Like a partner to me now. The guy's a genius with a spray gun.'

'He looks like he knows what he's doing. Have you always known sign language?'

'Few phrases, that's all. It looks as if I know a lot more than I really do. I went to – shit, I don't even know what you're supposed to call it these days – a special school. Had a couple of deaf kids in my class. I wasn't the brightest boy. Suppose that's why I get a little bitter with Charli sometimes. She must've got the bigger slice of brains when we were in the womb, but she's never done anything with them.'

I froze, with the coffee at my lips. 'I didn't realise you were twins.'

He shrugged. 'Since before we were born.'

I was quiet for a moment, reflecting on what Patch had told us about Roy Macey and his mysterious twins. The Meadows twins? It seemed highly unlikely, not least on the incongruity of race. Adopted? Equally unlikely … Wasn't it? I must've been staring quite intently because Delroy rolled his eyes and shook his head.

'Before you ask,' he said, 'the answer is no.'

'No?'

'No. We can't read each other's minds and we don't share bruises or none of that.'

'Oh.' I smiled. 'Well, I did wonder.'

He took another long sip of coffee, breathing heavily through his nose. 'Look, if I came across a bit abrupt the other morning ...'

'It must be a stressful time.'

'You don't know the half of it. It's like your car over there, in a way. To me, that car's just another job on the worksheet. For you, those wheels are your way of life. Vice versa – to you, my sister is another couple of weeks in the courthouse. For her, for us all, it could be her life. You understand that, don't you?'

'I do.'

'She's not a bad woman by any means. She's a *great* mum. Just got herself a habit for making crap decisions. Men, mostly.' Over his cup, he gave me a shrewd look; so he knew about my visit to the allotment last night.

'She lied about him,' I said. 'Deacon. You both did.'

'Her decision.'

'Doesn't look very good from where I'm standing.'

'No,' he agreed, 'I suppose it doesn't.'

I had half an urge to seize him by the overalls, to scream all manner of obscenities regarding what I would like to do to his prospective brother-in-law. 'She said nobody else had access to that car,' I managed coolly. 'I can't see it being too difficult for this Deacon to have got hold of her keys.'

Delroy shook his head. 'That's where you're wrong. At the time it happened, it would've been pretty damn difficult for him to get anywhere *near* that car.'

138

'Why's that?'

He swirled his coffee, contemplating. 'She didn't tell you how they met?'

'No.' It took another few seconds for the pieces to come together. 'Not the Scrubs?'

He nodded regretfully. 'Deacon only got out last month.'

'Drugs?'

He blinked: yes.

'That explains her reluctance to introduce him from the beginning,' I said.

'Can't blame her, can you?'

I shrugged. 'Financially, he appears to be doing rather well since his release. Would it be so unreasonable to suggest that she might've been taking the Spice in to him all along?'

He turned his whole body to lean back against the window. 'What do you expect me to say to that? She's my sister.'

'She doesn't seem to be demonstrating much caution towards their relationship. I've only been up to her home once and I've already met him by chance. There's no mention of him in the prosecution's case, nothing that has been disclosed so far at least, but if they *do* become aware of this relationship, well, I'd say it writes a rather convincing story.'

'And are you obliged to tell them?'

I met his eye. 'Is that a legal question? Or an ethical one?'

He bowed his head over his drink, preparing to take another mouthful, then a sharp knock on the glass behind caused him to jump and spill coffee onto his overalls. He spun round so that his employee could read his lips when he shouted. 'For fuck's sake, Danny!'

139

Danny was standing on the other side, looking deeply concerned. With his left hand he was holding up a mass of twisted metal that dangled from his grip like a pheasant's carcass. It took me a second to recognise what it was: a mangled fusion of exhaust pipe, chain and a single bicycle pedal.

'Jesus,' Delroy said. 'We're not going to find one of these kids underneath there, are we?'

I left the car there along with my phone number and walked a block north to Hackney Wick Station, passing the Lord Napier, the nineteenth-century pub that was now also obscured by graffiti. One of the most noticeable pieces read *Shithouse to Penthouse*. I was feeling quite the opposite.

From the station, I had to take the Overground west to Stratford, where I would then be able to change onto the Central Line heading back east towards chambers. It was eight o'clock now and the platforms were crowded. I managed to get a seat on the Overground, but my sheer size pressed against strangers on either side, and when my phone rang in my pocket I almost couldn't get my hand down to reach it. For a split second I imagined it would be Delroy Meadows telling me that they had indeed found part of a child tangled up in one of the wheel arches, and that the Met was on its way.

Thankfully, it was Zara. Conscious of my elbows, I slid the phone up to my ear. 'Yes?'

'How did it go?'

'Well,' I said, 'they found one of that little shit's bicycle pedals caught up in my rear wheel, so I'll be amazed if I'm not in handcuffs by the end of the day.' At this, those sitting nearest glanced up from their phones. I resolved to keep my voice down. 'Where are you now?'

'Just coming up to chambers. Are we still going to Belmarsh to meet this drug dealer?'

'Isaac Reid. Yes, I'm on my way to meet you now.'

'How are we supposed to get there?'

I sighed. 'I can think of a number of unattractive options involving public transport. Black cab, I suppose.'

'Uber's cheaper.'

'As is using slave labour instead of paying the London living wage, but my conscience votes for black cab.'

'If only our legal system shared your conscience, then I might actually have an income.'

13

I was watching the taxi meter closely, which mounted higher and higher every several seconds until it was surely bound to equal the Greek deficit figure.

'Have you learned anything more about Reid?' Zara asked.

'Very little,' I said. 'Already convicted of double murder and given a life sentence with a minimum of thirty-five years to serve before he's eligible for parole. His family are paying us privately, a modest amount, to advise on whether or not he has any realistic prospect of appealing the conviction.'

'He was given to you through Percy?'

'Not quite. I was actually recommended to him by, ah – by Billy Barber.'

'Oh, awesome! I *love* meeting the fascists of Belmarsh.' She lowered her voice, grumbling. 'And my ex used to moan about her job at Primark ...'

We arrived at the prison and, after paying the taxi driver almost the sum I was being paid to advise Reid, I moodily surrendered myself to the familiar torturous groping of Belmarsh's security staff.

It was twenty minutes before we were led through the legal visitors' corridor to the cell where Reid was waiting for us. He was a powerfully built black man of around fifty with dreadlocks as thick as rope. He greeted the two of us with an open, engaging smile; in that smile, his teeth were stained deep yellow.

'Mr Reid,' I said, taking a seat across the table. 'I'm Elliot Rook. This is Zara Barnes.'

'Isaac,' he replied softly. 'And just like that, we're all friends. So, my good-good people, what are my chances of appealing this shit?'

'I'm sorry,' Zara interrupted, raising her hand like a pupil in a classroom. 'If you don't mind, there's one preliminary matter I'd like to ask you about ...'

'Go on, little one,' he said. It didn't seem patronising. His tone was rather warm.

'Our services were recommended to you by an ex-client named Barber, is that correct?'

'That's right,' he said. 'Billy Barber. So?'

'So ...?' She looked between us, frowning. 'William Barber is a white supremacist, a racist to the core, and you're – you're –'

'A Black man?!' Reid shouted. Then, after holding out for a second or two longer, he exploded into booming, almost deafening laughter. 'I'm sorry, little one, but you should've seen your face!' He wiped a knuckle across one leaking eye as the hysterics quietened to a chuckle. 'Priceless.'

Zara didn't seem so amused. Her front teeth were set into her lower lip, hands gripping the edge of the table to keep from being huffed and puffed into oblivion.

Once more, Reid was smiling. 'In here, a man is just another con. Barber was all right by me. We padded together until he was taken into high security, but he told me he was going to get this Rook onboard. Next thing I know, Barber's a free man. You must have the golden touch, my friend. The question is, will you be doing the same for me?'

'I hope so,' I replied. 'Why don't you tell me a little more about the night in question. You *were* somehow connected to the killings, weren't you?'

'Unwittingly. I cruised over to Margate with a mate of mine from London to meet a couple of ladies off Tinder. You know how that game goes. Tinderellas, I call them.' He glanced to Zara and waggled his eyebrows. She didn't respond. 'Only, when we got to Margate, this mate of mine started giving me the business. He wanted driving here, he wanted driving there. I must've looked like I was *Driving Miss Daisy*.' He sat up straight, imitating Morgan Freeman with the steering wheel in both hands. 'Um, yes'm, boss! Lord knows! I used to rassle hogs down yonder!'

I blinked. 'Your friend was white, I take it?'

The act quickly vanished, his face flinching as if he'd given too much away. 'Long story short,' he said, 'this supposed mate of mine had promised these Tinderellas a wild night.'

'What sort of a wild night?'

'Well, I don't want to use the term "coke-fuelled orgy" in front of a little one, but …'

'He wanted drugs,' I said.

'You got it. Now, I was pretty baked. The next thing I knew, I was giving a lift to two of his mates I didn't know. All there was to do, they said, was drop them off back at their place, where my boy would pick up the sniff, and then we'd be nothing but a couple of princes on our way to the ball. The sexy ball, you feel me?'

144

'Yes,' Zara said. 'I think we got that.'

He grinned softly. 'We turned up to the place and I waited outside while they went in.'

'And let me guess,' I offered, 'instead of collecting the drugs, the dealers were killed.'

'Of course,' he said, the grin somehow remaining. 'I couldn't even tell you how long I was sitting out there behind the wheel. Hours I guess, but the sirens woke me up. The police said I went in with one of those, what do you call them? Zombie knives. This thing was still sticking out of some fool's chest.'

'And this mate of yours?' I asked. 'The one you'd driven from London.'

'Slipped out the back door and left me behind.'

'So,' Zara said, 'one more time, if you don't mind. This friend of yours wants drugs. The local dealers aren't home, so he presumably makes a phone call and you have to go and pick them up. These two dealers willingly get into your vehicle and show you to their place. Then, as soon as all three men are inside, your friend turns around and kills them both?'

'That's it. That's been my argument all along. They had this dog, you see. Big fucker. Pure white. An Argentino, they call it. Mexican or something. I don't know how anybody could pull a knife with that fucker around and still get out of there without either wasting the dog first or getting torn up enough to leave a hefty trail of DNA behind.'

'The dog was loose in the same room at the time?' I asked.

'Yep.'

'How can you be certain?'

A grim chuckle, darkening his eyes to something far less friendly. 'By the time Old Bill got there, the animal had turned hungry and been at one of the bodies. Guts everywhere. A real mess. The first pig to walk into the place lost half his left hand. He's scarred up to the shoulder now. He managed to put a taser into the dog and gave it a heart attack, which killed any chance of being able to prove that the mutt wouldn't recognise me.'

'Why would these two dealers have done that?' I mused. 'I mean, why would they invite their own killer inside? A rival from London, no less?'

'Isn't that obvious?' Reid leaned forward. 'These players weren't rivals. They were part of the same game. Word is these two dealers, they were sort of, like, end-of-the-line pushers.'

'For a county lines operation?' Zara asked, briefly catching my eye.

'If that's what they're calling it.' He shrugged. 'They get given a place to live, an area to run, and even their own dog to hold the stash. It's like a franchise. Only, these fools decided to cheat the system. They had their hands in the till. Management aren't into that, so they sent someone down from head office to have a word. Start afresh.'

'Did the men talk between themselves in your car?' I asked. 'Did they seem amicable?'

'That's the fucked-up thing,' he said. 'My mate – former mate, I should say – acted like he didn't know them at all. He was making out he got this number from somebody else, but he *had* to have known them, right? Shit, this dog's territorial enough to rip a cop's hand off, but it lets a stranger put a knife through its owners.'

'Maybe the dog was scared of the knife?' Zara tried.

'I doubt it,' I said. 'I've seen the breed and I don't believe they'd back down from anything. Not unless ...' I fell momentarily quiet.

Yes, I had seen them. They'd been savage, incredibly so, right up until Jacob Werner had arrived. But was it really Werner they were afraid of? Or was it something he'd said?

'Obey ...' I muttered to myself.

Reid tipped his head. 'Come again?'

'What if it wasn't the face they recognised?' I asked. 'What if the management, as you call them, have a keyword already trained into the animals?'

At my side, Zara snapped her fingers. 'Of course! This guy walks in and pulls a knife. The dog rears up, but before anything happens your mate says the magic word and the dog falls onto its haunches!'

Reid shook his head in disbelief. 'Holy shit. You *are* worth the money. Does this mean you could get me out?'

'The story is logical enough,' I said, 'but there's a gaping flaw, as far as your defence is concerned.'

'Which is?'

'The prosecution could simply suggest that you *were* the killer invited inside. That there was no mate to begin with. You made it past the dog the same way your so-called friend must have, because *you* were the assassin sent there by management. Then, when you pulled the knife, you said the magic word.'

His face sank. 'What I just told you is the truth. I wouldn't even know the damn word!'

'That may be so, but can't you see the hole? Unless you can somehow prove that you never left that car, then your appeal would be lost before it begins. Although ...'

147

'Although?' His ears perked.

'There could be another way,' I said. 'Tell the truth. The entire truth. Throw the real killer under the bus.'

Every bit of humour left the room. 'Are you serious?' he asked.

'Why not?' Zara joined. 'Your mate left you behind to take the fall. He's out there right now enjoying the freedom that should be yours.'

'I don't care. I won't roll on him.'

'So, tell us about the gang instead,' I pressed. 'You seem to know enough about their business. Do they have a name?'

'No. I don't know.'

'How about the E10 Cutthroats?' Zara asked.

That, apparently, was the final straw. 'What the fuck is going on here?' he snapped. 'I hired you for advice about my appeal, and here you are grilling me like a couple of cops! I think you'd both better get out of here before I lose my famous cool.'

'Mr Reid,' I tried, 'Isaac, I really do think we could help you, if you'd just be willing to give us –'

'No.' He held up a hand as large as a stop sign. 'You think I was born yesterday? You're into something, the pair of you, and I want fuck all to do with it.' He stood up and walked past us for the door; he banged on it and the warder opened it from the other side. 'I might not want to spend the rest of my life in this place, but I do want to have a rest of my life.'

Then he asked the guard to take him back to his cell, and our conference was over.

I had no choice but to let Zara order an Uber on her phone to take us back to central London, which was an hour's drive away, after promising to transfer the fee before it ever tried to leave her empty account. I hadn't slept much after the destruction of my car, so all I really wanted to do was get home.

'I'm going to take the dog for a walk,' I said. 'Try to clear my head and forget all about last night. Come along, if you want. I could use a designated scooper.'

'Wow, thanks, but no thanks. I've had Andre's bail application listed at Snaresbrook for tomorrow afternoon, and I'm still struggling to decide on the change in circumstances that will even justify me making it.'

'You'll figure it out,' I said. 'I've no doubt.'

'Yeah, right. And maybe tonight I'll get a lucky break, and his circumstances really will change.'

'Perhaps they will,' I said.

And overnight, they did.

14

I was back in Regent's Park the following morning, waiting patiently for Scout's first ablutions of the day, when my phone rang. Zara.

'Morning,' I yawned. 'You were wise to avoid yesterday's walk; my legs feel like they've been put through one of those –'

'The police have issued Andre with an Osman warning!'

It woke me like a slap to the ear. 'A threat to his life?'

'Yes!' She was panting, breathless, the line whistling as she raced through standing air. 'They've received intelligence of a threat on his life if he stays –' the blast of a car horn '– *it's a zebra crossing, dickhead!* – if he stays at the Scrubs!'

'Did they say who wants him dead?' At this, two fellow dog walkers glanced in consternation and gave me a wide berth.

'Don't know. Haven't spoken properly!'

'Where are you now?' I asked.

'Just left home, I've got to be at Snaresbrook in an hour. They've moved the hearing forward and they're bringing Andre from the prison!'

'I'd say this is a good enough change in circumstances to warrant that second bail application.'

'My thoughts exactly. Where are you? What are you doing?'

'Walking Scout, but I could be at Snaresbrook in an hour if you wanted me there.'

'Do it! I'm off underground. Meet you there!'

And she hung up.

Snaresbrook Crown Court is a rather magnificent Grade II listed building in north-east London dating from the Victorian era, constructed in an Elizabethan style. On first glance, it's hard to believe that this former orphanage is now the busiest Crown court in the country, with twenty courtrooms hidden inside its picturesque turrets and limestone ashlar. It is surrounded by eighteen acres of landscape gardens, complete with a lake called Eagle Pond.

It was across these grounds that I saw Zara pelting, canvas shoulder bag flapping, boots flattening the lawn like a pair of leather pistons. I'd been waiting by the entrance for ten minutes or more when she eventually came to a skidding halt before me; from the colour in her cheeks, it looked as if she'd waived the Underground in favour of a sprint all the way.

'Come on!' she wheezed. 'Queue!'

'Catch your breath. The queue isn't going anywhere.'

She shook her head and pushed past me to join the back of the line for security checks; ahead, the morning's lawyers were placing the contents of their pockets into plastic trays and filing through the metal detector.

'I wish I'd worn my court clothes!' Zara moaned, tugging at the laces of her boots.

I couldn't blame her for being agitated. An Osman warning, so named after the 1998 high-profile legal case of *Osman* v. *United Kingdom*, is no trivial matter. They are issued by British police in the event of a serious and immediate threat to life when there still isn't enough evidence to actually arrest the malefactor.

'When did the police issue the warning?' I asked.

'Last night. Two officers showed up at the prison. All they told Andre, as far as I know, was that they'd received intelligence of a threat on his life and to be on the lookout for anything suspicious.'

'Anything suspicious in *prison?*'

'That's what I said.'

As we came out of security, I checked my watch. Ten minutes late. 'Where are we going?'

'Meeting Lady Allen in her chambers,' she replied, marching ahead. 'Evelyn Allen! Only one of my role models, and look at the state of me!'

'Allen?' I caught her by the shoulder and spun her round. 'This way.'

Sitting in chambers used to mean a conference in the judge's private chambers, but these days it tends to refer to a courtroom with no public access.

'They can't refuse bail after this,' she said. '*Surely* they can't! God, I wish I wasn't so late. For fuck's sake!'

'You're all right,' I told her, striding along. 'The courtroom is just ahead. It's fine.'

'It doesn't *feel* fine,' she groaned. 'At least they haven't started without us. That's Andre's solicitor waiting by the door.'

I looked up and saw the solicitor tapping her feet impatiently, clutching a stack of papers to her chest. After the luck I'd had this week, I should've seen it coming.

'Elliot!'

'Morning, Lydia.'

'You know each other?' Zara asked, coming to a winded stop.

'Lydia is the solicitor in another case I'm working.'

'Another case?' Zara was readjusting the folds of shirt that had billowed out from her waistband. 'What other c—' She paused. Despite her stress, a slanted grin began to unfold. '*The* solicitor?'

'Shall we?' I blustered through the door into the courtroom.

The Resident Judge, responsible for the large Crown court centre at Snaresbrook, was Evelyn Allen QC, an indomitable woman of around sixty-five who was famously fine company outside of the courtroom, and infamously formidable at the bench. She was wearing the violet robe with lilac trim of her office, with a short horsehair wig and a red sash over one shoulder. She was also wearing an impatient, austere frown on her jowly face when the three of us came charging into her silent courtroom. 'Rook,' she said sharply across the room. 'I'm not supposed to be hearing your case until next week, am I?'

'Correct, My Lady.'

'What business brings you here?'

I gestured to Zara. 'Miss Barnes is coming up to the end of her pupillage at Miller & Stubbs. I'm here to observe her performance.'

'Ha.' This dead laugh had come from the right-hand side of the room. It was followed by a drawling voice. 'It's no great surprise, My Lady. These days, one seldom sees anything of Rook or Barnes without the other in tow.'

I glowered across and saw Ted Bowen, an old adversary from our own set, sitting on the prosecution's side. The last time Zara and I had faced him in court he'd lost, and he hadn't lost particularly well.

'You didn't tell me Bowen was prosecuting,' I grumbled quietly as we made our way into the well.

'I didn't know,' Zara replied. 'Makes no difference to me.'

I was planning on sitting a row behind her to avoid stealing her thunder, but our solicitor dived into that row before I had a chance, so I slunk in alongside Zara while she was still stuffing her bag down at her feet.

I looked around the room: Bowen was sitting hunched and crooked, a spindly plucked vulture alongside a short woman whom I vaguely recognised as Claire Morton from the Crown Prosecution Service. There was also a man of around thirty-five sitting on their side, with messy hair, stylish stubble, blue jeans and a tan suede jacket; a plain-clothes officer if ever I'd seen one. Andre Israel was in the dock. It had only been five days, but his bruises had healed surprisingly well, which was rather unfortunate considering this morning's hearing.

The prosecution introduced both parties, then it was over to the judge.

'Morning,' Lady Allen said. 'His Honour Peter Bromley, who will be hearing Mr Israel's upcoming trial, could not be here at such short notice because of prior commitments, though he has been made aware of these latest developments. As Snaresbrook's Resident Judge, I will be hearing this particular matter.' She glanced briefly at her paperwork. 'Miss Barnes, this case is listed for a bail application.'

'It is, My Lady.'

'As the defendant has already made an application for bail, which was refused, there needs to be a change in circumstances in order to make a second application.'

'There does, My Lady.'

'And what is the change in circumstances?'

Zara's voice sounded high and shaky and I felt a knot of both empathy and pride tighten my chest. 'The defendant has been served with a Threat to Life warning notice.'

'I see.' The judge turned to the prosecution. 'Mr Bowen, do you accept that this constitutes a change in circumstances?'

Bowen rose slowly to his feet. 'Not exactly.'

Lady Allen raised her eyebrows. 'Are you being serious, Mr Bowen?'

'I am. What troubles me most, My Lady, is that the defence had this case listed for bail yesterday morning, the hearing originally scheduled for this afternoon, and yet this Threat to Life notice was only issued late last night. It all seems a tad convenient.'

'I am not concerned about what troubles you,' the judge replied. 'It doesn't trouble me, even if Miss Barnes does possess a remarkable gift of foresight. From where I'm sitting, this clearly amounts to a change in circumstances. Do you intend on calling any evidence?'

'Yes, My Lady.' Bowen coughed lightly into his fist, apparently crestfallen. 'I call the officer in the case, Detective Inspector Jack Linford.'

The plain-clothes officer was on his feet with soldierly speed. He marched into the witness box and was sworn to give evidence. Linford looked like a young father, the sort that still makes it to the Sunday league and runs the occasional marathon for fun.

'What can you tell us about this warning?' Lady Allen asked him.

'The warning was issued to the defendant within hours of receiving our intelligence, which came from a source that has repeatedly proven itself to be credible. Because of several ongoing investigations, I can't reveal that source to the court at this time. Suffice it to say I believe the threat to be genuine, and to involve alleged organised criminal activity within HMP Wormwood Scrubs. Both the message and motive were simple enough. These criminals do not wish for Mr Israel to make it to court. I believe they will do almost anything to stop that from happening.'

Lady Allen scribbled notes onto paper. 'Thank you, DI Linford. Do the prosecution have any questions for the officer?'

Bowen shook his head. 'No, My Lady.'

'Defence?'

'Yes.' Zara rose to her feet. 'I have several questions, My Lady.' She turned to face the witness. 'DI Linford, were you present at the raid at the Princess Alexandria?'

'I was.'

'Is it correct that you were in charge of that operation?'

'Yes.'

'When six men, including my client, were arrested for drug offences?'

'That's right.'

'What about the seventh man?' she asked. 'What can you tell us about him?'

Linford winced, scratching his left temple. 'The seventh man?'

'Yes, the seventh. The man you allowed to escape. Your participating informant.'

Linford shrugged. 'I'm not sure what you're talking about.'

'You're not?' Zara returned the shrug. 'DI Linford, do you not recall a young man by the name of Omar Pickett?'

Instead of answering, Linford hastily turned to the bench. 'My Lady, I need to have a word with Mr Bowen.'

Allen shook her head. 'Mr Bowen cannot speak to a witness in the middle of his evidence.'

'Ah, My Lady!' Bowen was up on his feet. 'I actually must address you as a matter of urgency.'

The judge sighed. 'All right, I see where this is going. Take the defendant back to the cells, please.' She waited while Andre was escorted from the dock and then continued. 'I assume this concerns a matter of PII, Mr Bowen?'

'Yes,' he said. 'I intend to make an *ex parte* application in the absence of the defence.'

'Very well. Miss Barnes, Mr Rook, I'm going to have to ask you to step outside with your solicitor for a minute or two.' She glanced back to Bowen. 'What about DI Linford?'

'He needs to stay,' Bowen said.

'Fair enough.'

Zara, Lydia and I shuffled out of the court to wait in the corridor outside. PII, or public-interest immunity – once referred to as Crown privilege – is a principle under common law that allows a court order to be granted to withhold the disclosure of evidence between litigants.

'In other words,' Zara said to neither Lydia nor myself in particular, 'I'm about to have a big old strip of tape slammed over my mouth.'

'I suspect you may be right,' I said. 'You seem to have ruffled some feathers.'

'I don't understand,' Lydia interjected. 'Who the hell is Omar Pickett?'

'Some drug dealer,' Zara explained. 'I'd heard he was Linford's informant and, going by that reaction, I'm guessing it's true. I think he either helped to set up the raid, and then Linford let him walk, or these drug dealers were actually banking on the raid, in which case Omar Pickett must've been working both sides to begin with.'

'Banking on the raid?' Lydia shook her head. 'I'm missing something, aren't I?'

'I think we all are,' I said.

A few minutes later we were ushered back into court and Andre was returned to the dock. DI Linford was still standing in the witness box.

'Miss Barnes,' Lady Allen began, 'based on the application I have just received, and subject to my ruling, Detective Inspector Linford does not need to answer your last question, and you are not to ask any more questions of a like nature. With that said, do you have any further questions of the witness?'

'No, My Lady.' Zara returned to her seat with a sigh.

'In that case, we shall return to the bail application. Mr Bowen, do the prosecution still oppose bail?'

Ted Bowen got to his feet with a dry smile. 'We certainly do, My Lady, on the same grounds as before. We believe there is a substantial risk that the defendant would fail to appear. We say that because these are serious offences. The nature and strength of the evidence against the defendant is overwhelmingly strong, and he has a history of absconding. His trial is due to begin in a matter of days. Release him today, and the prosecution strongly doubts that we shall see him at court on Monday.'

'Yes,' Zara muttered, 'because he might be dead by then.'

'Regarding this apparent threat to his life,' Bowen added pointedly, 'there can surely be no safer place than within the walls of Her Majesty's Prison.'

Lady Allen sat back, tapping her pen close to the microphone. 'Defence?'

Zara stood tall and took a slow breath. She tried to shove her hands into her pockets but forced herself to stop; instead, she clasped them behind her back.

'My Lady, DI Linford stated that the threat to my client's life came from within the prison itself. I think it is therefore worth highlighting the shocking toll of violent acts currently being perpetrated between inmates behind the walls of Wormwood Scrubs. The prosecution claims that there is no safer place than Her Majesty's Prison? Well, with the most recent report citing a staggering forty to fifty violent incidents every month at the Scrubs alone, I don't see it as being beyond the realms of possibility that a serious, perhaps even successful attempt might be made on my client's life at any given moment. It is not a safe environment, and we mustn't forget that Mr Israel is only awaiting trial. A fair trial. He is innocent until proven guilty; even then, no matter what outcome the jury eventually decides upon, it is our country's sworn duty to protect him. The Scrubs has been the setting for so much tragedy before today – tragedies that could have, and indeed *should have*, been avoided if only the warning signs had been heeded in good time. We have been given our warning. We mustn't let our collective inaction cost another young man his life. We mustn't let that prison claim one more victim. Not ever.'

She stood stock-still for another moment, catching her breath, and then sat down with a bump.

The judge placed her pen flat onto the bench. 'Mr Rook, do you have anything you'd care to add?'

'No, My Lady. I am here as an observer only. Miss Barnes has said it all, much more eloquently than I ever could.'

'Very well.' Allen leaned forward, studying Zara. 'Miss Barnes, this is the first time we've met, isn't it?'

'Yes, My Lady.'

'Then I should start by saying that your enthusiasm is invigorating, your passion thoroughly commendable. I suspect that you will have a fine future here at the Bar.'

'Th-thank you,' Zara stammered. 'That means so much coming fr—'

'That said, please make no mistake that this court regards an Osman warning with the utmost seriousness. Contrary to the implications of your speech, no life is *ever* simply left to chance.'

'No, My Lady. Of course not.'

'However, on this occasion, all the passion in the world cannot change the fact that your client has been granted the trust of our courts once before, and he chose to abuse, exploit and breach that trust. I consider *any* failure to surrender to bail as utterly inexcusable. Taking the defendant's prior convictions for absconding into account, and given the serious nature of the charge and the strength of the evidence against him, I must continue to entrust Mr Israel's safety to what I consider to be the thoroughly competent employees of the Prison Service. Your second application for bail is refused.'

Zara thanked the court for its time once more, though now it was little louder than a mumble.

She picked up her bag, dropped it, clenched her shaking fists and picked it up again. Then she hurried out of the room, banging her knee on the door as she went.

I sighed as I got to my feet. I looked up at Andre, who was already being taken away. It would be another hour's drive back to the Scrubs. A two-hour round trip for a hearing that had lasted twenty minutes. After being a barrister for so many years, I rarely felt sorry for defendants any more, yet I couldn't help but feel sorry for Zara.

I was almost out of the room when, from behind, a small hand alighted neatly onto my shoulder. It was Lydia, papers under one arm, smiling and entirely unfazed by the decision of the court.

'So,' she said, 'I'm still waiting to hear back about that drink. What are you doing tonight?'

And in that moment, a drink was the one thing I couldn't bring myself to refuse.

I found Zara in the corridor a couple of minutes later. I didn't tell her about Lydia. I still wasn't sure if there was anything much to tell. Besides, she looked like she wanted to grieve a little in silence and – after a sincere yet clumsy 'happens to the best of us' speech – I was glad to oblige.

On the Tube heading west towards chambers, she broke the silence.

'The car … Dare I ask?'

'Bad,' I replied.

'Write-off?'

'Waiting to hear back from Delroy Meadows.'

'Meadows?' She was standing up in our carriage, despite it being practically empty at this time; I was sitting, and she shuffled her boots closer. 'As in …?'

'Charli's brother. Charli's *twin* brother. He owns a garage in Hackney Wick.'

'And you took the car there?' With the hand that wasn't lassoed in an overhead strap, she reached up behind her glasses and pinched her eyes. 'Did you tell him how it happened?'

'No, of course not. I just told him it was vandalised.'

'It'll get back to his sister.'

'I'm sure it will, assuming her boyfriend hasn't already given her a first-hand account.'

'Did you report it to the police?'

'Honestly, if I report this to anybody in the Met they'll likely pop a bottle of champagne. Speaking of which, I didn't realise that we were sharing the same OIC.'

'Linford? He's in charge of your case too?'

'I'd have to double-check my papers, but I'm almost certain.'

She caught my eye but didn't say a word. Then she turned to face the glass behind me and watched the darkness of the Underground rush through her own reflection, shaking her head from time to time.

When I got off the Tube, I had a voicemail from Meadows informing me that, in short, I shouldn't dream of seeing my car again for at least a week. He asked me to ring back with my go-ahead, before listing the work that needed doing. Halfway through the list, I called him back and told him to do it.

I was to meet Lydia in Soho at six o'clock. By five, I was rifling through shirts at home. I chose what I thought to be a slimming striped one and did a substandard job of neatening it up, using the carpet for an ironing board and brushing dog fur from the cotton as I went. For the first time in years, I combed my hair back, trying to hold the rebellious waves in place with a quarter-pot of old pomade; it looked as though I'd grown an inch more forehead than the last time I'd done it. I tried on two different blazers and discovered that neither would meet at the middle any more. Eventually, I turned to Scout, who was watching idly from the other side of the room.

'What do you reckon?'

She didn't answer. I asked the mirror instead, but it didn't answer either.

'Christ almighty,' I said. 'I look like Ray Winstone in *The Departed*.'

I was still grimacing like a tough guy in the mirror, entertaining myself with impersonations of Winstone's loose Boston-cockney accent – 'Cranberry juice! Craaaanberry juice!' – when there came a soft knocking upon my front door and the dog began to bark. I shepherded her into her cage, locked it, and then hesitated. I could probably count on one hand the amount of times the basement door had ever been knocked upon, and I had a sickening feeling that I'd misunderstood our meeting, and this would be Lydia come early to collect me.

Improbable, I told myself. Impossible. She didn't know where I lived, did she?

I opened the door and froze. It felt as if I'd dropped something, a fleeting sense of falling, but there'd been nothing in my hand to begin with.

'Hello, Elliot.'

I'm not sure how long I stood there. In the end, I managed no better greeting than her name.

'Jenny.'

15

On a drizzly September evening in 1993, ten years after my trial for fraud and induction into the straight life, I fell in love with Jennifer Tilden.

It was the beginning of my year at Bar school.

After graduating from Bristol University, I'd returned to London and discovered a setback on my journey towards qualifying as a barrister. To get into Bar school, one first had to join an Inn of Court, one of London's four ancient legal societies. These were Gray's, Lincoln's, the Middle Temple and the Inner Temple, and there was an old rhyme about them: *Inner for the rich, Middle for the poor, Gray's for the scholar, Lincoln's for the bore.*

Throughout my time at university I'd been consciously burying my working-class roots, developing the highbrow persona that would – for better or worse – remain with me for the rest of my life. I'd trained myself to talk with a BBC accent and convinced so many people I'd studied at Eton College that former 'classmates' would introduce themselves, claiming to remember me being there. I even went back to Eton to represent the Old Boys against the school field.

After enjoying this new persona for a couple of years, like Joyce's Jimmy Doyle, I saw no reason to stop now and so I applied to the Inner Temple. When the application form asked if I had a criminal conviction, I answered honestly, not wanting to build my house on shifting sands.

I was miserable when I posted my application, confident that I'd be rejected outright, but I wasn't. I was invited to an interview to explain the situation, where the members of an admissions board sat like extras in a *Shawshank* parole hearing, and, somehow, I left that interview as a member of the Honourable Society of the Inner Temple.

Unfortunately, the society didn't board its students; I was now twenty-eight and homeless again.

During my first year on the streets of the capital back in '87, there had been hundreds of vagabonds occupying Lincoln's Inn Fields, which was the largest public square in London and conveniently situated between the Inner Temple and Bar school. I'd slept there once or twice before leaving the city for college and had planned to nest there for at least my first term at Bar school. What I hadn't counted on, however, was the fine folks of Camden Council who, with the backing of local businesses and non-governmental organisations, had in the early half of 1993 raised enough money to surround the area with high spiked fences and gates that were to be locked at every sundown. While these measures worked in deterring a good number of the square's former residents, there was still a more resilient proportion that would simply scale the gates after dusk, and so this was what I ended up doing in between my seminars on the merits of law and order.

For the first couple of weeks I exploited the facilities of the Inner Temple's changing room, bathing there every morning and stashing my belongings on top of the lockers during daytime lectures, but the weather was already turning and completing homework without a home was becoming problematic. I spent most nights working in the Inner Temple tea rooms, loitering there until asked to leave, then I'd join the queue for soup and a hunk of bread from the Salvation Army van.

One afternoon, as I was settling down in the tea rooms with a fresh stack of paperwork, I overheard a lecturer on the next table boasting to his cohorts about a recent trip to the Whitechapel Gallery. There was an exhibition on, he told them, of works by figurative artist Lucian Freud, grandson of Sigmund. From the way he told it, his night had been a staggering, once-in-a-lifetime melange of fine art and consorting with the most cutting-edge creatives in the city over free wine and canapés.

While fine art did nothing much for a man of my pedigree, the promise of free food and a complimentary piss-up was plainly too good to pass on. Within two hours I'd had one of my four shirts washed and dried at the usual launderette, had stuffed my camping bag into the depths of a familiar bush on the Fields and had started on the forty-five-minute walk east to the Whitechapel Gallery.

As a trainee cross-examiner – not to mention a well-practised bullshitter – I probably should've realised that the tea room's boasting lecturer had either been extraordinarily lucky on his visit to the exhibition or was, like most braggarts, a liar. There were no *comestibles* to speak of at the gallery, and the only stars I'd seen were those punching through momentary gaps in the swollen clouds by the time I'd made it onto Whitechapel Road.

The gallery was crowded enough for me to go unnoticed, with smaller groups talking appreciatively among themselves, and I wasn't *entirely* oblivious to art; I'd lived in Paris, after all, and had roamed the Louvre six or seven times to wait out rain or snow. I couldn't say much about composition or the use of negative space – and as far as some fine art went, I wouldn't have been able to differentiate between a beloved masterpiece and an infant's scrawl – but I had enough about me to recognise the technical skill in Freud's work. The paintings were mostly harsh, uncompromising nudes; I sidestepped from one to another, stroking my chin and nodding thoughtfully at the naked portrayals of performance artist Leigh Bowery while keeping a careful eye out for any sign of the elusive wine.

I only paused at the final piece, which appeared to be the main talking point of the whole collection. Entitled *Painter Working, Reflection*, it was precisely that: an enormous self-portrait of Lucian Freud standing on a bare studio floor wearing absolutely nothing except for a pair of boots, sans laces, while holding a palette in his left hand and a paintbrush in his right. The attention to detail and undeniable technical skill was only half as staggering, in my opinion, as the candidness behind the sunken dips in his collar, the sagging folds of flesh, his receding hairline and, yes, even his unexaggerated genitals. I might not have understood a great deal about art, but this struck a deep chord; here I was, disguised behind my false persona, staring back at a man in all his honesty.

And there, while I was still marvelling at a seventy-one-year-old man's cock, she spoke to me.

'Discomfiting, isn't it? Reality.'

That was the first thing she ever said to me.

I pulled my eyes away from the canvas, glanced to my right, saw her standing there, and found no immediate response; it seemed that my trained badinage had boarded the last chopper out and left me to fend for myself. I checked over my other shoulder to ensure that she hadn't been talking to somebody standing on my left. No, she was looking right at me. Eleven years earlier, the blade of a flick knife had cut me open from one side of my chest to the other, and that was the closest comparison I could find to this current sensation.

She was twenty-two, as I would soon discover, but had the piercing grey eyes of an older, wiser woman. Her dark blonde hair was long and naturally wild, almost dancing in a defiant bouffant reminiscent of a young Brigitte Bardot. Much like Bardot, all of her outward abrasiveness could not hide her bourgeois grace. While I'd tried hard to look smart in my freshly tumble-dried shirt, she'd done the opposite, dressing in an oversized Pearl Jam T-shirt, tattered jeans and black combat boots; there were flecks of paint on the cuffs of her leather jacket, blue, violet and red. All at once the gallery and its art were only fog behind her colour.

She hadn't come alone. Sniffing at her heels was an entourage of four young men, each one deliberately shabby and yet reeking of wealth.

I cleared my throat and said something worthless. 'Yes, it is a rather good painting.'

'Good?' She raised her eyebrows. '*Good*, he says. Look at the shades he's discovered in his own skin, the clots of paint on his genitals. It's so reminiscent of Bacon.'

I found the comparison peculiar, but with this beautiful stranger I wasn't going to stand there and argue. 'Yes, bacon, I know just what you mean. It is sort of *meaty-looking*, isn't it?'

She blinked at me three times and then started to giggle. The sound was stunning.

Her followers were not amused. They narrowed their eyes, and all at once those eyes said fraud, usurper, unworthy of her amusement.

'Francis Bacon,' one of her cronies, the one with a goatee, interjected sardonically. 'Do you even know who he is?'

'Francis Bacon? I should certainly hope so,' I replied. 'I studied him for an entire term at university. Attorney General, Lord Chancellor, he was the original Queen's Counsel designate, appointed by Queen Elizabeth herself as her personal legal counsel in 1597.'

What had started as a giggle now exploded into laughter that drew frowns from across the room.

'Jennifer!' Goatee hissed. 'They'll think you're laughing at the painting!'

'Oh, let them think what they want! Sir Francis fucking Bacon!'

From that moment on, my disguise was worthless: she had me sussed. It wasn't long before I had her figured out in return.

She was an Old Dolphin, a former pupil of the illustrious Godolphin and Latymer School in Hammersmith, with a family listed in *Burke's Landed Gentry* that could be traced back through all manner of lords and barons with its own coat of arms. She must've been the only out-of-work illustrator that could comfortably afford to keep her own spacious apartment in Kensington, but she was never overtly snobbish about it. Perhaps it was because of her conflicted feelings regarding her privilege and new-found socialist attitude that she ever thought to give me the time of day to begin with. Maybe she just liked me. For some reason, she even loved me.

Of course, I didn't come right out and tell her about my living situation, even after we'd been seeing each other for a month or so and she was becoming irritated and suspicious about never being invited back to my fictitious flat. It came to a head in November, when the weather dropped below freezing point and I had no choice but to seek out shelter. Centrepoint was a charity for homeless youths that had originally started out in 1969, offering refuge in a disused basement in St Anne's Church on Dean Street, Soho. By the nineties, it had three nightly shelters and nine semi-permanent hostels in the capital, with links across the country thanks in part to the work of its new patron, Diana, Princess of Wales. I reluctantly turned up at Centrepoint's Soho office on a bitterly cold Sunday evening with my rucksack on my back, where I was greeted by a troop of new volunteer workers. One of the volunteers was Jenny. That was how I ended up moving in with her.

Later, after we were married and had moved into what she called our 'forever home', she purchased a huge print of Freud's *Painter Working, Reflection* and hung it in the downstairs loo. I wasn't especially keen on doing my business under the gaze of that naked figure, but I told her again that it was a rather good painting.

Later still, the print was torn in two, and on a drizzly September morning in 2016, twenty-three years after my induction into the world of art, our divorce was done and dusted.

16

'This is cosy,' Jenny said, peering round my right shoulder with those huge, dove-grey eyes.

I was too busy looking at her to answer. I stepped out of the basement and pulled the door half shut behind me to block her view.

Jenny at forty-six was now a middle-aged, middle-class socialist: curvier, more conservatively dressed, but still stylish. An old grey blazer over a new white turtleneck, jeans and heels and a Stella McCartney shoulder bag; a touch of eyeshadow and pale lipstick; deeper lines and darker hair tied back with a few hanging, wavy tendrils. At once so familiar and so different, like a childhood home after a change of owners; you know the rooms and every flaw, but the wallpaper and furniture have changed. Had it really been eighteen months since I'd seen her last? It seemed impossible, yet I couldn't decide whether that was because the time apart felt a lot shorter or so, so much longer.

'I went upstairs first,' she said. 'They told me you were down here. Nice couple.'

'I've never really spoken to them,' I replied, clearing my throat with an unpleasant hack.

She raised her eyebrows as she so often had before. 'He's still a hit with the neighbours.'

Jenny's habit of talking in the third person, a habit I'd learned to love and grown to hate.

'I couldn't see your car parked on the road,' she said. 'Don't tell me it finally died?'

'Murdered, I fear. Although the jury's still out on whether it can survive.'

'I'm not surprised.' Her eyes were clocking me, making fast deductions. 'How's your head?'

'Still sore if I press it hard enough.'

'I read about what happened in the news, of course. The attack. Then your sister messaged me at New Year. You went there for Christmas?'

'Had to go somewhere,' I said.

'About time you made some sort of effort with them.'

Down at my side, I lifted my thumb from my fist; barb number one.

'Dad kept the newspaper clippings,' she went on. 'Another story for the Rook book he'll never get around to writing.'

'How is Phillip?'

'Dying.'

That hit me like a hook to my ribs, stealing my wind. Phillip Tilden had been more of a father to me than my own ever had. Even after those nights when Jenny would storm out to stay at her parents', he'd always kept me in good favour. He was a decent man. Now I felt appalling for not calling him since the divorce. 'Why? I mean, how?'

'Cancer. Pancreatic. Advanced.'

'Shit.' I assumed this was the reason for her visit. I relented and opened the front door. 'You want to come inside?'

She breezed in and then stopped as if she'd hit a brick wall. 'Jesus. It smells like stale smoke and sour piss in here.'

'That's the name of this new aftershave I'm trying.' I closed the door behind us. In her cage, the dog started to growl.

'He has a dog now!'

'Scout,' I said.

'You always disliked pets.'

'You always disliked opening your mouth for the dentist, but I'm assuming that isn't such an issue any more,' I couldn't help replying. 'How is Tom?'

'Ever the acid-tongued barrister,' she muttered, circling the futon. 'Tom is fine.'

'I take it he made it through the winter without needing me to come and show him how the boiler works.'

She looked back over one shoulder, those damn eyebrows rising again. 'Elliot, I'm not sure you *ever* knew how the boiler worked.'

Atop my head, I could feel a single curl of combed hair fighting the pomade, lifting upwards into a more wilted imitation of alfalfa. I flushed, brushing it back down.

'At least you're not still wearing that stupid hat,' she said. 'Drink?'

She turned and stared at the kitchenette with an expression of horror. 'I'll pass, thanks. You know, you could've taken the coffee machine.'

'Your father,' I said, getting myself a lager from the fridge. 'How long …?'

'Does he have to live? Realistically, we're talking about a length of string, but the string is more like stretched cotton. Cotton snaps. So probably sooner rather than later.' She always spoke like this.

I opened my can with weak hands. 'And your mother? How's she handling it.'

'About as well as can be expected.'

'He's still at home with her?' I asked.

'Where else?'

'I wasn't sure if he'd gone to a ...' The word formed on my lips – *hospice* – and dissolved there. 'I should give him a ring.'

'He'd appreciate that.' Her eyes drifted down to my left hand, the fingers wrapped around the beer.

'I don't wear it,' I told her after a huge, cold mouthful.

'I read in the paper –'

'Don't believe everything you read.'

'Hmm.' After lapping the entire room twice over, she perched on the nearest arm of my folded futon with narrowed eyes. 'What have you been fucking around with now, Elliot?'

'Excuse me?' My stomach lurched; for one bizarre second, I thought she was referring to Lydia. 'What do you mean?'

She swung her bag onto her knee and opened it. From inside, she produced a clear plastic wallet, which she held between two fingers as if it might erupt into flames at any moment. It looked sort of funny, like something out of a corny old spy film, until I saw the single sheet of A4 paper inside.

There were seven words. Printed, not handwritten. Large, plain font.

YOUR TRIAL OR YOUR LIFE. LOSE ONE.

I swallowed. 'What's this?'

'*This* was lying on my doormat this morning.'

For a moment I couldn't speak. I could feel sweat spreading across my forehead. I emptied half of my beer. 'It came in the post?'

'Does it look like it came from the Royal Mail? Delivered by hand in the night, I assume.'

'Did Tom see it?' It sounded like a stupid question, but it seemed a matter of personal embarrassment.

'God no. He'd have had the police over in minutes.'

I nodded. This wasn't the first threat that had found its way to that address – at one time they'd been terribly frequent – and I was glad to see that Jenny had remembered my preferred way of handling things. That said, their former frequency had undermined their severity and they tended to go straight into the recycling along with the circulars and takeaway menus. This was different, not least because I was no longer the one at risk. The threat was clearly aimed at me, but it was Jenny who could be in danger, and only hours after the Osman warning had found its way to Andre Israel.

'I thought this shit would've left after you did,' she said. 'How are they still coming to my house?'

'Same way they always did, I suppose. Our address was no great secret, considering you worked from home and advertised it on three separate websites.'

The grey in her eyes turned red before she was up on her feet. 'You're saying this is *my* fault?'

'No.'

'That's exactly what you're saying!' She threw the plastic slip wallet at the floor with force; it drifted casually, almost brazenly, which annoyed her even more. 'Where's your car, Elliot? What happened to it?'

176

'Vandals.' With one eye I checked my watch, which was the equivalent of throwing a can of gas onto a fire.

'Oh, I *am* sorry,' she snapped. 'Do you have somewhere more pressing to be?'

'As a matter of fact, I have a date.' I told myself not to say it smugly, but like a door slammed in her face, it had the impact I was looking for.

'Right. Well. Don't let me take up any more of your precious time.' She was already storming for the front door, opening it, a fireball with a designer handbag swinging wildly behind her.

'Jenny –'

'It's Jennifer.' She stopped at the bottom of the steps outside. 'Keep the note. And if I find another, it'll be *you* answering to the police.'

And as she thundered up the staircase, I could feel my heart leathering against my ribs. Not because I was angry, I realised. It was because I'd missed our fighting as much as everything else.

The last thing I wanted to do next was meet the solicitor, but a stiff drink was definitely on the agenda. I took the death threat along with me, folded in my coat pocket, for light conversation.

I was already late by the time I hailed a black cab, and it took another twenty minutes to get through traffic to the Dog and Duck, a tiny pub on a corner in Soho that had once hosted the likes of John Constable and George Orwell and boasted these facts to this day. The Thursday crowd was piled deep outside, spilling off the kerbs onto Bateman and Frith Streets, and I couldn't see her standing among it. I had to elbow my way into the building, which was incredibly old and still decorated with its original glossy tiles, mahogany panelling and enormous Victorian mirrors.

Lydia was there waiting. She'd managed to secure for herself one of the copper-topped tables at the rear of the bar, and she appeared to be as relaxed as I was rattled, arms stretched across the back of her seat.

'Over here, Elliot!'

She was wearing a crimson dress that spoke nothing of business; against so much red, her strawberry-blonde hair seemed blizzard white. Her goblet of gin was a fishbowl. Raspberries and ice floated like sailors overboard.

I tugged my shirt straighter and pointed to her glass. 'Do you want another?'

'I wouldn't say no. Just tell them I'm having the usual.'

It took me almost five minutes to get served, so I took two pints and another fishbowl back to the table with me. She finished off her first and moved the same plastic straw into the new glass. 'Two pints?' she noted.

'It's a two-pint kind of night,' I said, and then slid the plastic wallet out of my pocket and onto the copper table-top for her to read.

She choked around her straw, eyes bugging out, and put her glass down. 'Where has this come from?'

'No idea. They could've at least signed it, so I know who wants me dead this time.'

'Jesus!' Her eyes were darting around suspiciously, as if anybody in the bar might be responsible. 'Did it come to your office?'

'My wife's doormat.'

If her eyes could've only widened further, I think they'd have tumbled out into her drink. 'Your *wife*?'

'Ex-wife,' I swiftly adjusted. 'I'm still getting used to the idea.'

'You get used to it, believe me. So, this was posted?'

'Sometime last night, I presume, to the house I used to live in.'

'Jesus,' she said again. 'How could they find the place?'

'Quite easily, I suspect. The former Mrs Rook works from home. Art studio in the loft. She keeps the address, and our surname, as her place of business online.' I drained half a pint and felt better for it. I needed to belch but managed to hold it down, albeit with watery eyes. 'The more pressing question is: who the hell stands to gain from Charli Meadows going to prison?'

'I've no idea.'

'I did have my own suspicions, but I can't see what he could gain from her being incarcerated.'

'*He?*'

'Oh, nobody. Nothing.' I drank some more.

'Elliot, I hope you're not holding out on me.' She looked down into her glass and swirled the liquid, imitating a starlet's pout, breaking up the raspberries and ice. 'We're in this together, aren't we?'

Her confidence was obvious. In her younger days, Jenny had been confident in her own purposely outrageous sort of way, but this was different. Lydia's was a confidence in people she hardly knew, and its effect was at once beguiling and oddly unnerving.

'I'm not holding out on you,' I said, stuffing the note back into my pocket. 'That would require me having some idea of what was going on.'

'But there is a *he*, isn't there?'

I nodded. 'Charli has a boyfriend. A younger man by the name of Deacon. Did she ever mention him to you?'

'No.' She frowned. 'She explicitly told me she was single, in fact.'

'Probably because this Deacon is a former inmate at the prison.'

'Now that *is* interesting,' she said. 'You suspect he put the drugs in the car?'

'He was inside at the time on a drugs charge. Perhaps he was coercing her into bringing what she assumed was tobacco onto the grounds for him.'

'Plausible,' she said. 'Highly plausible. I'll nose around, see if I can find anything out about this Deacon and his convictions. Are you certain that this note is actually referring to the smuggling case? Is there not another trial you have lined up?'

'It's the Meadows case. I'm sure of it.'

'It isn't hard for somebody to get hold of a printer and a sheet of paper. What about this drug-dealing case you've been assisting Zara Barnes with? Is she your pupil? I didn't think silks took them on.'

'Not mine, no, she's –'

'Oh God! The railway case last year! From the papers, *she* was your junior! So, she was there the night that ...'

'Yes.'

'Wow.' She whistled and took another long pull on her straw, leaving cherry-red lipstick on black plastic.

'This Israel case,' I said briskly. 'How many of the defendants did you represent from the raid?'

'All of them.'

'The whole lot?'

She hummed around the straw, then smacked her lips dry. 'Almost didn't bother going when I got the phone call at eleven o'clock on a Thursday night. What a mistake *that* would've been. Thirty cells at Leyton Custody Centre, and six were occupied thanks to that raid.'

'This may sound peculiar,' I said, 'but have any of the other defendants mentioned a gang that calls itself the Cutthroats? E10 Cutthroats, I believe.'

'No!' She laughed, which caught me off guard. 'What are they, pirates?' Her laugh simmered to a smile. 'Elliot, as much as I'd like to chat about the pirates of the East End, are we really going to talk about work all night?'

This made me feel a little embarrassed, and I hesitated. 'No, not at all.'

'Good,' she said. 'So, what else is going on in the life of Elliot Rook?'

I considered it for a moment, sure that something other than work still existed in my world. 'I got a dog this week,' I said brightly.

'A dog?' She raised her brows, eyes shining playfully. 'That's cute.'

'You haven't seen the thing.'

And the conversation went from there.

Over the next couple of hours, I felt very much like a chauffeur behind the wheel of an unfamiliar car; as a professional orator I could keep conversation going, but not without the occasional stall. Lydia didn't seem to mind. In fact, for somebody who didn't want to discuss work, whenever the threat of silence loomed she simply talked for the both of us, filling empty air with gossip about various judges and solicitors, which I enjoyed much more than I probably should have.

Between us, Lydia and I were a little more than tipsy when we staggered out of the Dog and Duck. The evening had turned cold, and she tightened a thin jacket over her dress while I lit myself a cigarette. Her green eyes glowed as she tracked her Uber's advance on her phone. There was dead air between us again, but it wasn't so awkward now. Still, I found myself wanting to fill it.

'This was nice,' I said. 'Thank you. I appreciate it.'

She looked up from the phone and rolled her eyes. 'You don't have to thank me, Elliot. This isn't charity. I asked for *your* company, remember?'

'Yes,' I said. 'I suppose you did. In that case, you're welcome.'

She laughed softly, 'Wow, thanks,' and pointed to approaching headlights. 'This is my car.'

'I'll walk you to it,' I said, and when we got there I opened the door for her.

'The perfect gent,' she chuckled, climbing into the back. A moment passed, something electric between us, but it had gone almost before I'd even noticed it. She held the handle from the inside, preparing to close herself in. 'So, where will your evening take you now?'

I checked my watch and smoked. 'I'd like another look through the case papers before I turn in. Apart from that, just trying not to get myself killed will keep me plenty busy.'

'Good idea.' She shook her head, started to close the door and paused. 'The case isn't going anywhere. You should give yourself the rest of the night off. Life's too short, Elliot.'

I smiled, nodded, and patted the pocket with the death threat inside it. 'Yes,' I said. 'It's getting shorter every day.'

I closed the door and waved her off, and she slipped away into the night.

I held the smile until she was gone, and only then did I really start to worry about the warning on my life.

17

With Snaresbrook hearing approximately seven thousand criminal cases every year, it came as no great surprise that both Zara and I would be there at the same time on Monday.

Across England and Wales, court listings are published electronically via CourtServe. Even if a case has been scheduled for months, the trial details – including court number, judge and position in the court list – are only confirmed on the database in the listing officer's 'final list' the workday before starting. This information is then also displayed on large electronic boards for those arriving at the court. Fixed trials – as ours were – tend to start on Mondays, whereas 'floaters' are listed to float over a two-week period and depend upon another trial finishing short, which can happen on any day. Our final list had been published on Friday afternoon: Zara's case with Andre was scheduled for a courtroom in Snaresbrook's outer annexe, while mine was in the main building.

The two of us agreed, quite optimistically, to rendezvous while changing trains at Oxford Circus on Monday morning. I walked the four blocks from my front door to Baker Street and entered the Underground via the Station Arcade, which had survived since the nineteenth century and was now crammed between a Boots and a Yo! Sushi. Zara had messaged to say that she'd be taking the Victoria Line up from Brixton at a little past seven o'clock and would be changing onto the Central Line at Oxford Circus from which I was only a three-minute ride away on the Bakerloo. We managed to find each other on the crowded eastbound platform below Oxford Street, and then had to squeeze ourselves into a stifling, packed carriage that stank of countless deodorants working hard to cover human sweat.

It was half an hour from there to Snaresbrook, and the only sounds apart from the screech of tracks were the over-spill of earphones, the occasional chesty cough and Zara's low, muttering voice as she went over and over the evidence in her case. I watched her knuckles whiten around the near-est handrail, occasionally loosening only to ensure that both her usual canvas shoulder bag and blue damask barrister's bag hadn't vanished from her side. I wasn't in any sort of a position to offer advice, being blasted as I was by a suited chap's coffee breath from about an inch away, but I hoped that my presence was providing her with at least a little comfort.

The courthouse opened its doors at eight, and we were in the security queue a few minutes after that. Court hours are generally in session from 10.30 until 4.15, unless there's a sick juror or the judge has something else to do, but we had both arranged early conferences with our respective clients. We got ourselves coffees in the Bar mess and waited quietly for our defendants to arrive. Charli would be able to walk freely onto the premises, as a defendant on bail only has to surrender themselves as their case is called; they walk into the dock, the door is locked behind them, the guard takes them out to a small anteroom to be searched, then they return to the dock. Andre, on the other hand, would be brought directly from the Scrubs to one of Snaresbrook's twenty-two cells.

In legal aid trials, it's quite rare for solicitors to actually come into court, but Lydia had told me she was planning on flitting between our two trials as well as those of the additional defendants on her agenda. She walked into the Bar mess sometime after our coffee cups were empty, struggling to carry a weighty stack of loose paperwork under one arm, and cheerily asked how our weekends had been.

'My weekend?' Zara replied blankly. 'Thanks to the prosecution opposing bail, I spent almost every minute of it checking my phone to see if my client was still alive. So yeah, you know, I've had better.'

Lydia pulled a *wish I hadn't asked* sort of face, then turned her smile on me. 'Elliot?'

'Nothing much. Work.'

'Ah, of course.' She repeated the same expression. 'Work and the dog.'

'Looks like you have a lot on yourself this morning,' I noted, gesturing to her paperwork.

'It's ridiculous, isn't it? Trials are organised online with access to the case papers via computer, but the defendants aren't allowed to have a computer in the dock. Every week I have to print them all off and dish out hard copies. I'm developing biceps like Schwarzenegger. Still, every client is another bill paid.'

Zara's eyes jerked towards her; I knew that cold look well enough by now to recognise the danger, but Lydia didn't notice. She was still grinning when she walked away and left us in our thoughtful silence.

For the entire weekend, I'd been debating whether or not to tell Zara about the threat finding its way into my former letter box. After seeing the concern already behind her eyes, I decided not to add to it.

It was about nine o'clock when I changed into the familiar silk and horsehair. I bundled the rest of my belongings into a locker and then clocked in for the day on the robing room's computer. Zara had gone down to the cells to see Andre, while I'd agreed to meet Charli in a small conference room outside our court before anybody else arrived. She was already waiting by the entrance when I got there, gazing vacantly down at her shoes. She looked miserable. As soon as I saw her, any longing I might have had to rant about Deacon withered to a feeble choke.

'Charli?'

She looked up gradually. She'd dressed smartly in a dark grey suit, but her eyes were raw, glassy and crimson as if she'd been crying all weekend. She didn't speak. I swallowed and opened the door and she followed me at a shuffle.

'It always comes in threes, doesn't it?' was the first thing she said upon sitting. I had the strangest idea that she was referring to my car; if she hadn't heard about it first-hand from her boyfriend by now, then she would almost certainly have found out from her brother at the garage. But, of course, she was not. 'First, I'm arrested for a crime I know nothing about,' she said. 'I lose my job because of it. And now, right before I'm due in Crown court, *this* ...'

I bent forward to sit my briefcase between my shoes. 'Has something else happened?'

She nodded, just a twitch, and then sighed. 'Biggie, our dog. He died over the weekend.'

'Oh.' My stomach lurched, thinking of Scout. 'I'm sorry to hear that. Was he old?'

'Only a puppy.'

'Jesus. What was it? Traffic?'

'No, nothing like that. He got poorly.'

'Poorly?' Something about this word struck me as peculiar. I assumed it was simply because I'd seen this dog, albeit through a frosted door, and such a sweet, juvenile expression did not correlate with my memory at all; then my thoughts turned to something a great deal more sinister. 'I must admit that Biggie didn't strike me as being particularly sickly when he was trying to take your front door off its hinges last week.'

'No, that's the worst thing about it. We've never had a problem before. With his health, I mean. Not one. It was all so sudden. It happened so ... so quickly ...' She began to cry but the tears were small, as if her ducts were almost spent. She reached into her bag and retrieved a tissue, with which she dabbed the make-up from her face in dark umber patches. 'He must've got hold of something in that damned allotment. I had him tied up out there on Saturday. All I did was take my eye off him for five minutes to nip into the house. *Five minutes ...*'

In my stomach, a lump was growing heavy. 'Something in your allotment?'

'That's all I can think of. It has to be. I don't know what. Some poison, I guess.'

'Poison?'

Charli blew her nose into the tissue. 'Leeks, onions, garlic, they're all poisonous to dogs. Grapes, even. Chocolate, but the kids know better than to leave it laying around. I'm sure they do. Slug pellets, maybe. All those weeds at the back behind the fencing, it wouldn't surprise me if half of those were toxic, but I've always made sure his chain couldn't reach that far. Always. Then again, it wouldn't surprise me if it was one of the neighbours. They all hated him. But he was harmless. He was part of the family, even though we've only had him for a few weeks. He was family, and to die like that ...'

'Where did it happen? At the vet's?'

'No. I came back across the road and he was on his side, shaking in the plants. *Convulsing*. He started throwing up blood. I screamed for Deacon, and the kids came across, hysterical. He was dead in minutes.'

'Sounds horrendous.'

She nodded, catching the last of her tears, and then scrunched the tissue to a ball and returned it to her bag. As she did, the cuff rode up her right forearm and I could just see the tail of what appeared to be a deep gash there. She caught me looking and sharply yanked the cuff down to cover it. 'His claws,' she explained. 'He was damn strong, even in the end.'

'I bet he was.'

'We buried him there, under my plot. He always liked it out there. Well, I say we, but I couldn't do it. My brother came over. Him and Deacon. They got the kids involved, made a ceremony of it. Roland was so brave, bless him. They all were. And I finally got those paving slabs down, just to stop the foxes from ... from, you know, getting at him ...' She sighed. 'Some start to the week.'

189

I forced the image of her animal dying aside. 'Could it have been one of those breed-specific illnesses? What breed was he?'

'Some kind of mastiff, I think. A cross-breed. Deacon got him for us. He loved that dog.'

'Deacon,' I said. 'You lied about him. He was an inmate?'

'Yes.' She tugged at her lashes, picking away the gluey mascara.

'You must know what I'm thinking. Does he live with you?'

'No,' she said quietly. 'He lives in Leyton. One of the estates.'

'Does he keep any of his belongings at yours?'

'Nothing more than a toothbrush and a change of clothes. Why?'

I shrugged, thinking about dying dogs and cuckoo birds. 'He appears to do quite well for a man of his age, especially one who has been free only a matter of weeks.'

'Expensive habits, but it's mostly on credit. That's why I get so mad about him spoiling the kids. He's younger than I am, you could probably tell that much. Young and stupid with money.'

'He must have a pretty good job though, to afford a car like that. Not to mention those trainers.'

'I think he was borrowing the car. Since he got out, he's been doing a bit of driving for Uber, so he's often loaning his mates' nicer cars. He isn't dealing any more. I know it looks so obvious, but I believe him.'

'You'd have to be some friend to lend him a car like that. What else does he do for a living?'

'He's a music producer. Only independent stuff. Nothing big, but he does OK. That's how he got used to the nice clothes, I guess. Sponsorships through the label. That kind of thing.'

'A producer ...' I already knew before I asked. 'What sort of music does he produce?'

'I don't know. My Roland is into it, but it goes over my head. Showing my age.'

'What genre?'

'I guess you'd call it grime, a bit of dance, and this drill stuff. They were releasing it through Spotify, and they had a channel on YouTube called –'

'Banged Up Records?'

She looked at me, slow and puzzled. 'You know it?'

'Only a little.'

Her eyes moved up to my wig. 'Wouldn't have thought it was your sort of thing.'

I managed a shrug.

'Deacon didn't have anything to do with this,' she said. 'I'm not going to sit here and tell you that me and Deacon are *meant to be together* or anything stupid like that. I'm not fifteen years old. He's just – a nice lad. Most of them aren't.'

I nodded, my thoughts reeling around Deacon and the dog now buried under paving slabs. 'Come on,' I said. 'It's almost time.'

We left the conference room and walked straight into our prosecutor, further souring the moment. I had not been at all shocked to discover that Harlan Garrick QC would be stepping up against me; if Zara was facing Ted Bowen, it only made sense that his former lead counsel would have gone out of his way to get onto my trial. Not all barristers would take a defeat to heart, but rumour had it that Garrick had felt cheated ever since losing the Barber case last autumn to a new silk and a pupil, and he had been trying to get onto my listings ever since. Of course, that could've been nothing more than hearsay; in the courts of London, encountering the same prosecutors by chance is very common. This morning Garrick was already wearing a face like thunder, though perhaps that was only an impression created by his disposition. Even by my standards the man was a moody old sod.

He passed us and entered the courtroom with barely a glance, and I distinctly heard Charli swallow. 'Do you think I've got time for one last fag?'

'Sure,' I said. 'Go ahead.'

She smiled, but as she rummaged through her bag I saw that her hands were trembling. She paused. 'Shit, my phone! What do I do with it? Should I have left it at home?'

'No, that's all right. You can keep it with you in the dock, but it has to be switched off, just like mine. Then, if you are con—' I caught myself before finishing, not nearly soon enough.

'If I'm convicted ...?'

'If you are convicted and sent to prison then it'll become part of your confiscated property.'

'Of course. That used to be my job. Life's weird, don't you think?'

She wandered off without waiting to hear my answer, though as it turned out, yes, I did think so.

Reluctant to spend any more of a Monday morning with Harlan Garrick than necessary, I wandered the corridors to see if I could spot Zara before her trial started. What I found instead was Lydia coming up from the cells, sashaying now that she was no longer weighed down with papers.

'How's Meadows?' she asked after waving me down.

'Not good. Her dog died.'

'Christ, that's an ominous start. Old age?'

'Poison, she thinks.'

'Poison?' Lydia's face whitened, just as mine had probably done. She looked around and leaned in, lowering her voice. She smelled of perfume, something sweet. 'You don't think it had anything to do with the trial, do you? That note you got ...'

'It had crossed my mind, though surely not. Either way, short of digging the poor thing up from under her allotment for a post-mortem, I don't think we're likely to find that out.'

'The allotment? Shit. This is turning into a mess.'

'You can say that again.'

'What are you going to do?'

'Do?' I considered it for a moment. Around us, the lawyers were rushing off to various courtrooms to make their opening plays. 'If somebody really *is* behind this, then they're trying to drag the fight out of the courtroom. So that's precisely where I'm going to keep it. As far as I'm concerned, the key to this case is Deacon. I just need to find a way to expose him. And when I do, we can win this case.'

That was what I said to the solicitor in the courthouse, but I didn't believe it myself. Things seemed to be repeating in an ominous fashion; Garrick, Bowen and all the same cursed stars of last year were aligning once more.

It didn't matter what I told Lydia or what I told myself, because I couldn't ignore the feeling that this was going to end in violence, and nowhere near any court of English law.

18

Half past ten came around and court was in session.

I hadn't managed to catch up with Zara, which I was a little sorry about, though I had enough faith in her ability by now not to let it worry me too much. Sooner or later, we are all sent plummeting out of our nests. I knew that, in her moment, Zara would fly.

The clerk started off the trial of *Regina* v. *Charli Meadows* with the usual formalities.

'All persons who have business before the Queen's justices draw near and give your attendance. God save the Queen.' We stood for the entrance of Judge Evelyn Allen QC, who was kitted out in her full violet and lilac robes with a red sash, and then Charli was asked to confirm her identity. As prosecuting counsel, it was Garrick's job to introduce us both to the court.

Trials, and their traditions, take time. After the protracted jury swearing come the legal arguments, case opening and agreed facts; witness statements have to be read and live witnesses to be called. While televised legal dramas have the luxury of being able to dip in and out of the action for pacing's sake, a genuine trial is a meticulous, occasionally arduous affair that stretches over days, weeks and even months. This is mostly because of the judicious care required, but it's also because barristers really do like to talk. We are professional orators, after all. The prosecution have to fight a tactical trench war, covering every conceivable defence, painstakingly laying any plausibly relevant evidence before the jury. They carry the burden and standard of proof; the defence only need to cast doubt on a single element of their case. A defence campaign, then, should be a blitzkrieg; we hold back, look for the weakest point, and then smash through it. At least, that's the idea, but the odds are always in the prosecution's favour for one simple reason: *they* choose the fight. The CPS considers the evidence and only charges people when the evidence reveals a realistic prospect of conviction.

We adjourned for lunch after the jury had been sworn, and ten minutes later I was sliding a plastic tray along the length of the counter in the Bar mess, peering down at the selection of food dehydrating under heat lamps. I settled on chips, bread and butter and, after noticing her unpacking her meagre lunch onto a table in the back corner of the room, an extra cup of tea for Zara.

'Thought you could use this,' I said, placing the steaming mug in front of her.

She glanced up from a noticeably dry cheese sandwich and smiled. 'Thanks.' She'd removed her wig but still looked older than usual in her professional black court suit; if it wasn't for the rather pitiful lunch of one sandwich and only half a KitKat, it would be quite hard to believe that she still lived in a shared student house in Brixton. 'Don't they do anything stronger than tea?'

'That bad?' I dropped into a chair, and used my teeth to rip into two sachets of sugar. 'How was Bowen? Do you need me to rough him up a little bit?'

'He's been all right. As boring as ever. His opening speech had all the flair of being lifted word for word from the CPS guidelines.' She lowered her voice to a pompous drawl. '"Intentional obstruction of a police constable exercising his powers to search and obtain evidence, contrary to Section 23(4) of the Act. There is a strong public interest in prosecuting those who destroy or conceal evidence of serious drug offences, blah, blah, blah ..." I swear, the man could kill Shakespeare.'

I had to chuckle, tapping my teaspoon dry on the edge of my mug. 'And Andre?'

'Alive, which is a bonus. Not especially happy that he has to share a cell while he's here.'

'Who's he sharing a cell with?'

'I don't know. Just some bloke. Belmarsh, I think. This Osman warning seems to have messed with his head a little. He's ... *scatty*. Not that I can blame him. They warn the lad that somebody is going to try to kill him, then lock him in a cramped, dirty cell with a morally ambiguous stranger. Seems backward to me.'

I started fashioning my food into a butty. 'Did you submit the Section 8 application? The disclosure request?'

She nodded, chewing her sandwich. 'Not that I expect anything positive to come of it after that PII ruling. It's so stupid. A participating informant set up the crime in league with the police, and somehow that's not disclosable to the defence!'

'Maybe Bowen will have a change of heart.'

'He'd need to have a heart first. What happened with Meadows?'

I shook my head, still not quite managing to believe it myself. 'You may want to strap yourself in for this one.'

Her eyes lit up and she froze with the sandwich halfway to her lips. 'Go on.'

'Deacon, former drug dealer, inmate of the Scrubs and potential cuckoo of the Meadows household … is also the proprietor of an independent drill label by the name of Banged Up Records.'

She slammed the sandwich down onto its foil. 'Get the fuck out of here!'

'At this rate, I almost wish I could.'

'He produced for Andre *and* Omar Pickett.' She squeezed her eyes shut. 'What have we got ourselves into?'

'There's more. You recall the Meadows family dog?'

'Oh, you mean the county lines guard dog of choice? Yeah, I think I do recall that.'

'My client got it from Deacon.'

'Inevitable, really. How did you find that out?'

'Charli told me all about it this morning, when she was explaining how it died.'

'It died?'

'Poisoned, it would appear.'

'*Poisoned?*'

'And it is now buried under the very allotment where we sat last week.'

She gawped at me for a moment, then slid the last of her sandwich away across the table. 'They're not still going to eat those tomatoes she was growing, are they?'

I couldn't say.

The afternoon brought Garrick's opening speech. I'd been staring at the strangers gathered in the public gallery when the judge invited him to start, and he got to his feet and turned to the jury, notes sprawled before him on our shared row.

'From ten o'clock on the morning of Monday 15 January this year, a joint operation between the Prison Service's Anti-Corruption Investigation Unit, the National Crime Agency and the Metropolitan Police's Organised Crime Division was undertaken at Her Majesty's Prison Wormwood Scrubs, a Category B local jail in the Hammersmith and Fulham borough of London. Code-named Operation Triptych, this strategic manoeuvre consisted of searches on all members of staff as well as every onsite vehicle in response to drugs-related fatalities within the prison. Specially trained canines were employed for the task.

'At approximately 10.35, Operation Triptych uncovered a large quantity of synthetic cannabinoids, generically referred to as Spice, concealed within the boot of a vehicle in the prison's private staff car park. These drugs, which were disguised as ten individual packets of rolling tobacco, were estimated to have a combined prison value of £10,000. The vehicle in which they were discovered was an unassuming Vauxhall Corsa, a dark blue model from the year 2000, registration number X326 ADM. This vehicle was owned by Charli Meadows, the defendant brought before you today. She was the only suspect to be arrested and charged under the efforts of Operation Triptych that day.

'Charli Meadows was a trusted employee of HMP Wormwood Scrubs. Her role, officially titled Operational Support Grade, was one tier below officer level, but no less integral to the running of the prison. For more than four years, her responsibilities included everything from direct contact with countless inmates to having control of the very locks designed to hold them on the premises. It would be no hyperbole to say that Charli Meadows quite literally held the keys to Wormwood Scrubs in the palm of her hand.

'The single count on today's indictment is one of smuggling psychoactive substances, as defined by the Psychoactive Substances Act 2016, into a custodial institution. This is in direct violation of Section 40B of the Prison Act 1952, which concerns the unlawful conveyance of List A articles into one of Her Majesty's Prisons. It is the Crown's case that the defendant, Miss Charli Meadows, did knowingly smuggle these drugs onto the premises.

'But who is Charli Meadows?' Garrick's eyes turned briefly and indifferently towards the dock, his hollow expression revealing that he didn't really see anybody inside it. 'A single mother to three children, she has by all accounts been a hard-working woman before now. The sort that you will, perhaps, recognise from your own lives, your own families. And make no mistake that the defence will attempt to use that to distract you. To cloud the fact that this crime has been committed, committed knowingly, and committed by the defendant alone. The drugs *were* found in that car. This fact is agreed upon, meaning that it is presented before you *unchallenged* by the defence. The sole individual who has access to that car is its owner, Charli Meadows, another hard fact that the defence has not even bothered to deny. You will hear that the defendant chose to *drive* the two-hour round trip from her home in Walthamstow to the prison every single working day for more than four years. What was so important about braving the city's congestion to have her vehicle onsite in that prison car park is answerable only by the conclusion of her time there.

'The defence may suggest that Miss Meadows simply did not know that she was committing a crime. That, as far as she was aware, the packages contained nothing worse than ordinary tobacco. As Her Ladyship Lady Allen will direct you on the law as to what constitutes *mens rea*, you shall discover that ignorance does not legally excuse any such actions. It may even be suggested that Miss Meadows did not have a choice in the matter whatsoever. That she was being coerced into her crime. Well, the answer to this is that we all, always, have a choice.

'In her interviews, the defendant was given ample opportunity to explain where she acquired the drugs. Her solicitor suggested that she reply "no comment" to all questions asked, but, to her credit, Miss Meadows *did* respond a little. She denied knowing anything about the drugs. No excuses, no theories, no alternative explanations. The Crown says that she could offer no alternatives, because there is only one possible explanation: Charli Meadows was smuggling Spice into those prison walls for financial reward. True, it might not have been for a lavish, millionaire's lifestyle – it might simply have been to make a better life for her family – but the fact remains that she broke the law, and intentionally so. The trafficking of drugs is never a victimless crime.

'On that note, it will become quite obvious to you, as the trial progresses, that Operation Triptych was conducted almost immediately after the tragic, drugs-related deaths of thirteen inmates on the night of Tuesday 9 January. Though the relationship is undeniable, it is vital that you do not allow the horror of those fatalities to impact your eventual decision. The pathologists were not able to legally link the drugs seized to the deaths prior, and the proof of intent to supply does not prove past supply. Therefore, those deaths should not be considered when judging this defendant. The charge brought against Charli Meadows is one of smuggling drugs into Wormwood Scrubs. Through the course of this trial, I shall make you absolutely certain of her guilt. There can be no doubt – there can be only justice. It is every bit as simple as that.'

Garrick returned to his seat, and a single word was muttered in the public gallery – it carried on a draught through the silence of the room, a gust so quick and cold that nobody turned towards it. But we all knew what had been said. Everyone.

'*Murderer*,' the whisper called.

We adjourned for the evening twenty minutes earlier than expected, and while changing out of my robes I sent Zara a text telling her to meet me at the Toby Carvery a block away from the court, where I would treat her to dinner; the thought of her going home to the other half of that miserable KitKat after her opening day had been playing on my mind. I was conscious of the number of hours Scout had been alone and, strangely, I was looking forward to getting back to her after dinner. I resolved to make it quick.

I arrived at the pub and purchased the tickets for two roasts, one king-sized and one vegetarian, before commandeering a table away from the bar to wait for Zara. She arrived at half past with a face like thunder, slamming her bags down under the table as she dropped into an empty seat.

'As soon as the prosecution received my disclosure request, they once again applied for public-interest immunity and Judge Bromley granted it.'

'They really aren't going to disclose what led them to the raid?'

'They aren't going to disclose *shit*, Section 8 application or not. They're claiming that if they were to reveal their source then it could affect a number of ongoing investigations, so it's in the public's interest to withhold the evidence.'

'Omar Pickett.'

'Has to be, but I can't even approach the topic in a court of law. I can't get answers to the fundamental questions supporting my own case! It's a damn gagging order, that's all it is. A sham!' She removed her glasses, folded them and closed her eyes. 'Without a miracle – without Omar Pickett magically popping up to testify at some point during the next few days – it's just a losing battle.'

I sighed, then slid the meal ticket over the table towards her. 'Let's get some food in our stomachs and have a think about this.'

'You shouldn't have,' she said, 'but thank you. *Again.*'

'That's all right.' I pushed my chair out and got to my feet, feeling thirsty. 'You get us a place in the queue, and I'll get the drinks.'

The inexplicably enthusiastic barman drummed his hands across the beer pumps as he approached, grinning broadly. 'Good afternoon, sir. What's your poison?'

And after the day I'd had, the image that word brought to my mind was almost enough to put me off my dinner altogether.

19

Zara's case didn't seem to be going much better by the time I met her for lunch the following afternoon.

We were walking towards the Bar mess, her hands stuffed into her pockets, when Ted Bowen appeared ahead of us and she grunted.

'Let's go to the public canteen instead,' she said quietly. 'I can't be arsed to look at his face while I eat.'

'Any particular reason?'

'You've been in a courtroom with him and you still need a reason?'

The public canteen was extremely crowded, and we just managed to win the race for a table that was still littered with someone's tray and leftovers. As soon as we were seated, Zara had her nose to the screen of her iPad. I recognised the dull beat leaking from the speaker; she was watching the last music video of Omar Pickett, aka Post Mortem.

'Any luck?' I asked, knowing the obvious answer.

'No. Nothing. I had an idea about this skatepark, but, I don't know ...'

'The one from the video?'

'Yeah.' With one hand she shoved the tray of leftovers to the edge of the table and then laid the iPad in its place for me to see. There was Post Mortem, gesticulating with both hands against the backdrop of spray-painted convex walls. I tried to pay attention but couldn't keep from glancing around, acutely conscious of the members of the public bustling through the room. Zara didn't seem to care. She paused the video, freezing the masked youngster. 'I was looking for skateparks in Leyton last night.'

'On *foot?*'

She rolled her eyes. 'Online. There aren't any that fit the bill in Leyton itself, but there are plenty in the surrounding areas ...' She produced a pocket notebook and flicked to a page of handwriting, a list that looked noticeably more chaotic than her usual neat script. 'Walthamstow Skatepark, the closest, is way too small to match this one in the video. Hackney's Concrete Bumps and Victoria Park aren't right either – no graffiti in the photographs online ...' She moved her finger down the page. 'At first I thought it might be Mile End Concrete Bowl, but that's about five miles south of Leyton. White Grounds in Bermondsey is underneath a railway arch that looks a lot like this one, and –' She glanced up; whatever she saw on my face made her frown. 'What?'

'Nothing. It's just making my head spin a little, that's all. What good is a skatepark going to be?'

'I was thinking that Pickett might go back there. You can search by area on Instagram, which brings up all the photographs tagged in that location. A lot of people skate in these parks, they might know him. I could message *them* and see if they have any idea where he might be hiding.'

'But if the people he runs with haven't yet been able to find him ...'

'You don't think it's a good idea?'

'I didn't say that.'

'This could be my whole case!' Her voice turned quiet and earnest. 'This public-interest crap has got me clutching at straws. All I know is that *this* idiot is supposed to be sitting in Andre's place, and Andre still won't tell me anything about him!'

'And do you really believe that Omar would take Israel's place willingly?'

'I *know*, but I'll never be sure unless I talk to him.'

'It sounds unlikely. My advice is to take a step back. Fight the case to the best of your capabilities and trust in the system. You don't need to do this independent research.'

'A little rich coming from you.'

She wasn't wrong there.

'Speaking of independent research,' Zara went on, 'I did a bit of digging into Banged Up Records. The producer is shown on their website as Deacon Walker.'

'We already knew that.'

'Not the surname, we didn't. Don't you think it's strange? Walker.'

'It isn't the strangest I've ever heard.'

'Not the name.' She rolled her eyes again. 'The initials. Think about it. If his initials are DW, then why is he driving a car around with the registration DM1?'

'Meadows told me that he's an Uber driver. Apparently, the car belongs to a friend.'

'You believe that?'

'I don't know. She lied about his existence in the first place. If it *is* his car then DM1 could've simply been the closest thing available. Deacon Music, maybe.'

'Or maybe his real name isn't Walker at all.' Now she was fully whispering. 'Maybe it actually stands for Deacon

Macey! Think about it. He could be the mystery heir that Patch was telling us about.'

'It's a theory.' I sipped my tea. 'Of course, Patch also believes that Elvis Presley is alive on the moon, eating cheese and riding around on the back of Shergar.'

'Fine,' she snapped, 'but until you come up with something better, I'm keeping all possibilities on the table.'

That afternoon brought my first attempt at challenging a witness for the prosecution. There was nothing in his witness statement that I disagreed with and, generally, you would allow the prosecution to read such a witness's statement as agreed evidence, but I had an inkling that I could get a little more out of him than he'd told the police. The oft-quoted rule of advocacy is never to ask a question unless you know the answer. Sometimes, however, you have to take a gamble, especially when the weight of evidence is against you.

The aged black man in the box kept leaning too close to the microphone when he spoke, which gave his voice the tinny resonance of a cheap DJ. Sporting a fuzz of white hair and an ancient brown suit, he introduced himself as Russell Chapman and told the court that his role at the Scrubs amounted to sitting in a booth by the entrance gates for forty hours every week, watching vehicles roll in and out of the prison grounds. Upon reflection, I remembered seeing him on the day we visited Andre Israel.

'Not what you'd call stimulating,' he chuckled, 'especially since they installed those automated barriers, but it gets me by.' He seemed to be enjoying the attention of the room and kept smiling warmly towards the jury; for some witnesses, this was the most excitement they were likely to see all year.

'Do all of the vehicles that enter the grounds belong to members of staff?' Garrick asked.

'Most, and that's not just guards. We've got nurses, administration, cleaners, counsellors, handymen, employers in the workshops. More staff than I could count, cars coming and going all day long. They either scan their tickets, or they don't get past, it's as simple as that.'

'Tickets?' Garrick replied. 'Are you saying that every employee has a permit?'

'Uh-huh, that's right. We've got the red-and-white barriers up, you know, one in and one out. There's a machine there that scans the ticket and lifts the barrier.'

'And with all this automated machinery, what exactly do you do?'

'Well, we get a lot of vans, deliveries and linen. They're scheduled in advance, but I've got to get out and check them off. I get a list at the start of every week and make sure those drivers have got their paperwork in return. Course, they could just send the lorry drivers a ticket out in advance, but don't tell *them* that or I'll be out of a job!' The tiniest titter from the jury, which made the man beam with pride. 'Never get too many issues, except for you lawyers trying to park onsite.'

'Is there any public or legal visitor car parking onsite whatsoever?'

'Uh-uh, none. Visitors park out there at the roadside.'

'To clarify, the only vehicles that ever get past your booth are authorised in advance, one way or the other?'

'All authorised, yes.'

'Were you working on Monday the fifteenth of January this year?'

'Eight until four.'

'You were onsite when the staff vehicles were searched?'

'I was.'

'And are you familiar with the vehicle registered to the defendant?'

He nodded. 'Vauxhall, dark blue, a bit of a rattler.'

'Do you happen to know the registration number of the defendant's Vauxhall?'

'You must be joking. I don't even know my own car's registration number.'

Lady Allen leaned to her microphone. 'Is this evidence disputed, Mr Rook?'

'No, My Lady, the defence accepts every word of Mr Chapman's evidence. My learned friend may lead him through all of it.'

Garrick bristled. 'If Mr Rook accepts this witness's evidence unchallenged, then why has he been fully bound to attend court? Why couldn't we just read his statement?'

'Mr Rook?' The judge raised an inquisitive eyebrow.

'I have a few supplementary questions for the witness.' I smiled. 'A few points I hope he can clarify.'

'Very well. Continue, Mr Garrick.'

After a hard stare, he did. 'The car in question would be a Corsa, registration X326 ADM?'

'Sounds about right.'

'And on these days, was it always the defendant behind the wheel?'

'As far as I recall. I would've noticed and stepped out if it wasn't.'

'Do you keep a record of the times that each vehicle enters and exits the premises?'

'My Lady,' I interrupted, half raising my hand. 'The car's presence on the morning in question is already agreed upon, as is the CCTV footage of the defendant arriving in said vehicle and driving through the barrier a few minutes before nine o'clock. The defence has no dispute with any of this.'

Again, she raised her brow. 'You did just invite the prosecution to lead the witness through every word of his statement.'

'That's all right,' Garrick snorted. 'That's all I have to ask, Mr Chapman. Please wait there while Mr Rook decides upon which supplementary questions he'd like to ask you.'

In Garrick's stead, I got to my feet. 'Mr Chapman, your booth is positioned on the inside of the outer gates, is it not?'

'It is.'

'For those present in the court who are not so familiar with the layout of Wormwood Scrubs, could you give us a basic description of the approach to the prison by vehicle?'

He ran a hand across his cheek, bemused. 'I suppose I can, yes. The car comes along Du Cane Road, turns in through the outer gates and past my booth to the barriers, where it gets its ticket checked, like I said. Then it's a straight drive forwards to the gatehouse.'

'Those would be the iconic towers that I'm sure we're all familiar with, correct?'

'The same.'

'Do the cars continue ahead through the gatehouse?'

'No. Staff cars don't. They turn either left or right, following the outer wall around, and the parking is down there on both sides.'

'Once they are parked up, can you personally see the vehicles from your booth?'

'Not directly, no, but I have a monitor relaying the CCTV from along the perimeter.'

'And do these cameras focus on the staff vehicles?'

He paused, thinking about it. 'They actually don't. They're aimed more at the walls.'

'Why is that, do you think?'

'Huh ... Well, I've never really considered it, but I suppose you'd have to have some real big balls on you to break into a car in a prison car park, wouldn't you?'

Another titter from the jury. I didn't mind; this was going well enough.

'Yes, Mr Chapman, I believe you probably would. What I also find interesting is that you said the cars follow the outer wall to either the left or the right and park up there.'

'I did.'

'All right, let's see. So, if *this* represents the prison itself ...' With my left hand I held up a sheet of paper from my pile. 'And this is a car ...' With the index finger of my right, I traced a path coming up to the paper from the centre underneath, then followed the perimeter of the paper over to the left and parked it there. 'Wouldn't that mean that the parking areas themselves are actually *outside* of the prison walls, even for members of staff?'

'They are situated on the property, inside the outer fence, but security couldn't have cars coming in and out of the main walls all day long. It'd be a nightmare.'

'I'm sure it would.' I returned the paper to the pile. 'On the morning in question, do you recall whether the defendant turned left or right upon reaching the gatehouse?'

'Left.'

'You're sure about that?'

'Course. Even in prison, it isn't every day you have dogs closing off half the car park. The Corsa was parked up in the south-western corner, close to my own car.'

'Again, that is *outside* of the actual prison walls, yes?'

'Yes.'

Garrick sighed; it must've been as loudly as he could manage. 'My Lady, it seems as though the defence intends to suggest that the defendant's car, as well as the contraband inside, could not have been in breach of smuggling laws because they were not actually discovered within the prison's walls ... Perhaps a reminder is required to refresh my learned friend on what constitutes prison premises?'

'A considerate offer,' I said, 'but no reminder is necessary, thank you. Prison property begins at Mr Chapman's booth and barriers, and by all accounts the defendant's vehicle was most definitely onsite at the time of the discovery. The point I was trying to make is that it was parked up in the south-western corner of the grounds. Nothing unusual there – it is one of two parking zones reserved for staff – but would it be fair to say that this area is something of a dumping ground, Mr Chapman?'

'In what respect?'

'Well, I have seen the area for myself in the past, and would you agree or disagree with my observation that it is nothing more than a patch of loose, potholed concrete with a few industrial Biffa skips and piles of scrap metal and rubbish?'

He nodded. 'I'd say that's a good enough description, though you missed out the weeds. At the end of the day, it's only a place to leave your car.'

'Indeed. One can only assume that those enormous bins require emptying from time to time?'

'Once a week. There's a gate in the fence up there, padlocked. Every Tuesday I unlock it, let the wagons come in, then lock it back up again when they're done.'

'The gate leads back out onto Du Cane Road?'

'Right.'

'And are there any signs on these gates?'

He frowned a little. 'Private property signs, mostly. An arrow pointing in the direction of the main entrance down the road. Nothing out of the ordinary.'

'But it's a prison, hardly an inconspicuous structure. Why the signs?'

'Oh, that's easy,' he said, brightening up. 'They're for the fly-tippers.'

'Fly-tippers?' I cocked my head. 'As in, members of the public dumping rubbish?'

'Uh-huh, sure. There's a low point at the very end of the fence down that side, must be about four feet high, which backs onto Wulfstan Street, the residential area to the west. People who can't be bothered to hire a skip have a bad habit of just hopping over the fence there and dumping their crap into the Biffas.'

I heard the softest rustle of silk as Garrick straightened up beside me.

'You'll have to forgive me for sounding like a broken record, but just to elucidate ...' I spoke more slowly. 'To gain vehicular access to this car park, which is securely enclosed between the prison walls and the outer perimeter fence, a member of staff would have to show their credentials at your barrier, yes?'

'That's what I've been saying.'

'But there are *no* cameras whatsoever covering the area where the defendant's car was parked, despite a problem with fly-tippers?'

'Right.'

'And you just told the court that these fly-tippers are able to hop over into the car park, did you not?'

'Right again.'

'So, wouldn't it be possible for somebody to enter that car park, unseen, and gain access to any number of staff vehicles at any time of any day? Size of genitalia withstanding, of course.'

The judge cleared her throat and levelled me with a stern look.

The witness thought about it. Nodded. 'It's possible.'

'Are the vehicles regularly checked for contraband?'

'In the staff car park?' He shook his head. 'Never during my years at the prison.'

'You personally don't give them a quick once-over upon arriving?'

'No.'

'Then, hypothetically, couldn't the drugs have been inside that car for hours, days, or even weeks before that morning?'

He shrugged, then considered the idea. 'I just work the booth, but ... for all I know, they could've been, yes.' He leaned forward until his lips were actually touching the microphone, then started to speak low and confidential as if the two of us were alone in our conspiratorial gossip. 'Hey, come to think of it, it could just as easily have been some old con, couldn't it? Someone looking to get back at the screws! He hops over the fence, gets into the first car he sees and dumps that crap under the boot. Maybe he's planning on chucking it over the wall and he bottles it! Christ, *my* car was parked up there as well. It could've been me!'

'It's possible,' I said, feeling a huge smile coming on. 'Thank you for your time, Mr Chapman. No more questions.'

Did I honestly believe that an unknown assailant had snuck over the fence, broken into Charli's Vauxhall and stuffed the drugs inside? Not really, not nearly as much as I suspected the involvement of her boyfriend, but that was beside the point. Doubt was the most crucial part of any defence.

Once again, we were adjourned a little early, and like a child released from school I practically bounced out of the courtroom. That's where I found Zara, sitting on a bench in the corridor. Her glasses were off, face buried in her hands, and she didn't look up until I placed a hand on her shoulder.

'Good day, I take it?'

'Hopeless,' she replied. 'Without a miracle, Andre is certain to be convicted.'

I wasn't smiling any more.

20

As we got back into chambers a little after five o'clock, Percy flagged us down through the open door of the bustling clerks' room. He'd been smiling, but one look at the pair of us and his expression wilted.

'What happened?'

Zara flapped her mouth, but nothing seemed to be coming any time soon.

'Tough day at the coal face,' I answered for her.

'The drug dealer from Newham? The silver lining is that, as we're prosecuting *and* defending in that case, it's a win–win situation for chambers.' When she didn't react, he sighed. 'Look, don't worry, young lady. My advice is to push on through to the end, then move on to the next case.'

Her eyes turned up to him, their infinitesimal movements revealing a series of conflicting emotions: irritation, distrust, weariness, even gratitude. 'Just like that? Serve up your client's head on a platter and then it's on to the next one?'

'I wouldn't be so morose about it, but yes, almost like that. The wheels of the system keep on turning. As a part of that system, you must learn to move forward. If not, you risk losing a little of yourself to every failure. That is the nature of our justice.'

'Justice?' she muttered. 'Do you honestly believe that?'

Percy blinked softly. 'Miss Barnes, I believe that our legal system is the closest thing we have to justice on this good earth.' And he left us to climb up to the third floor.

Chambers was officially open until five thirty, but already there was a steady stream of junior barristers squeezing past us on the narrow staircase. Zara hadn't said much since I'd found her waiting outside the courtroom. Up in my room, I reached into the compartment beneath my desk where I kept a few emergency drinks, which I'd been venturing into less and less just lately. I opened a couple of warm lagers, banging the caps off on the dented edge of my desk, and handed one to Zara, who was sitting in her usual spot by the bureau.

'It's just unravelling so fast,' she said, taking the bottle. 'The prosecution case is racing along. They're on to their last witness tomorrow morning. That's DI Linford, and I'm not even allowed to ask him any questions. I just can't stop thinking that Andre should have got himself a real barrister. A tenant, not some useless pupil.'

'Don't do that to yourself,' I said. 'Percy might be a twat from time to time, but he isn't wrong. You cannot win them all, especially when the evidence is so overwhelming.'

'You're saying I never had a chance to begin with?'

'No. There is always a chance at trial. You haven't lost anything yet.'

She looked tired and close to tears, hands wringing the neck of her bottle. 'I might as well start packing this crap up out of your bureau.'

'There's no use in being dramatic about it.'

Her eyes swelled and then narrowed straight at me. 'I am *not* being dramatic.'

We were interrupted by a loud ringing; it took me a moment to realise that it was coming from the phone on my desk, which I'd had for some months and rarely bothered to use in favour of my mobile. A flashing red light told me it was a local call from inside the building. Percy. Annoyed by the interruption, I lifted the receiver and put it down again, cutting it off.

A few seconds later, it rang again. This time I slammed the receiver down. After months of absorbing Zara's good moods, it seemed that I was succumbing to her foul ones as well.

'Now who's being dramatic?' Zara said. 'You should answer.'

'He has legs, doesn't he? If it's so important he can climb the bloody staircase.' As if someone had heard my suggestion, there came a timid knock at the door. 'What?' I called.

It opened, revealing a lad of around twenty years old, an intern from the clerks' room. He cleared his throat, simultaneously flushing and flinching. 'Um, Mr Peck sent me up with a message.'

I lowered my voice to something almost apologetic. 'Which is?'

'There's somebody downstairs asking to see you. He's been told that we close in ten minutes and to make an appointment, but he seems quite … insistent.'

'Did he give a name?'

'Oh.' The young man turned from pink to purple. 'Not you, Mr Rook.' He pointed to Zara. 'He's here for you. He says his name's Fred.'

'Fred?' She frowned. 'I don't know any Fred.'

The clerk tugged at his skinny tie. 'I've got to be honest, he doesn't *look* much like a Fred. He says you messaged him at the end of last week asking him to come in and see you. On Facebook, apparently.'

'That's ridiculous,' she said, 'I wouldn't message anybody on –' Her jaw dropped. She looked towards me, eyes wide behind her glasses. 'It can't be.'

'Surely not,' I said.

It was.

We made it to the bottom of the staircase in a queue of shuffling barristers and sidestepped back into the reception area.

Zara coughed. 'Fred?'

He turned round sharply, a teenager dressed in a mismatched combination of wraparound sunglasses and an oversized winter coat, a snapback cap and scarf; all that was missing from his ludicrous disguise was a novelty fake moustache. He assessed Zara for a moment, then gestured to me. 'Who's this?'

'Elliot Rook,' Zara said, 'another barrister. It's OK. We're on your side.'

I wasn't entirely sure that we were, but I nodded in agreement all the same.

I took the two of them back up to my room and closed the door behind us; the elusive 'Fred' had lowered the brim of his cap a half-inch further with every barrister we'd passed on the staircase, and now it was pressing straight down against his sunglasses.

Zara offered him a seat as she perched lightly on the edge of my desk. 'You can lose the disguise, Mr Pickett.'

Even through the shades, he appeared to be looking up at the corners of the rooms.

'There are no cameras in chambers,' I said, taking my own chair. 'The majority of our clients wouldn't approve.'

He removed his shades, cap and scarf slowly, cramming them into the pockets of his massive coat, but didn't take the seat. Instead, he picked up the Rubik's cube that had been forever rolling around my desk and paced in a jittery circle. With the puzzle in his hand, he looked very young, a college-aged boy with a strong nose and soft skin, incredibly dark eyes and hair shaved at the back and sides. I could see why he didn't want to go to prison; he probably weighed as much as my right leg.

'How do I know I can trust you?' he asked. 'Either of you.'

'I think you want to,' Zara said. 'Otherwise you wouldn't have come here.'

He shrugged, fiddling with the cube.

'Would you like us to get you a solicitor?' I asked.

'No. No solicitor. I came to see *her*,' pointing at Zara, 'I don't know you.'

'You don't know her either.'

'Yeah, well, she looked fit on Facebook.' He eyed me up and down. 'You don't.'

A glower crossed Zara's face like a passing cloud, but she pulled it back; it was obvious from the quake in his throat that his bravado was fuelled by chronic nerves. 'What do you need from us, Omar?' she said.

'Or should we call you Post Mortem?' I asked.

'You can call me Fred if you like. I need to get into that witness protection. I need someone to speak to the feds.'

'Feds are American,' Zara replied, 'and this isn't *The Sopranos*.'

'But you do want me to snitch on my crew, don't you?' he asked sharply. 'Why else would you get me here?'

'*Your* crew?' Zara leaned forward from her perch, hands clasped on her lap; she looked much shrewder than she had only half an hour ago. 'That's just the thing, Omar. Are the Cutthroats still *your* crew at all?'

'Cutthroats?' He laughed coldly. 'That was just a stupid name the kids used. They're my neighbours. E10. We came up in the same tower. Schoolmates. Safety in numbers.'

'Safety in numbers?' I said. 'Those numbers seem to be growing exponentially, don't they?'

He continued pacing, eyes on the puzzle in his hands. 'The whole scene's blowing up. We were brothers, you know? Tight. Now, I don't even recognise half our crew. It was meant to be a way to earn a living, like, independently. None of that nine-to-five managerial bullshit.'

'And let me guess,' Zara said, 'now you're getting ordered around and you don't like it?'

'Such as the order to get yourselves sent to prison,' I added.

He stopped pacing. Instead of answering, he tossed the Rubik's cube onto the desk, where it rolled to a stop behind Zara. I did a double take; the thing was solved.

'Who's giving these orders?' Zara asked.

He shook his head. 'I tell you that and we're all dead, believe.'

'But that was the plan, wasn't it?' I said. 'To get yourselves sent to prison?'

Again, he didn't answer. His eyes had fixed onto the beer I'd opened earlier, which was still effervescing quietly. 'Got one of them going spare?' he asked.

'Here.' Zara impatiently crossed the room to her own bottle, passed it to him, and returned to her spot on my desk.

Omar checked the level of the liquid – untouched – and sniffed at the bottle like an animal at a trap. Then he drank thirstily and belched. 'That's the game,' he said. 'You go inside, do a bit, come out and you're on top. No more college. No dole. No more tins of ravioli.'

'It'd be hard to continue your music from inside a cell,' Zara noted.

He looked up at the ceiling and shook his head, half smiling. 'You know how much equipment I could buy after one single stretch? I'm talking about some of that top-of-the-line, professional Jay Z shit. Not to mention the rep. That sort of reputation *pays* in drill. A man can't be writing about doing time and hustling if he's never had to hustle.'

'And when did you start working for the Met?' I asked.

His face tightened, reluctant, and then relented. 'Christmas. Some undie snatched me with enough crack to send me down until my thirties.'

I nodded, reaching for my own drink. 'Not quite the short, glamorous stretch you had in mind?'

'We made a deal,' he said. 'It'd all go away if I let a few details slip here and there. I'd even make a bit of cash. It sounded like suicide to me, but I didn't have much choice.'

'Who was he?' Zara asked, eyes widening. 'This under-cover officer.'

Omar took a bigger mouthful of lager before replying. 'Man called Linford.'

'I knew it!' Zara slapped her hand against the desk. '*Sod your PII.*'

Omar blinked. 'Huh?'

'Nothing,' I said quickly. 'This raid at the Alex. Was that Linford's plan?'

'No.' He started moving again, tracing his own path over the rug. 'Those orders came from the bosses.'

'Your own bosses ordered you to organise the raid with Linford?' Zara said. 'They knew you were a paid police informant, and they were willing to let you live?'

He paused to empty his bottle, then wiped his lips dry on his sleeve. 'I did what they asked, walked out of that pub, and by the time I got home, they'd already booted my mum's door in and trashed the place. There was a dead rat in my bed. I grabbed some clothes and went ghost, man. Had nowhere else to go. Couldn't trust anyone, and now I'm sleeping in bushes and shit, freezing for weeks, getting hypothermia or something. I go anywhere near my end and it'll *be* my end, you get me?'

'I do,' I said, 'though one might argue that you've encouraged their disapprobation. You've still been posting videos about them online, haven't you? What was it again? "Cutthroats pulling them strings / Unlucky number's feeling the wrath."'

His eyes flared with surprise as Zara joined. '"Gaza Strip caught up in things / Sorry, Palestine–Israel's off."' She shook her head. 'After a look on your Facebook, it seems that your family are mostly Palestinian. So, *you're* Palestine, of course. And you are friends with Andre Israel, aren't you?'

'I don't know about friends,' he muttered. 'Used to be on the same scene. He's quiet. Straight.'

'Yes,' she said, 'and I take it from those lyrics that you're aware of his current trial? You could go so far as to say he's been charged in your place.'

'If it's protection you're after,' I added, 'then you're going to have to offer something in return. We're going to need you to testify in court.'

He considered this for a while longer, though he must've already been considering it for weeks. He shuffled over to the bureau in the corner and dropped into Zara's usual chair. He bowed his head, passing the empty bottle between his hands, and mumbled, 'What would I have to say?'

'Well,' I told him, 'you'd have to testify about Andre Israel's involvement, or lack thereof, for a start, as well as the actions of your fellow Cutthroats, and whatever they're up to in that prison.'

'Is that all?' He laughed weakly, staring down at his trainers; they looked expensive, but tattered by the streets. 'Will I be safe?'

I hesitated. In asking this question, as he had with the Rubik's cube in his hands, he looked much younger. 'I don't know. We'd do our best to make it so.'

He nodded slightly. 'How would it work?'

'First, we'd need you to see Andre's solicitor, tomorrow, so that she can take a statement from you.'

'Tomorrow? You need me to help you out, but you're going to send me back out to sleep on the streets? Some deal that is.'

Zara shrugged. 'We don't run a hotel, Omar.'

'No,' I agreed, 'I'm sorry to say that we don't.' I fell quiet then, thinking about it. I clenched my eyes shut, realising what I had to do, and sighed. 'I need to go and make a personal phone call.'

Omar braced in his seat. 'To who?'

'Somebody,' I replied, getting to my feet. 'If we're going to keep you alive, then you're going to have to trust me.'

Whether I had his faith or not, he didn't say. I could feel his suspicious gaze as I went out onto the landing, closed the door behind me and took my phone from my pocket.

I leaned back against the wall a few yards from my door and listened to the sounds of the building. Ernie's vacuum cleaner was already at work a floor away. In a room nearby, somebody coughed and stiff keys clicked across a laptop. I took a deep breath and scrolled through my contacts to the listing I'd never changed: *Home*.

After precisely seven rings, it was answered. 'Hello?'

My stomach tightened at the sound of the voice, pushing hot blood into my ears. 'Is Jenn— *Jennifer* there?'

'May I ask who's calling?'

I had to clamp my jaw: I was the man who had kept that king-sized bed warm for fifteen years. Thankfully, I heard her voice before I had to force a civil answer. '*Who is it, Tom? They're about to start the final chase.*'

'It's for you, dear.'

'*Oh, for God's sake. Hang on, I'll pause it ...*' There was the fumbling of the receiver changing hands, then a deep, feminine breath beside the mouthpiece. 'Yes?'

'You know that those game shows are all fixed, don't you?'

A fuming sigh. 'What do you want?'

'How's Phillip?'

'Still dying. Is that what you called for?'

'I need your help.'

Her voice lowered to a hiss; the lack of background air suggested that she'd cupped her hand around the microphone. 'If it's to do with that threat then think again.'

'It's not. Do you still help out at Centrepoint?'

A few seconds of silence. 'Why?'

'I've got a young man here that could use your help.'

Twenty minutes later, Omar was back in his ludicrous disguise and cautiously following Zara and me along Chancery Lane.

I led them both through the gate of Lincoln's Inn, which was unlocked every day until seven at night. Across those grounds, I retraced the same shortcut that used to take me from waking up on Lincoln's Inn Fields to the baths down at the Inner Temple. Omar seemed to be surveying the society's ancient stone buildings with distrust, though it was hard to be sure from the outside of his sunglasses. Beyond the gated grounds of Lincoln's Inn itself, we passed the fields that I'd once called home, then crossed Kingsway.

Altogether it was only a ten-minute walk to Bruce House, the massive five-storey red-brick building that occupied more than half of Kemble Street at the front and a considerable chunk of Drury Lane to the side. It was classed as a charitable lodging house, another of the city's Grade II listed buildings, and had been hosting the homeless since before George Orwell wrote about his stay there in *Down and Out in Paris and London* in 1933, in which he described the place as 'excellent value for one and a penny'. Now it was run by Centrepoint, and cost its residents £13.44 a week.

'Here?' Omar asked after I'd come to a stop.

'Here.'

I'd never stayed here during my own 'down and out' period – it had been undergoing a major renovation that saw it closed between the late eighties and early nineties – but its proximity to chambers made it the obvious choice, and its sheer size was the reason Jenny had suggested it, in the hope that Omar could become lost among the tenants. The entrance was comprised of wooden double doors set beneath a stone semicircular arch. Two residents were smoking there; Omar tensed as we passed them by, but neither paid him any mind.

The woman behind the counter looked up and smiled as we entered. She had a face that was vaguely familiar from Jenny's charity events of yesteryear. 'Elliot! Long time, no see. I literally just got off the phone with Jennifer, she said you'd be coming down.' She turned her smile to the teenager and his ridiculous outfit. 'You're extremely lucky, young man. Ordinarily there's a waiting list, but the Rooks have done a lot of good for our cause. It's the least we can do.'

'I really do appreciate it –' I paused; thankfully, she was wearing a name badge. 'Sally. How have you been?'

'Oh, just swell, thanks.' She was gathering up forms but paused before handing them over. 'Look, I'm sorry to hear about you and Jen ...'

I reached across for the forms, avoiding her eyes. 'He just fills these out, yes?'

'That's it. I just need one reference, a form of identification, and the name of his employer.'

'Employer?'

'House policy. Residents must have an employer, even if it's just part-time ...' She raised her eyebrows to Omar. 'You *do* have an employer, don't you?'

'Of course,' I said, forcing a reluctant smile, reminding myself that I was doing this not for him, but for the young woman beside us. 'Omar here is working with us. An intern at chambers.'

'Oh.' She smiled, but the smile was puzzled. 'Well, it's good to see you branching out.'

Omar wasn't happy about surrendering his identification. I almost thought he wouldn't do it, but after a few grumbles he relented. A few nights on the city streets will do that to a young man's resolve.

Sally made two photocopies of his provisional driving licence and stapled one to the original form, which the hostel would keep for its files, and the other to its carbon copy, which she told Omar to keep safe. As soon as her back was turned to source him a room key, I caught him preparing to tear the form into pieces.

'What are you doing?' I asked, catching his hands.

'I can't have this shit lying around,' he hissed. 'What if somebody breaks into my room and finds it? As long as I'm here, I'm Fred.'

'Nobody is going to break into your room,' I replied, though my own years of homelessness had taught me that honour among thieves was rare. On second thought, I whipped the paperwork out of his hands.

'Oi, what're you doing, man?'

'Holding on to this,' I told him. 'I might need your details when I apply for witness protection and it'll be more than secure in chambers.'

He glowered. 'That's my life in your hands.'

'Yes,' Zara said. 'And when the time comes, you'd better remember that, Fred.'

21

Negotiating a deal for witness protection is no simple feat.

While it is possible for an informer to receive total or partial immunity from prosecution under the Serious Organised Crime and Police Act 2005, sentence discounts ordinarily come at the discretion of the judge, and that is only *after* they have pleaded guilty and evidence has been given. True to the Hollywood trope, these so-called 'vulnerable witnesses' can be granted new homes and identities but, with a typical individual's protection costing up to half a million in taxpayers' money, the circumstances must be near to exceptional.

Omar Pickett's problems in qualifying for witness protection were manifest. His circumstances did not appear to be exceptional. He also hadn't been charged with an offence and, most importantly, he was to be giving evidence for the defence, not the prosecution. The situation seemed impossible, but I'd somehow gone and given away my word, and the following morning found me already robed and intercepting Ted Bowen and Claire Morton inside the entrance of Snaresbrook before my own trial continued.

'Ted, Claire.' I nodded as politely as I could manage while stepping out to block their progress. 'Could I have a quick word with you both?'

'About what?' Bowen asked, coming to an irritable halt. His breath smelled of an Embassy Number 1 and his eyes rolled onto Zara, who was standing behind my right shoulder. 'I'm hoping to begin cross-examining her drug dealer this morning, and I personally like a large cup of coffee to ensure I'm fully awake when I stick the boot in a young man's backside.'

'Really? Well, when you've finished your sadistic and apparently sexual shoeing of Miss Barnes's innocent client, she has a defence witness to call.'

'Fine by me,' he snorted. 'If they come up with the same sort of bull as we're likely to hear from Israel, then they'll get a good toeing as well.'

'Gross,' Zara muttered, then cleared her throat and spoke up. 'I only wanted to inform you that this particular witness is afraid to give evidence, and I'll therefore be making an application for special measures.'

'What special measures?'

'Screens, to shield him from the dock while he gives evidence.'

'What sort of a defence witness needs hiding from the person he's defending?'

'This one,' Zara said. 'It's Omar Pickett.'

Bowen's eyes widened. 'You are joking, aren't you? You're not seriously hoping to call a witness who has already been subject to not one but *two* PII rulings by two different judges!'

'I'm entirely serious,' Zara replied coolly; she rummaged through her canvas bag and produced a document. 'For you, I have this fresh Section 8 application requesting that Judge Bromley revisit disclosure in light of these new developments.'

Bowen snatched the paper from her hand. 'Where is Pickett now?'

'He's in hiding. Associates of these drug dealers want him out of the picture.'

'I'm hardly surprised.'

Zara glowered. 'We're talking about an eighteen-year-old's *life* here.'

Bowen almost yawned. 'Yes, yes, and just last Friday you were talking about *another* young man's life, but he will be here today, alive and well, I'm sure. I fear that you take the hollow threats of these hooligans far too seriously, Miss Barnes.'

'All right,' I said, taking her by the arm. 'Don't forget to deal with her application, Ted,' and I led Zara away in the general direction of the public canteen.

'Well,' she seethed, 'I don't see how that does Andre any favours whatsoever.'

'It may do yet. It may do yet …' I checked the time. 'Fifty minutes until court commences. I want to catch Meadows before she's locked inside the dock.'

'I'll join you,' Zara said, 'if you wouldn't mind coming down to see Andre with me afterwards. I don't … I don't quite know what the hell I'm supposed to say to him.'

'Of course.'

We found Charli outside the canteen, wandering aimlessly from one side of the corridor to the other like a yo-yo. Whether it was because of our frosty encounter with the prosecutors, or the result of an emotional hangover after the evening I'd had pandering to Omar Pickett, this morning I wasn't in the mood for wasting time or mincing words. 'Charli, where's Deacon?'

'D-Deacon?' She was holding a cup of tea; I could hear the liquid sloshing around.

'We've tiptoed around the subject for long enough,' I said. 'Another man in this very courthouse could be sent down through pride or fear or something as stupid as both put together, and Deacon is tied into it somehow. I may not know why, not yet, but I trust my instincts and your boyfriend's name is the one that keeps on cropping up. *He* talked you into bringing that tobacco into prison. You weren't just meeting up for stolen kisses by the prison lockers. You were handing him contraband, the same drugs he once supplied through his so-called record label.'

'No!' On tiptoes, she raised an inch higher. 'You're supposed to be my defence, Mr Rook!'

'I am, and that's the problem. I believe you're a good woman, Charli, and I don't want to see you go down on somebody else's orders. I don't want to see your children end up in social services because an inmate pulled the wool over your eyes!' This outburst came as a surprise, even to me, but it felt right. It felt like the truth.

'But I've told you so many times, I didn't smuggle any –'

'Where is he now? Where is Deacon?'

Her heels returned to the floor, quickly followed by her eyes. 'I haven't seen him. Is that what you want to hear? Ever since the ... the weekend. The dog. He got this idea into his head that ... It's crazy ...'

'What idea?'

She shook her head. 'He thinks the dog was poisoned on purpose. Something to do with this trial. He said something about a threat, a note he'd been sent, but he wasn't making any sense.'

'And you didn't think it necessary to tell me this?'

'What was I going to say? That another man has walked out on me? On *us*? He hasn't answered any of my messages. He's gone, Mr Rook. Are you happy now?' Without another word she marched off towards our courtroom, the place I'd be standing to defend her within the hour.

'That was short,' Zara said, 'not quite sweet.'

'No. Not quite.'

'I don't buy it. Not one bit. I'll bet he's sitting on her sofa watching *Jeremy Kyle* with a round of toast as we speak. A *note*? What, like some anonymous letter? Who's she trying to fool?'

'Yes,' I muttered. 'Quite.'

'Right, next.' She swallowed a heavy, rattling breath. 'Time to see Andre.'

But the next person we encountered was not Andre Israel; it was Lydia, who we found at the entrance to the cells, the usual stack of papers under her arm.

She was smiling. 'Elliot! Zara.'

'Can we talk?' I asked quietly.

She looked at her watch. 'Maybe later, I've got clients here to see.'

'We've spoken to Omar Pickett.'

This caught her attention. 'You're joking. The mystery informant? When?'

'Yesterday evening. He got in touch with us.'

'The two of you?' Her eyes narrowed. 'Why on earth would Omar Pickett have come to you?'

'He'd heard about Andre's defence,' Zara replied quickly. 'He felt guilty, I guess, and wanted to know if he could help him out.'

'Oh.' A beat. 'And you didn't think to drop me a message?'

'It has all been rather touch and go,' I said.

'Where is he now?'

'I don't know.' The lie came out so smoothly that for a moment I forgot I really did. 'I've told him that he needs to see you so that you can take a witness statement from him.'

Her frown suggested that Lydia didn't buy it. 'So how am I supposed to contact him to take a witness statement if we don't know where he is?'

Zara answered before I could. 'He's staying in a homeless centre, but he's agreed to come back to us in time for further details. He didn't say where.'

A moment passed between us; I could've sworn the solicitor looked hurt.

'Right,' she said briskly. 'Well, you'll be in touch as soon as he shows up, won't you?'

'Of course,' I told her. 'You'll be the first person I call.'

She began to walk away, heels clacking on the ground. She paused and looked back. 'You remember what I said, don't you, Elliot? About us all being in this together?'

I nodded. 'The first person I call.'

She was gone.

Zara slapped a hand on my back, as playful as it was uneasy. 'You're a real hit with the ladies this morning, aren't you, champ?'

'I always am.'

She started to follow Lydia's route to the cells. I caught her by the shoulder.

'What's wrong?' she asked.

'As his counsel it is ultimately your decision, but I would advise you not to tell Israel about Pickett's appearance. Not yet.'

'Why not?' she asked. 'You just told his solicitor.'

'Do you remember what I told you last week about my own time in prison? The dangers of hope?'

She thought about it. 'That the idea of being convicted was terrifying, but hope for acquittal was even worse?'

'Exactly. Giving him such hope before we know that we can rely on Pickett, well, I'm just not sure it would be the kindest thing to do.'

'I think he deserves to know.'

'As I said, it's your call, but your client is in a uniquely desperate position. His hope is not my only concern.'

She sighed, tapping her feet. 'OK. I guess I'll play it by ear.'

He was facing the wall of his cell when we entered; the door was snapped shut and the silence came down around us. I was the first to break it. 'How are you doing, Mr Israel?' It was a pointless question, but somebody had to ask.

As it turned out, he didn't have to answer.

'Omar Pickett has shown up!' Zara blurted. She'd taken one look at her weary, broken client and crumbled.

I winced, briefly clenching my eyes, and when I opened them again Andre was facing her. 'What?'

'Pickett,' she repeated. 'We're hoping that we can convince him to submit evidence about the night of the raid. He could testify that you were never there with drugs in the first place.'

'Why would he do that? He don't owe me shit.'

'Because he's running scared,' Zara said. 'You know what these people are like, Andre. What they'll do to him.'

Andre shrugged. 'The way I hear it, he tried to play the game from both sides and got played. Serves him right.

Omar's let me sit inside for months now. Fuck his scared little bitch-arse.'

'There's more to your case,' I said. 'It's more intricate than we first imagined, but it ties into a case of my own. Pickett can bust it all wide open. The whole story. Cutthroats, the lot. I just need your help with a couple of questions.'

'You said you'd get me bail.'

'I didn't say that.'

He glanced to Zara, sulking. 'Fine. What do you want this time?'

'What can you tell us about Deacon Walker?' I asked.

His expression brightened a little. 'D? He's a sick producer, that's what. Helped me out big time with my tracks.'

'That's not his only business though, is it?' Zara said. 'He deals drugs.'

'So? He's given a lot of kids work that way.'

'Do you consider that a noble thing to do?' I asked.

He rolled his eyes. 'Man coming down here, talking about nobility and shit. Where I come from, in ends, kids are more concerned with filling their bellies than filling their big fat egos, old man. What the fuck would you know about that?'

'More than you think,' Zara bit. 'I was brought up on an estate, just like you were, Andre. I'm standing here today because I worked my arse off to better myself.'

'Whereas I grew up in a slum without hot running water,' I added, surprising myself. 'By your age, I'd already been down the mines. You're not the only kid who's had it hard.'

Andre was quiet. He eyed us both, narrow and suspicious. Then, when he'd apparently decided that we weren't lying, he leaned back until his head was on the wall. 'Deacon's done some bad shit, all right, but he really has done a lot of good. It's just, like, perspective. He treats his kids well. Some of them, these trappers, they don't. They keep the young ones in line with beatings and rape and all kinds of nasty shit. D spoils his kids.'

'I'll bet he does,' Zara said. 'I'm sorry to tell you this, Andre, but in a court of law they call that grooming.'

'What about a man called Roy Macey?' I asked. 'Ever heard of him?'

Andre nearly smirked. 'Jesus, how old *are* you, man? My grandad used to tell me stories about that guy. He must be like, what? Eighty?'

'Thereabouts,' I said. 'You haven't heard anybody mention him lately? That surname?'

'No. But if half of what my grandad said about that man was true, then shit – it isn't the kind of surname people would be stupid enough to shout about.'

'You think he's still dangerous?' Zara asked.

'Everybody is dangerous. If you don't realise that soon, then you're both going to end up in the ground.'

22

That afternoon's witness was the drugs expert, a man named Johnson.

I hadn't asked for him to be fully bound – meaning the witness must attend court and give live evidence – but Garrick had decided to call him anyway, presumably for the effect on the jury. Prosecutors often do that. Evidence on paper rarely has the same impact as evidence in person. I once conditionally bound a witness in a fraud trial where my client had allegedly scammed a number of gullible investors in a foreign exchange fraud. My client had offered a higher rate of foreign exchange than normal – about ten times higher, in fact – on the condition that they waited one year for their funds. The case involved tens of millions of pounds, so my client needed the twelve-month delay in order to spend his ill-gotten gains. One victim was a soldier, a war hero who'd lost both legs to a landmine in Afghanistan. He'd been told that, to minimise arthritis, he needed to relocate to a warmer client. With that in mind he'd invested all he had, about £100,000, in foreign currency. Within a year he was expecting around a million and a half euros in return, enough for an early retirement in a Spanish villa. What he ended up with was nothing, just like all the other hapless investors. I told the prosecution that I was happy for his evidence to be read. 'Not on your nelly,' was the

239

reply. As soon as the jury caught sight of the witness being wheeled into court, uniform adorned with medals, it was all over for my client.

This drugs expert wasn't quite of the same calibre, but he certainly brought life to a relatively dull subject in front of Charli's jury. He ended his evidence in chief with no further damage done to our case, and then I was asked if I had any questions. I didn't really, but I was clutching at straws, and sooner or later I might've been able to fashion a bale of hay.

'Only a couple,' I said, rising to my feet. 'Mr Johnson, is it true that Spice, or the synthetic cannabinoid so-called, is often designed to look like cannabis, though the substance itself is actually nothing more than a combination of liquid chemicals that can be sprayed onto almost any existing product?'

'That's correct. Of course, because of these particular circumstances, the drug wouldn't have been engineered to look like cannabis.'

'Why is that?'

Johnson shrugged. 'If a person was planning on smuggling the drug into a prison, then they wouldn't want to disguise it as another drug, would they?'

'Probably not. And yet the prosecution are suggesting that the drugs were disguised as tobacco, another form of contraband. Would that be a better method?'

He considered it. 'No, now you mention it. I suppose that would be almost as conspicuous as counterfeit cannabis.'

'How would *you* do it, Mr Johnson?'

A single laugh rang out from the public gallery; Lady Allen did not look amused.

'I-I wouldn't do it,' he replied.

'Of course not.' I smiled. 'What I mean is, armed with your expert knowledge, you must be able to think of more convenient ways to smuggle it in. As, presumably, would any smuggler, unless they genuinely believed that they were trying to smuggle regular tobacco beyond those walls.'

'Ah.' He nodded slowly, a little rattled. 'Yes, I see what you mean. Tobacco would be a rather unusual choice. As I said, you can spray it onto practically anything. My Lady may recall a rumpus when Mr Grayling was Justice Secretary, and he tried banning prisoners from having books sent into prison. That policy wasn't as draconian as it appeared. Many items were being sprayed with cannabinoids.'

'Really?' I replied. 'So, you're saying that the common convicted drug dealer wasn't really interested in reading Proust's *À la recherche du temps perdu*?'

'I don't think so,' he said.

'Mr Rook ...' The judge raised her brow in my direction. 'Any more questions?'

'No, My Lady. I just wanted to clear that up.'

'Then you may be on your way, Mr Johnson, thank you.' Lady Allen said. 'Who is your next witness, Mr Garrick?'

'As Your Ladyship knows, I have a case in the Court of Appeal tomorrow, so we won't be sitting. Since it's three o'clock already, we'd be unlikely to finish examining the witness today. Rather than having his evidence only partially heard before a break of two nights, might I be allowed to call him on Friday morning?'

'I'm sure the jury won't object to an early day. Members of the jury, since the Court of Appeal requires Mr Garrick tomorrow, we won't be able to sit. So, not only do you have an early finish today, but you also have an entire day off tomorrow. I suggest that you enjoy it.'

'Them and me both,' I muttered, packing my things away.

Zara's trial was still being heard, so I was walking out of the courthouse alone when I spotted Delroy Meadows in full overalls, accompanied by Charli's three children, walking through the grounds towards me.

'You go ahead, kids,' Delroy said, patting Roland on the back as I approached. 'I'll meet you up there by the doors.'

The middle child – the eight-year-old – stomped the plimsolls of her school uniform. 'No, Uncle Del, I don't want to! It's haunted!'

'Shut up, Zoe,' her big brother snapped, moving her on with a sly kick to the rear. Roland had been eyeing me with the familiar hatred. He was wheeling a pink buggy in which the third child, a toddler, was sound asleep, and once again I was reminded of his wretched claim to the title of man of his house.

'I was sorry to hear about your dog,' I said, but he was already passing and didn't pause to respond.

The uncle shook my hand, then waited until the children were some yards off behind me. 'You're out a little early. I hope that's not a bad sign. How's she getting on?'

'Hard to say at this stage. Always is. I thought I had something yesterday but ... I really don't know. We'll have to bide our time. I haven't seen you in the gallery.'

'Can't afford to give myself the hours off. Not yet. There's just no way.'

'You must have some real rust buckets on your hands.'

He laughed softly. 'You better believe it. Danny has been closing up, which is a big help. Gives me chance to pick the kids up – get their dinner. They just need somebody at the minute, you know?'

'They'll appreciate it in the long run, I'm sure.'

He shrugged, hands in pockets. 'You heard about Biggie then. The dog.'

'I heard. Were you there when it happened?'

'No. Charli rang me up after it was, you know, *over*. Me and Deacon buried him. Weighed a ton, the poor bastard.'

'Have you seen Deacon since?'

The lines on his face, so much like his sister's, formed a grimace. 'No.'

'Sounds as if he's left the scene.'

'Looks that way. Ro's in bits about it, hence the face like thunder. Won't go into school, not that there's anything new there.' He sniffed, turned his face and spat onto the grass. 'You know how these things are.'

'What brings you here now?'

'Kids wanted to surprise their mum. Take her out for dinner, cheer her up a bit. I hear there's one of those carveries up the road.'

'It's not bad there,' I said. 'You're all going? Straight from here?'

'That's the plan.'

I nodded, the scent of opportunity tugging at my shoes. 'Well, your sister should be out at any moment. I won't keep you.'

'I'll be in touch about the car, just as soon as we get those parts. It's an old model, and they don't make them like they used to.'

'Yes, yes, whenever you get round to it, that's quite all right.'

'I'll see you then?'

'You will,' I said, already on my way. 'You certainly will.'

I meant to text Zara to apologise for not waiting around but forgot. I had a new plan, and the clock was already ticking.

Snaresbrook Station, which is basically across the road from the court, serves only the Central Line, its options limited to either east or west. I negotiated the entrance barrier, broke into an awkward version of a jog for the west-bound platform and jumped onto the first train headed in the direction of the city, chambers and home. But I wouldn't be going that far. Not yet anyway.

Three minutes later, the train made its first stop at Leytonstone, by which point I'd already settled on my decision. After Leytonstone was Leyton itself. When the train stopped there, I alighted. Beyond the barriers, out of the station building, I found three black cabs parked up in a line. I clambered into the back of the car at the front, holding my hat in place, and leaned forward.

'The allotments on Low Hall Lane, please, mate.' I considered telling him to step on it.

The Meadows home was supposed to be empty. I was going there because I suspected the opposite.

It was a short drive north through Leyton, and I spent the journey wondering what I was going to say if – or rather *when* – Deacon answered the front door. It was something I was still pondering when I paid the fare, climbed out of the car and passed through the garden gate. I momentarily hesitated, watching out for the dog, before remembering that the poor beast was currently pushing up tomatoes several yards behind me. The thought didn't bring me any comfort.

I knocked.

I waited.

I checked my watch, extremely aware of every passing second. It had been more than twenty minutes since I'd stopped to talk to Delroy, and I couldn't help but wonder if Charli, almost certainly exhausted from another disheartening day in the dock, would even want to go out for dinner without notice.

If Charli returned and found me standing here now, whatever amount of trust remained between us would surely be obliterated. Then again, if Deacon answered, there'd be no remaining trust to lose.

He didn't answer. This time I clenched my fist tighter and let the frosted glass have it.

Nothing. The sound of birds singing somewhere in the allotments. The sweet aroma of onions frying in a neighbour's kitchen. But Charli's house was lifeless. I couldn't tell if I was more relieved or disappointed. Either way, I had to remind myself that this hadn't been a waste. If I hadn't come looking, the possibility would have played on my mind all evening, and the hint of resentment that had been developing after each of Charli's lies would have grown into something far uglier. It was better to know. For better or worse, Charli seemed to be telling the truth about Deacon.

I was turning away from the door, cursing myself for not asking the cab driver to wait and wondering how I was going to get back to the station, when from the corner of my eye I saw something move. It was at the downstairs window of the house next door, where the netting was still falling back into place. That's when I remembered the face that had appeared there at the very moment we'd watched Deacon pull up in the Audi.

Another furtive glance at my watch. Almost twenty-five minutes now. I climbed from Charli's yard straight over the low connecting wall, careful not to land my feet in any of the dozen potted plants, and then knocked much more politely on the neighbour's door.

I could see her outline already, a hunched shadow studying me through the translucent netting for an entire minute before she decided to venture to the door. When she finally opened it, she kept the chain on, revealing nothing more than a slither of incredibly creased brown skin and a single eye to match.

'What?' she grumbled.

'My name is Rook, I was wondering if you could spare me a moment of your time.'

One long, rickety finger wriggled out through the narrow gap and tapped a paper sign that had been written by hand and sellotaped to the outer door frame: No Jehovah's Witnesses.

I had to force a smile, repeating an earlier mental reminder to invest in a more stylish wardrobe. 'I'm not here from any church, ma'am. I was actually hoping to speak to you about your next-door neighbour.'

Her eye widened, aglow with new-found excitement. 'Are you the police?'

I hesitated, choosing my words carefully. 'I am an officer of Her Majesty's court.' I hoped it sounded just as good.

It must have, because the door was closed, the chain slid across, and then the door opened fully to reveal an elderly

Indian lady braced on a walking stick. 'You've come about the dog, have you?'

'Yes. Though I should warn you that my visit here must be held in the strictest confidence.'

'Confidence, yes,' she replied, bearing a remarkable likeness to Yoda in both voice and gait. 'Four times I ring the council. Four. Sending somebody today, they tell me, and here you are.' She rolled her tiny eyes up and down the street, then lowered her voice as if imparting a great secret onto me. 'No big loss, it was a horrible creature, but council property, that is. Well, half council, half charity, but belong to *her*? No. She says it's all right because she puts slabs down. Number 4, David, he grows his bloody carrots over there! Sanitary? I don't believe it. Nasty, rotting beast.'

'I'd have to agree with you. Did you witness the burial yourself?'

'Yes, sir, from this very window. Her, the brother and that fellow of hers. Putting flowers on it, the little ones were. More flowers than my own husband ever got!'

'You seem to keep a sharp eye on things around here, Mrs ...?'

'Sharma.'

'Mrs Sharma. This fellow you mentioned. What do you make of him?'

'*Make* of him?' She didn't so much as roll her eyes; she rolled her entire skull, creaking the fibres in her neck. 'Day and night, he's coming and going. Music blasting. Three, four o'clock in the morning. Used to be a nice road, this did.'

'How very inconsiderate.'

247

'Not just me saying it. Everybody in the lane has had enough. Take *that* back to the council.'

'How long has this been going on for?'

'Weeks. Month, maybe.'

'What about last year? The summertime, perhaps. Did you notice him coming round then?'

'No. No, I would've noticed.'

'Yes, I'd believe it. He has a rather recognisable vehicle, wouldn't you say?'

'Horrible noisy thing. *German.*'

I smiled. 'Yes, I hear they're quite good with the vehicles over there.'

'Eh?' She tilted her ear towards me.

'This car,' I said, increasing volume. 'Have you seen it around over the last couple of days?'

She thought about it, eyes shrinking further. 'No.'

'Not at all?'

'Since the weekend, no. Not since the dog. Right down there with Dave's carrots, it is!'

'Curious.' Thirty minutes. I was pushing my luck.

'Need me to point out the plot, do you?'

I looked up from my watch. 'I beg your pardon?'

'The allotment! What are you going to do about it?'

'I'll be passing it along to the necessary parties, and we'll go from there.'

'Rotting by now. Disgusting.'

'Yes, I suspect it will be.'

I made my excuses, thanked the lady for her time, and let her return to her living-room window.

Upon leaving the garden, I saw the paving slabs some way off behind the fence across the road. I pictured the

Meadows family standing out there on a warm Saturday, burying their puppy under the earth, and it made me feel nauseated. I wanted to get out of there fast, not only because I still had to walk until I could source a cab, but also because I now felt guilty for leaving Scout alone all day.

As I turned the bend in the lane on foot, a flatbed truck from Waltham Forest Council arrived and parked up behind me.

At least Mrs Sharma would be pleased.

I was halfway back to the main road when I rang Zara.

'Where did you run off to?' she asked suspiciously. 'I just went to the bloody pub expecting to find you there, and what did I find instead?'

'The entire Meadows family.'

'Good guess. How'd you know?'

'Because I'm walking away from Charli's house right now. I don't suppose Deacon Walker happened to be there tucking into a roast as well, did he?'

'No. I'm assuming you went over there to catch him out?'

'I did. No luck.'

'Even if he had been there, you really expect him to answer the door?'

'It was worth a shot. How did your latest Section 8 application go?'

'The judge was actually really good about it when I explained the situation. He lifted the PII and the prosecution confirmed that the raid had been as a result of information from an informant. I asked Linford about it in evidence, and he accepted that Omar Pickett was the registered informant.'

'About time.'

'Right. Only, when I suggested that there were supposed to be six dealers including Omar – which would mean that Andre was an extra body – he didn't buy it. He said that Omar hadn't given specifics on the number of dealers who would be sitting in the pub. So, as far as Andre is concerned, it was a bit of a bust.'

'The real fun will start when both Israel and Pickett give evidence against the Cutthroats.'

'Yeah, I'm not so sure I'd call that fun. How about your trial? How's it going?'

'As well as could be expected, but I think tomorrow will be better.'

'What makes you think that?'

'Because we're not sitting,' I said. 'Garrick is in the Court of Appeal.'

'No way! That means you can come and help me out!'

'That's not really the day off I had in mind …'

'Ah, come on. When was the last time you gave yourself an actual day off anyway?'

I sighed. 'All right, I'll see you in the morning.'

But I didn't get the chance.

23

Thursday started off strange.

I was approaching the outer gates of the court's grounds when my phone began vibrating against my knuckles in my coat pocket. I expected it would be Zara telling me she was running late, but it was Percy.

'Morning, Rook. I hear that you've offered to help Barnes out this morning. Have you left for Snaresbrook already?'

'Left? I've just got off the Tube – I'm walking up to the courthouse as we speak.'

'You shouldn't have bothered.'

'Why? What is it?'

'Her trial has been stood out for the day.'

'Stood out?'

'Apparently so,' he said. 'One of the jury is unable to attend.'

I came to a stop on the pavement. 'Sick?'

'Must be. Hospital, I think. The listings officer just called.'

'Does Zara know?'

'Yes, I just spoke to her. How else would I know where you were going? I don't have a tracker planted in that tramp's hat of yours, you know.'

'Goodbye, Percy.'

'Wait!'

I sighed. 'Yes?'

'If you're looking for something else to do with your day, I was thinking that you could come into chambers instead. Perhaps have a sit-down with the rest of the pupils and give them a few first-hand lessons on how a silk goes about organising and preparing for a major –'

'You're breaking up, Percy, I can't quite hear –' I hung up without finishing and dropped the phone into my coat pocket. Close call.

Pedestrians were stepping around me, flocking towards the court's gates ahead, but I remained there for a while, a static body with racing thoughts.

Something cold had settled in my gut. Something like poison. It was something I hadn't felt since that snowy night in Radcliffe. It accompanied me back into the station, and it was still there when I boarded the westbound train for home.

Yesterday had been the first sign of a break in Zara's case, and now a member of the jury had fallen ill? Hospitalised. What if our cases really were connected, only somebody didn't want that getting out? What if they'd got to Charli? Her children?

'*The next station is* Leyton. *Please mind the gap between the train and the platform.*'

I told myself that I wasn't going to repeat yesterday's trip to Low Hall Lane. This time I was going to remain in my seat, that's all I had to do. Even as the train came to its stop and the doors glided open, I was telling myself not to move.

'*This is* Leyton.'

No. I would have the whole day to myself. I would take the dog out for an hour, maybe two, and just unwind in Regent's Park like any ordinary person. I would read a novel. I would forget about work for a while. I might even enjoy myself for once.

These lies were still echoing in my head when I barged out of the sliding doors and landed with both feet on the platform.

Last night it had taken ten minutes to get to Charli's in the taxi. I estimated that I could check in on her and be back on the Tube within half an hour. A minor detour. Nothing but a courtesy call. Easy enough. So, why not ring?

It was just past nine o'clock, and Leyton Station was about as busy as it had been yesterday afternoon, its remaining morning commuters preferring the semi-calm that borders both sides of every rush hour. I approached the barriers with my contactless bank card ready in my right hand, still denouncing my own poisonous thoughts as paranoid nonsense. I was already swiping the reader when a small freckled boy with an oversized rucksack shoved his way into my barrier's lane from the other side. The gates opened and then snapped shut like mechanical jaws behind him and he walked straight into me, earphones blasting, apparently oblivious to me standing directly in front of him.

'Pardon me!' I said sarcastically, but he didn't bother to meet my eye. He just glowered and carried on walking, ten years old and ready to fight the world. 'Little bastard!' I called back, refusing to let my voice be lost under his music. 'Shouldn't you be in school?'

He didn't hear me, or more likely ignored me altogether.

I was still complaining to myself about the cheek of it all, and having to swipe twice, as I exited through the barrier.

I made it four steps before coming to a frozen halt. There'd been something in that scowl, in the blaze of his green eyes, that was impossibly familiar. I glanced back over my shoulder and caught sight of him once more before he got onto the staircase. I couldn't quite believe my eyes.

It wasn't just because I recognised his trainers. It was the rucksack. More to the point, it was the thing hanging from its zip, a very unique sort of lucky charm for a ten-year-old boy to be flaunting: a chrome jaguar.

'You've got to be fucking joking me.'

I tripped back through the barrier, that coldness in my gut now boiling, screaming for me to run up and catch him like a mouse by the tail. I somehow managed to summon restraint and instead followed him through to the platforms. Westbound. He stepped straight onto the waiting train and I shadowed his movements, entering the next carriage along and watching him through the connecting windows, now continuing in the same direction I had been going before. I was aware that my poorly practised, irresponsible stalking had already got me into more trouble than I could afford. I just didn't really care.

He got off a stop later at Stratford and, of course, I did the same. I maintained as much distance as I dared, though between his music and the course he was on, the boy seemed isolated and ignorant to much of anything going on around him. I wondered if, after a dose of full beams to the eyes, he'd be able to recognise my face anyway. I hadn't been wearing my hat at the time, and, though I was now grateful for the perpetual shadow it cast over my features, I knew it wouldn't look good for a large man to be seen following a small boy. This was an explanation I wouldn't ever want to be asked for.

Together, and yet not really together at all, we walked through the connecting shopping centre and into Stratford International, where the boy approached one of the large touchscreen ticket machines and started punching his selections in without discretion. He chose the 9.32 Southeastern train.

He was going to Margate.

He paid in cash and pocketed the receipt. Not just pocketed. He folded it carefully and placed it into his wallet, an unusually conscientious move for a boy of his age. My eyes moved to the weight of the rucksack on his back. The mystery prize.

Margate: the land of Isaac Reid's Tinderellas and two butchered drug dealers.

It was twenty past nine when the boy disappeared through the barriers for his platform.

It was twenty-five past when I purchased a ticket and followed.

Despite the run of fine weather, there weren't many Londoners bound for a Thursday at the seaside and the platform was almost empty. I waited on the staircase for the boy to board and then hurried for a separate carriage just as the alarms at the doors began to sound, signalling that the train was about to leave.

It was an hour and twenty minutes to the end of the line. I already knew who'd be waiting at the other end. I'd only been to Margate once before, on an early date with Jenny. I could still remember the Shell Grotto and Dreamland, the amusement park, but what I oddly recalled more clearly as the train got going was that T. S. Eliot recovered there after his mental breakdown.

'On Margate Sands I can connect nothing with nothing,' I muttered to myself. 'You and me both, Eliot.'

After sixteen minutes, the train passed through Gravesend, where my phone must have picked up signal, because it started vibrating with message alerts in my pocket. In fact, in those sixteen minutes I'd missed two calls from Percy, one from Lydia, and four from Zara. The last began to ring again, and I moved into the empty area that connected my carriage with the boy's before answering. Outside, London had disappeared, and open greenery was pouring past the windows.

'Is everything all right?' I asked.

'Where are you? Are you coming into chambers?' She sounded unusual. Offish.

'I'm on a train to Margate.'

'Margate?'

'I think I have a lead on Deacon. If I'm correct, there's a whole bagful of Spice heading straight towards him on this very train, and you'll never *believe* who's carrying it!'

She didn't try to guess. I heard her swallow. 'You haven't heard?'

'Heard what?'

'They … Deacon … saying it's …' Her voice was fading in and out. The floor rumbled underfoot.

'Hello? I'm between stations, I'm losing signal again.'

'You need … come back to London … get to chambers!'

'Chambers?' Here it was: all at once, the cold returned. 'What's happening?'

'Deacon! It's Deacon! The police have got him!'

And with that, the line died. 'Zara? Hello, Zara? Bollocks!'

Deacon had been arrested, and in circumstances that required me to return to chambers as soon as possible. It sounded as if the case was already over, and I was stuck on a train bound for the very edge of the country. I was missing all the action. I pocketed the phone, crept to the doorway of the next carriage and peered inside. I could just see the boy's blond hair sticking up above his seat. He was facing away from me. Through speakers overhead, the driver announced that we would shortly be arriving at Strood.

'*Please collect all personal belongings before departing.*'

All personal belongings. *My* belongings.

I pressed the button and winced as the door hissed open, but the boy didn't turn. There was nobody else in here except for an elderly man who was dozing at the far end. The train was slowing down. I got onto all fours and peered under the seats, hoping to hell that nobody would be watching a live feed of the carriage's CCTV. The rucksack was there underneath the boy's chair.

Reduced to crawling like an animal, I slipped into the footwell of the seats behind him and carefully reached under, my hands coming within inches of his stylish trainers, which were tapping rhythmically to whatever drill music was pounding through his headphones. Slowly, I pulled the bag towards me by the jaguar. I held my breath as I opened the zip, still undecided on how I would deal with the boy and the inevitable mountain of rolling tobacco in the bag.

I looked inside and saw ... nothing.

Nothing out of the ordinary, anyway. A scrunched-up jumper. A phone charger. A couple of snapped biros, some textbooks for Key Stage 2 SATS exams and a stack of papers with revision notes on them. Less cautious now, frantic with disbelief and rage, I opened the front and side pockets, rifling through the empty folds. Defeated, I undid the knot holding my jaguar emblem and pushed the bag back to its original position.

The train came to a standstill and, as my phone caught the town's signal, it began to vibrate again. I got up, clenching my fists only inches behind the head of the boy who had ruined my car, and stormed off the train just as the doors began to close. They locked behind me and the mechanics under the carriage hissed back into life. My phone was still jittering as I walked along the platform, but before I answered it I got to the window where the boy was sitting and pounded my fist against the safety glass. He looked around, startled, as the train began to pull away.

I was holding up two hands. In one, my jaguar roared. In the other, I returned the two-fingered salute he'd once flashed in my rear-view mirror. The look on his face was worth it. He scrambled down under his seat, yanking the rucksack out, but before he had chance to spit his dummy out proper the train had whisked him away and I was left on the empty platform, howling with laughter.

Yes. Absolutely worth it.

My phone stopped ringing and started up again.

I took it out of my pocket, swinging the jaguar from my other hand, and answered more brightly than before. 'Zara! So, they got the bastard, did they?'

'Deacon? Yes.'

'Where is he now? Where are they holding him?'

She was quiet for some time. 'At Waltham Forest mortuary, I think.'

I froze, the car's emblem hanging limply from one dead arm. 'What?'

'They found him … Shit, they found him dead under the allotment, Mr Rook. It's Meadows. Charli Meadows has been arrested for his murder.'

PART THREE

OLD HABITS

24

When it all fell apart, it fell apart fast.

I was back in Snaresbrook on Friday morning, with little more information than the scant facts that had kept me up for most of the night. Charli wasn't brought up to the courthouse. She was still in police custody being interviewed not just about the murder of Deacon Walker, but also the killing of the thirteen inmates at Wormwood Scrubs.

Fourteen murders.

That would put her neatly into the list of Britain's most prolific serial killers, up there between Dennis Nilsen on fifteen and Peter Sutcliffe on thirteen. If it was the all-female chart, then she'd beat Rose West's twelve to go straight in at number one.

Zara's juror was still unwell, so she wasn't around either; I drank coffee alone in the public canteen before walking into the courtroom at 10.30.

The only obvious way to proceed, as I saw it, would be with an application from the prosecution to discharge our jury and abort the trial. Not for the first, second or even third time this week, things didn't follow my expectations. While the jury waited outside, Garrick greeted Lady Allen with an excited, almost gossipy smile. 'Good morning, My Lady. I presume you are aware of yesterday's events concerning the defendant, who will not be attending this morning as she remains in police custody being interviewed.'

'For fourteen murders.' The judge nodded. 'That will take some time.'

'Though perhaps not as long as you might expect. She has been advised by her solicitor to answer "no comment" to all questions asked. I am told that interviewing will conclude by tomorrow at the latest.'

'I see. The jury are here this morning. The defendant does not need to be present for them to be discharged. I can only assume that that is your application.'

'It is not, My Lady.'

She blinked. 'It isn't?'

I turned to face him. 'It *isn't?*'

'No. My application is for this trial to be adjourned until Monday, at which time it will continue as planned. Most of the evidence has been agreed and the issue as to whether or not the defendant is guilty of smuggling drugs into HMP Wormwood Scrubs would undoubtedly have an important bearing on the future murder trial.'

'Monday,' I quietly echoed, aghast.

'Mr Rook,' Lady Allen said, 'what do you say about this proposal?'

I clambered to my feet. 'I say it is preposterous, My Lady. My client will not be in a fit state of mind to give evidence on Monday! She's just been arrested for fourteen murders!'

'Noted,' she replied. 'But is there any *legal* reason that this trial cannot continue?'

'How about in the interests of justice? It would not be just for my client's trial to continue as if nothing has happened.'

'On the contrary,' Garrick said. 'If Miss Meadows is convicted of the drug-smuggling charge, then all the prosecution would have to do in the murder trial is seek an admission of that conviction, subject to a successful bad character application.'

'So that's the plan, is it?' I spat. 'Get the woman convicted of drug offences then use that conviction to bolster the murder charges?'

Garrick shrugged. 'What's wrong with that?'

'I'll tell you what's wrong with that ...' I snarled, fists clenching; thirty years earlier I would've told him in the car park.

'No, you won't, Mr Rook,' Allen intervened. 'You will tell *me* what is wrong with it, and you'll do so calmly. Unless you can cite me a precedent that such a course of action would be wrong in law, then I'm afraid I must side with Mr Garrick.'

'My Lady,' I groaned, 'a fair trial is a right of law. Given the publicity likely to result from my client's arrest and almost inevitable charge to the biggest mass-murder case in modern history, how could she possibly expect to have a fair trial?'

'That's a simple matter to resolve. I can impose far-reaching press restrictions that would ensure no reporting on the matter until further notice. The trial will continue as scheduled on the coming Monday morning.'

By eleven o'clock I was walking back out of Snaresbrook as dazed as a heavyweight champion floored. There was no precedent concerning Garrick's course of action because no defendant had ever been arrested for serial murder in the middle of a trial. I couldn't begin to imagine what sort of a state Charli was going to be in by the time they dragged her into the dock to condemn her for a paltry handful of drugs only days after her partner had been found dead and her entire world had come crashing down around her.

I took the Tube back to Chancery Lane, and before I'd even made it down to Took's Court I saw two uniformed officers walking back to their parked patrol car, flicking over the pages of their notebooks and muttering between themselves. I braced myself for more bad news as I rounded the corner to chambers.

Percy was standing outside the front door alongside Rupert Stubbs, our head of chambers. They were talking between themselves, Percy shaking his head, Rupert looking particularly grave in a white shirt and black braces, his grey hair slightly ruffled with stress, fingers interlocked behind his lower back.

Percy sighed. 'What's going on in this city, Mr Stubbs? The man's almost seventy, for God's sake.'

'I cannot say,' I heard Rupert reply in his soft, aged voice. 'Though I fear we encounter so much crime in our business, we often forget how it feels to have somebody we care about on the receiving end.'

'What's happened?' I said, approaching more briskly now.

Rupert turned to face me with mild surprise. 'Ernest Richards, our caretaker. Last night he was mugged upon leaving the building.'

'Ernie?' I swallowed. 'Is he all right?'

'Not especially. The assailants beat him up rather badly. They broke his right wrist and two of his fingers.'

'Fucking animals!' I spat. 'He's an elderly man, for fuck's sake!'

'Language, Elliot,' Rupert replied, his voice hardening. 'I prefer to think of our generation as experienced. However, you are not wrong. Animals indeed. We shall be taking donations from all barristers, and there will be a card I'd like every one of you to sign. Ernie has been with us for a long time, longer than most, and I want him to know that we are all wishing him a swift recovery.'

'Of course,' I said. 'You don't even have to ask.'

'We'll have to get a temporary cleaner in,' said Percy. 'In fact, I believe we had a rep from an agency here enquiring about contracts just the other day. So it isn't all bad. Perhaps we can have them in before the start of next week to pick up the slack.'

'Oh,' I said, 'well, I'm sure Ernie's family will be so bloody relieved.'

'Your current case ...' Rupert said, diffusing the tension. 'I hear it has taken quite a twist.'

'You heard right.'

'What happened in court?' Percy interjected, characteristically blind to the offence he'd caused only a moment ago. 'Jury discharged, I assume.'

I laughed bitterly. 'You'd think so, wouldn't you?' I explained what had occurred at Snaresbrook.

Percy whistled. 'Christ, that's quite the move. I wonder if Harlan Garrick would ever consider joining us ...'

At that, I left the two of them standing outside and stomped up to my room, which is where I found Zara waiting.

She took one look at my face and swallowed. 'Please tell me your trial's been adjourned until the middle of next century ...'

'Try Monday,' I said, collapsing into my chair and flinging my hat across the room.

'That's insane!'

'I thought so at first, but I'm starting to think that it might not be such a bad thing after all.'

'How do you work that out?'

I picked up the Rubik's cube from where Omar Pickett had left it completed and rolled it between my hands. 'It isn't ideal, but it does mean that I get two bites of the cherry. If I win, the drug-smuggling case that puts an end to thirteen of the fourteen murder charges. If I lose, I've still got another chance at winning the mass-murder trial in front of a jury.'

'That's a pretty good way of looking at it, all things considered.'

'What about you?' I asked. 'Any word on your sick juror?'

'Nothing yet. Hopefully I'll be back in court on Monday.'

'I see. What's happening with Pickett?'

She shrugged. 'I *was* going to arrange for him to meet me here so that Roth could take a statement, but she's tied up at the station with Meadows and I can't get through. I'll drop Omar a message and let him know we might have to wait until the start of next week ...' She turned to her iPad on the bureau and opened Facebook. She leaned closer to the screen, blocking my view. 'No fucking way.'

'What is it?' I rolled the Rubik's cube onto the desk.

'Someone is posting a video of Omar on Facebook! The idiot is rapping!'

'So? There must be hundreds of those videos floating around on social media.'

'Yes, but *this* video is a live stream from outside the hostel! It's from his account, but somebody else is obviously filming!'

'For Christ's sake. We'd better get over there before anybody else sees it.'

We rushed it, and I could feel tension radiating from Zara's shoulder onto mine. Halfway up Kemble Street, I saw a collection of people standing outside the hostel's double doors. Closer still, I heard Omar. He'd stopped rapping and was laughing now, apparently in his element with seven or eight of his fellow residents. One, I realised with a pinch of horror, was still filming Omar on what must have been his phone.

Omar, who had his back to our arrival, nodded to the girl with his phone. 'All right, let's try another, yeah?'

Instead of replying, she gestured towards us. Omar turned round and blanched. He took a long drag on the cigarette he'd been holding. His audience were surveying us warily.

'Hey, guys,' he said to them, 'give me a minute, yeah? Meet you in the common room.'

As soon as they were gone, Zara had her finger aimed directly into Omar's face; any closer and she might've claimed an eye. 'Are you for *real*?' she began. 'We got you into this place so you could keep your head down! Not only are you out here smoking on the street, that girl was *filming* you!'

'Whoa, chill out!' he cried, the surprise on his features close to terror.

'I will not *chill out*! You were streaming it to Facebook! How *stupid* are you?'

'All right, I'll take it down.' He turned to me. 'Jesus, what's the matter with her? She on the rag or something?'

'You need to watch your tone,' I said, 'and you need to be more cautious. She's right – the Cutthroats are going to see that video.'

269

'And? There are thousands of these red-brick buildings in this city. I made sure there was nothing in the shot that'd give the place away. These guys all think I'm Fred.'

'It's a risk you can't afford to take.'

He leaned back against the wall, sulking, then flicked his cigarette into the gutter. 'What do you want, anyway?'

While Zara was still fuming, I explained as best I could. 'One of the jurors in Israel's case has fallen ill.'

'How?' he asked, eyes widening. 'What are the, like, symptoms?'

'I've no idea.' I frowned. 'Why'd you ask?'

He shrugged, glancing away. 'I dunno. Just wondered.'

'We still need a witness statement from you,' Zara said bluntly, not quite managing to find her cool. 'The solicitor is busy with another case today, so it'll have to be early next week. If court is back in session on Monday, will you be able to take a taxi up to Snaresbrook?'

'If you leave me a bit of cash, maybe. I'd rather you just sorted one of them armoured cars or something to come and collect me.'

'We're all out of armoured cars,' Zara glared. 'They're hard to come by at this time of the month.'

'You'll be safe once you're in the building,' I said. 'There's no safer place in the whole country.'

'Do they know I'm going to be there? E10.'

'They might do,' I said.

'In that case I'll probably never make it to the building.'

25

It was another hour before Lydia got in touch, and she insisted that we meet at the Dog and Duck to discuss what had been happening at the station. After the week I'd had, I wasn't in the mood for another social, but I had to hear about Charli. A drink would surely help me stomach the news.

I turned up to the pub shortly after six o'clock and found Lydia sitting at the same table as before. This week she was dressed in her work attire, a fitted blazer and pencil skirt, presumably having come straight from the station. She looked exhausted, but still got up and greeted me with a kiss on both cheeks, which caught me off guard.

'What a couple of days,' she said, returning to her seat. 'I've never known anything like it.'

'Are you having the usual?' I asked.

'Make it two. I'm going to need both for this.'

With four drinks between us, I invited Lydia to start filling me in on everything that had happened.

'It was a neighbour that reported it,' she said. 'An elderly Indian lady. Anjali something or other.'

'Sharma,' I said.

'Yes.' She frowned slightly, adjusting her glasses. 'How do you know that?'

'Charli must've mentioned her,' I replied quickly. 'Sorry, go on.'

'Well, this neighbour had apparently called the council to complain about a burial in the allotments across the road. That ties back to Charli's dog story. The council sent a couple of diggers to check over the site on Wednesday, for fear of a dead animal being down there with the vegetables. Instead of finding a dog, however –'

'They found Deacon Walker,' I finished. 'So, where was the dog?'

'No idea,' she said. 'Not down in that hole, that's for sure.'

'Do they know how Deacon died? The cause of death?'

'That's where the fun really starts,' she said, and took a huge mouthful through her straw. 'So, first we have to go back to the thirteen inmates at the Scrubs. Hold on, I'll need to get this right ...' From her packed work bag on the chair beside her, she produced her laptop and opened it up on the table. 'Right.' She leaned closer to the screen. 'The coroner's original verdict was that every one of those inmates had smoked synthetic cannabinoids, which caused a severe reduction in respiratory function, bleeding in the lungs and vomiting, a soaring heart rate that initiated cardiac arrest, ending with total respiratory paralysis and multiple organ failure.'

'And Deacon Walker?'

'The findings were identical,' she said solemnly. 'Cardiac arrest, respiratory paralysis, multiple organ failure.'

'So he smoked the same bad batch of Spice.' I said. 'It's a blend of dodgy chemicals, for God's sake, how can that be classed as intent to kill?'

Lydia shook her head. 'He didn't *smoke* anything, and therein lies the twist. It was never the Spice that killed them. Any of them. Not exactly.'

'So, what did kill them?'

'Nothing very technical, as it turns out.' She turned back to her screen. 'An aconitine, an alkaloid toxin produced by the aconitum plant. More common names of the perennial aconite variants are wolfsbane, monkshood and the queen of poisons.'

'Wolfsbane,' I repeated. 'Sounds like something out of a *Harry Potter* novel.'

'Don't you ever listen to *Gardeners' Question Time*?'

'No, I can't say that I do.'

'All of these poisonous plants still grow wild throughout the UK, Elliot. They're astoundingly common. It was the purple flowering *Aconitum napellus*, the wolfsbane, that officers found growing freely to the rear of the allotments in which Deacon Walker was buried. The roots of these plants are the most poisonous parts and, if ingested, a single tablespoon of aconitine tincture is likely to be fatal. They think that Walker had swallowed close to *half a pint's* worth of this tincture, which had been disguised in a lethal cocktail of various alcoholic drinks including whiskey and gin.'

'Christ,' I said. 'But the inmates of the prison, they hadn't swallowed poison.'

'Which is precisely what I said down at the station. Apparently, these toxins are notoriously difficult to detect through conventional methods. The original findings came down to the fact that there are no existing reports on the effects of *smoking* the aconite plant.'

'Nobody has ever been stupid enough to try, I suppose.'

'Exactly. It was only through symptomatic similarities between the prison deaths and that of Deacon Walker that they've been able to retroactively classify the toxin hidden within the synthetic cannabinoids. The thirteen inmates didn't die as a result of misadventure. They were poisoned.' She took another huge drink, and I did the same. 'Do you remember me telling you before that Spice is often sprayed onto plants like oregano?'

'The Spice was sprayed onto this poisonous plant?'

'That's the theory,' she said, eyes bright behind her lenses. 'It looks like our client might be bang to rights, Elliot, unless you can come up with any brilliant ideas.'

I shook my head, momentarily closing my eyes. 'Nothing jumps to mind. As all criminal defendants are innocent until proven guilty, I always start my consideration of the evidence from that premise. However, it has to be said that the evidence against Charli Meadows is strong, relentless and, most worryingly, all one-way traffic. The drugs were found in her car. They were the same basic type that had killed thirteen inmates only days beforehand. Those men were poisoned in the same way that her boyfriend, a convicted drug dealer who ran the line with children, was poisoned. And the poison was found growing on her allotment.'

Lydia closed the laptop. 'Children? What makes you think he used children?'

I shrugged, swallowing a mouthful of lager. 'Just something I heard.'

'Heard where?'

'Oh, you know. On the street.'

'The *street?*' She smiled. 'OK, Columbo, you've snagged my interest. What else have you heard chasing hot leads on the mean city streets?'

'It all comes back to this county lines operation,' I said. 'These Cutthroats, the gang involved in Zara's drug trial, are organised, Lydia. Organisation is essential, but it can also be a weakness.'

She clasped her hands together, leaning closer and lowering her voice. 'In what way?'

'The dog,' I said. 'Charli's dog. Biggie. Did you ever see it?'

'God yes.' She rolled her eyes. 'Some kind of white pit bull, the size of a horse. I don't want to sound like a heartless bitch, but I think somebody did those kids a favour getting that thing out of the house. It wasn't exactly the sort of animal you'd want loose around a toddler. She had to lock it in a separate room when I visited last month.'

'Exactly!' I said. 'Only, it wasn't a pit bull. It was an incredibly rare, banned breed. A Dogo Argentino. Deacon Walker gave the Meadows family that dog as a gift. Now, under ordinary circumstances, it would never have struck me as important. But it's the *breed*, Lydia. This gang, wherever they go, however far their tentacles have already reached, there's always a big white dog waiting at the end of the line. It's like a calling card. A symbol of their power, perhaps, the mark of their organisation. Unfortunately for them, it's also the link connecting their operation. I suspect that they chose this rare breed to stand out, but anything so rare can be traced.'

She seemed genuinely amazed. 'Traced to where?'

'Jacob Werner.'

'And who on earth is Jacob Werner?'

'He's a sadistic little bastard operating out of Croydon,' I said. 'A worm. I've represented him a few times over the years, always for some low-grade, slimy shit. A few weeks ago, he was brought to me on a charge of breeding dangerous dogs. From what I gather, he breeds pit bull terriers for semi-professional fighting, but he also has some sort of contract to breed these rare Dogo Argentinos for county lines defence.'

'Wow.' She leaned back in her chair and finished the first of her drinks. 'You really *are* Columbo. But if you're right, and this particular breed of white dog is bred for county lines dealers, and Meadows *had* one of these dogs … Well, that doesn't exactly help our case, does it? In fact, it only suggests that she really was one of their dealers and enforcers, as the prosecution have been suggesting all along.'

'You're right. It doesn't help our case at all,' I said. 'Neither does the fact that Deacon Walker conducted his business from an Audi with the registration DM1, not DW1, which would have been the obvious choice for his initials.'

Lydia slid her second drink towards her, stirring ice. 'What relevance does that have?'

'Charli told me that this Audi wasn't really Deacon's car at all. That he sometimes borrowed it for part-time hours as an Uber driver. I didn't believe her at the time, but now I'm starting to suspect that it really was loaned to him, and for something more sinister than taxiing passengers.'

'Loaned to him by who?'

'DM,' I said slowly. 'Delroy Meadows.'

'Why would Delroy lend his car to his sister's boyfriend? And, even if he did, what does that matter to us? More to the point, why wouldn't Charli just tell you that the car belonged to her brother?'

'Perhaps Deacon Walker worked for Delroy Meadows,' I said, thinking out loud. 'Maybe he borrowed the car for running Delroy's part of the distribution line and, somewhere along the way, he fell into a relationship with Charli.'

'It's an interesting story,' Lydia said, wincing a little as if she was struggling to keep up, 'but where does it take us?'

I took a deep breath and checked the mirror behind her for anyone standing near. Then, satisfied that we had the corner to ourselves, I lowered my voice. 'Have you ever heard of a man called Roy Macey?'

'The name rings a bell. Some old villain, before my time. Krays era, I'd guess.'

'A little later than that,' I said. 'Seventies, early eighties. He used to run a huge slice of the drug trade in the East End until he retired to Spain.'

'Oh.' She shrugged. 'What about him?'

I leaned closer, quieter still. 'Well, I've heard it said that he's running things again.'

'He's back in the country? He must be in his eighties.'

'No, I don't think he's back over here. But, if rumours are anything to go by, he's attempting to unite all the postcode districts into the biggest county lines operation this country has ever seen.'

Lydia eyed me for another moment, then laughed. 'Spooky, Elliot! You're not serious?'

I sat upright, a little annoyed. 'Why not?'

'Oh, come on,' she said. 'Are you actually suggesting that we stand up in a court of law and tell the prosecution to release our client, because a drug dealer from fifty years ago is actually responsible for these murders? We'd be laughed out of the door!'

'No,' I said. 'I don't know. But I heard that this entire operation is being organised by a pair of twins. Roy Macey's twins. Apparently they're doing the groundwork over here for him.'

'Oh God.' She snatched up her drink. 'You're going to tell me you think it's the Meadows twins, aren't you?'

'Why not? The pieces fit!'

She cleared her throat. 'I don't mean to sound rude, but that would take more than a simple name change, Elliot. I don't remember much about Roy Macey, but I'm pretty sure he was a white guy, and, well …'

'I'm not suggesting that Charli and Delroy are actually Macey's children. But what if the story has been twisted through word of mouth? What if the Meadows twins really *are* behind all of this, and they've intentionally used the Macey name to create a sort of bogeyman for everybody to fear? What if they're acting under an existing brand, so to speak?'

'Then I'd say that we are well and truly up shit creek. Instead of providing us with a defence, Elliot, you have just postulated an almost airtight case for the prosecution.'

'Oh.' I looked down into my drink, thinking it through. 'Yes, it seems I have.'

She shook her head. 'Now, do me a favour, won't you? Take that planet-sized brain of yours and do the exact bloody opposite.'

Unfortunately, I couldn't.

26

As soon as I was clear of the pub, I phoned Zara and told her to do a little digging into her sick juror.

'Tell them to look for aconitine,' I said, puffing on a cigarette. 'It's a poison, often undetectable unless the hospital staff know what they're looking for, but if it's left untreated then it can be –'

'Whoa! Slow down, it's all right. Percy got word back about the sick juror after you'd run out on me this afternoon. Food poisoning. She's better now. The trial is going ahead as scheduled on Monday.'

'Thank God for that.' I flicked my filter off into the evening.

'Are you going to tell me what the hell happened tonight?'

So I lit another cigarette and did just that.

I spent most of that rainy Saturday with my head buried in the case, but it was a jigsaw that remained impossible to piece together without Charli's honest input. As Lydia had rightly pointed out, every bit of evidence I'd scraped together did nothing but incriminate my client. Things were starting to look rather desperate.

Zara took the Tube up to mine late on Sunday afternoon, and together we walked Scout through Regent's Park. The weather had turned cold again, the mercury crashing back down to almost zero, and we were wrapped up in layers and mostly quiet on our walk.

'This feels wrong,' I said, using all the strength of one arm to keep Scout in check as she lunged for another dog walker in the distance.

'The muzzle?' Zara asked, gesturing down to Scout's new mouthpiece. 'I know it looks sort of cruel, but if she's going to keep losing her shit every time she sees another dog then –'

'No, I mean the trials. Both of them. We're missing something major, something obvious. I feel as if it's at the outermost edge of my vision.'

'Yeah,' she said glumly, hands in the front pocket of her hoody, beanie hat pulled down to her glasses. 'It's like an eye floater.'

'A what?'

'Those little squiggles you get on your eyes sometimes. Like, translucent shadows moving around. Something that vanishes every time you try to focus on it.'

'Exactly.'

'You know what the most likely explanation is, don't you? To both cases.'

'Yes,' I said. 'Meadows did it. She did it all, almost precisely as her prosecutors are suggesting.'

'But you don't believe it?'

'No.' I sighed. 'For some reason I can barely begin to fathom, I don't believe it.'

'At least we've only got one more night until our final showdowns begin. I don't know how much longer I could handle sitting here on the last mile like this, just waiting around.'

'Yes, at least there's that.'

'I guess it'd be stupidly irresponsible of us to go out for a couple of drinks tonight, wouldn't it?'

'Outrageously so,' I replied. 'We'll have to drop the dog off first.'

'I'm game if you are.'

'All right, but before we get too bladdered, how would you feel about heading up to chambers?'

She laughed without humour. 'Why the hell would you want to go up there on a Sunday evening?'

'There's something in the original Meadows paperwork I'd like to check before we resume tomorrow,' I said. 'Her brother is paying the legal fees, which often requires the solicitor to do a check for laundered money. That'd include copies of his identification, as well as Charli's.'

'You want to check for a change of name, don't you? You still think they have something to do with Roy Macey.'

'Am I that predictable?'

'Yep. But if it'll help you sleep tonight, then whatever. At least that way we can go to the Templar on Chancery afterwards. Wetherspoon prices suit me fine.'

We dropped the dog off at mine and then took the Central Line back to Chancery Lane.

Instead of walking down Chancery itself, we took the shortcut through Furnival Street and onto the pedestrianised strip that connected to the bottom end of Took's Court. It was gone half past six, almost the exact same time that Ernie had caught me smoking in my room nearly two weeks before, but the changing season had already pulled the darkness of that night back to a cloudy, cold, indigo dusk; as we walked, I couldn't help but worry about Ernie. More to the point, I worried about it being my fault.

Around this end of the court there was a stand for bicycle parking and motorcycles. Parked up on this strip was a single moped with its engine running.

'I bet every barrister in the country has got their feet up at this time on a Sunday night,' Zara said, briefly checking herself out in the rider's reflective visor as we passed. 'Chilling out with their other halves, watching Netflix, ordering Chinese. Everybody except us, anyway.'

I turned the bend, unlocked the front door of our building and crossed the threshold into the reception area.

'Everybody except us.' I nodded, moving for the narrow staircase. 'Although it looks like there are lights on upstairs, so at least somebody else is here.'

It wasn't until I turned off the staircase at the third floor that I crashed into a total stranger and almost elbowed Zara back down the entire flight in my surprise.

'*Jesus!*' I choked, catching her before she went toppling backwards. I rounded on the man. 'You scared the shit out of me!'

Equally startled, the stranger had dropped both his phone and a heavy bunch of keys, and he hurriedly bent down to collect them from the hallway carpet. 'S-sorry, Mr Rook,' he stammered, stuffing the keys and phone into the pockets of his overalls. He straightened and tapped the logo of an iron embroidered onto his chest. 'I'm from the agency. The temporary cleaner.' He gestured to the Henry vacuum and his basket of cleaning supplies behind him.

'Oh, of course.' I pinched at my eyes. 'My apologies. It's been a long week.'

He nodded, chewing his lips. His skin was pallid and blotchy, and sweat rolled past his ears. His nails, I noticed, were long and filthy. He also smelled like something I hadn't smelled in a while. It was the smell of the homeless.

'Well,' he said, picking up the basket and dragging the vacuum cleaner along by its pipe. 'Best be getting on.'

'Yes.' I stepped aside, Zara did the same, and he passed us both and began to descend the stairs.

I was already walking the landing towards my door when Zara clicked her tongue. 'Well, well, well. The Rook fame strikes again.'

'Fame?' From my coat pocket, I produced my own set of keys. 'What fame?'

'*Your* fame. You know you're getting a bit too well known when the temporary cleaner knows you by name.'

I paused, thinking back on the brief encounter. 'He didn't know my name.'

'Course he did, he called you Mr Rook.'

'How could he possibly know –' I stopped talking. As I approached my room it became obvious I wasn't going to need my key. The door was hanging from its hinges and the light was on. 'Bastard!'

The room was trashed. Books had been thrown from the shelves. The drawers were opened, rifled through, and papers were strewn across the floor. Whatever he'd been looking for would've been hard to say, if he hadn't left it face up on the desk as if neatly positioned for a photograph. The forms with Omar Pickett's provisional licence. The address of his current whereabouts.

'Zara, wait!' I yelled, but she was already on the staircase, sprinting after the man.

27

'Oi!' she shouted, dodging around the vacuum cleaner that had been dumped in the middle of the staircase. From below, I could hear the cleaner's footsteps increasing to a sprint. I heard the front door go crashing open, followed by the revving of an engine.

We made it outside just in time to see the cleaner stuffing his head into a helmet while clambering onto the back of the moped. The bike went putting off over the pavement into Furnival Street, slowing only briefly to negotiate the concrete bollards before disappearing towards Holborn with a sound like a mosquito fading into the night.

'Fuck!' Zara cried. 'They're going for Omar!'

'Come on,' I said, already turning. 'I know a quicker way!'

We sprinted across Chancery and up to the Honourable Society of Lincoln's Inn. It must've been coming up to seven o'clock now, because an old custodian was sauntering up to the gate from the other side, whistling and selecting the appropriate key from his bunch. He fell backwards shouting when we barged through the gate.

I could hear Zara panting into her phone. 'Hello? Police! I need Detective Inspector Jack Linford! It's an emergency! There's going to be a violent assault! Bruce House! The back of Drury Lane! Just fucking send somebody! Anybody!'

By the time she hung up, we'd made it through Lincoln's Inn and were out of the gatehouse at the south-east corner, pelting along the perimeter of Lincoln's Inn Field, the fence they'd raised to deter the homeless back in 1993. This was no jog. It was a flat-out sprint. When I finally reached Sardinia Street, the buildings were disappearing around me. All I could hear was my own wheezing, like an astronaut floating in darkness, a deep-sea diver sinking into black. Screws turned in the backs of my thighs, ankles and knees. Sagging hair clouded my vision.

Ahead, Zara had come to an abrupt stop at the edge of Kingsway, the main road running from left to right with a steel barrier dividing its four lanes through the centre. She was listening for something. I paused, focusing hard, and heard it too. The moped was now coming down Kingsway from the right. There was a rally of horns as it tore recklessly through the lanes and then Zara was off again, zigzagging between black cabs and nimbly jumping the barrier. I followed, vaulting over, legs like concrete, and almost tripped in front of a northbound bus. Then we were on Kemble, which forked onto Wild Street to the right, and I saw the small bike rocketing towards us from that direction. I leapt with arms outstretched as if I might be able to tackle the riders from it, but there was no chance; they were several feet ahead already, whizzing up towards the sign for Bruce House Centre on the left.

And like a spill of petrol flowing beside an open flame, I saw what was going to happen before it ever did. From my distance of about thirty yards, I could make out the cluster of figures standing in the archway of the building's brown double doors, cigarette smoke rising idly into dusk; I didn't have to identify Omar for my gut to be sure that he was somewhere in the middle.

In unison, the smokers turned towards the bike, which had slowed to a crawl, then a halt. The passenger in the cleaning overalls was reaching for something, and the next thing I knew, Zara had turned on the spot and was running straight back towards me.

'Back!' she cried, pushing against my chest. 'Get back!'

A sharp popping sound; three, four, five cracks accompanied by small bursts of light. It took my brain another second to realise that the passenger with the handgun had opened fire on the smokers.

Now somebody was screaming. The glass in the hostel's doors had shattered. Two of the smokers were on the ground. One was crawling but the other wasn't. The remaining bystanders had lunged into the safety of the building.

A siren was coming. Maybe two. Still not near enough. I pushed Zara aside and started running again, shoes pounding. Ahead, the bike's red brake light went out. It took off up the remainder of the street and hurtled left instead of right onto Drury Lane, head first into the one-way system.

The blast of a horn; it looked as if the driver of the moped simply didn't hear it. The next screaming sounds were those of brakes. For a split second, the assailants glowed white in the headlights of an oncoming van, but the moped nimbly avoided the bonnet and left the van to swerve straight into a parked Range Rover. Then the pair were gone, only seconds after arriving.

I made it to Bruce House with nails in my chest, very nearly suffocating on my feet. The first thing I saw was a young woman sprawled on her back, unconscious. It looked as if she'd fainted; I hoped to God that was all that had happened to her. Omar was still moving, jaw clenched, using a single elbow in a sort of half trench crawl for the doors. Blood smeared behind him in a slug-trail across the pavement. I glanced back to make sure Zara was all right and saw her on the phone again.

Omar blinked up at me, almost casually. 'Hey, man. I think I've just been shot.'

'Try not to move,' I rasped, dropping to my haunches. 'Where are you hit?'

'Shoulder, feels like.' He frowned, his elbow wobbling beneath his own weight. 'Have I been shot?'

'Yes. You're in shock.'

'Oh. Right.' He gave up trying to struggle and simply collapsed down into a plank.

I didn't know whether or not to move him. I wished I knew first aid. To my right, diners were warily looking out of the Turkish restaurant on the corner. The sirens were loud now, but the street itself was unnervingly quiet. Even Omar Pickett, who must've been in agony, wasn't making a sound.

First came the paramedics, then the police, and before I knew it the whole street was swarming with uniforms amid flickering blue lights. I backed away to sit on the kerb with Zara, who was extremely shaken up and looked close to tears.

I'd only just sparked a cigarette when a familiar voice spoke down at us.

'Well, what do you know? Elliot Rook QC at the scene of the crime.'

I blew smoke and nodded. 'Evening, Detective Inspector.'

Linford looked furious. 'So, which one of you is going to explain to me what my missing informant is doing bleeding out in the back of that ambulance?'

We glanced at one another, and then we told him everything that had happened.

Instead of drinking in the Knights Templar, we spent our Sunday evening going over and over our brief encounter with this supposed cleaner, describing him as best as we could, while Linford's team moved back and forth between the cordon at Bruce House and chambers.

Rupert Stubbs was on his way to our building by nine o'clock and, as I was no longer required at the scene, I got out of there before he could turn up and pull my pants down in front of all the journalists and investigating officers. Zara desperately wanted to go to the hospital to see Omar, but Linford almost laughed in her face when she suggested it.

'I'll have armed officers on that ward all night,' he snapped. 'Nobody is getting into that place without a uniform. As for the two of you, I hope you're happy with yourselves. You'd better pray my informant makes it through the night.'

'See you in court tomorrow,' I mumbled; it was all I could think of in the circumstances.

28

As it turned out, I saw DI Linford slightly earlier than expected the following morning. After a long, exhausting night, I wasn't particularly thrilled to find him waiting for me on the courthouse steps with a manila envelope in his hands.

'You know something, Rook,' he sniffed, 'I never like handing these things out.'

He passed me the envelope. It wasn't sealed, and it contained a single sheet of paper, which I tipped out into my hand.

'Oh, Jack, you shouldn't have!' I said. 'My very own Osman warning, and it's not even my birthday.'

'There's something wrong with you,' he said, turning to walk into the courthouse.

'How's Pickett?' I called after him.

'He'll live,' he said brusquely, glancing back. 'You'd better take stock of that warning if you want to do the same.'

I found Zara sitting in the public canteen. She looked up and managed a thin smile as I approached, but her expression was almost empty. 'Let's hope today isn't as bad as yesterday.'

'It hasn't started out too well,' I replied, and sent the envelope skidding across the tabletop.

She slid out the warning to read it and her eyes grew larger with every word. 'When did you get this?'

'Linford just handed it to me outside.'

'Fuck! What are you going to do?'

'I don't know. Ignore it like I do the pictures on the cigarette packets. Maybe frame it. At least this one didn't end up on my ex-wife's doormat.'

'What?' she asked, returning the envelope.

I shook my head. 'Come on, we'd better get ready.'

A few minutes later we were changed into our wigs and gowns and had gone our separate ways. Zara's case was coming up to the time when her client would have to give evidence, followed by his witness, Omar Pickett – but that obviously wasn't going to happen. Zara had no choice but to apply for an adjournment. Her trial was listed to start at ten o'clock, whereas mine began at half past.

Her application must have gone well, because I spotted her in the public gallery before we'd even started for the day.

Lydia entered the courtroom only a couple of minutes before the trial was called on. She slid into the seat behind me, and when I glanced back at the sound of her arrival she mouthed a simple enough greeting: '*What the fuck happened? Are you OK?*'

I flicked her a casual thumbs up and felt stupider for it.

The most shocking moment of the morning – even more so than the threat to my life – was seeing Charli Meadows for the first time when she was brought up into the dock. She looked utterly catatonic. I tried to convince myself that she might be the mastermind behind all of this, but my heart still wouldn't believe it.

The final witness for the prosecution was Linford.

He almost seemed to physically steam when he caught my eye on the way to the witness box. It wasn't the first time he'd given evidence in this case – OICs are often called and then re-called at various apposite times throughout – but it would surely be the last.

'Good morning, Mr Linford,' the judge said. 'Mr Garrick?' which was her way of ceding the floor.

As ludicrous as it seemed in light of subsequent events, because this trial was still only regarding the drugs in the car, Garrick asked Linford simple questions, mostly surrounding Charli's original interview, and why she'd answered 'no comment' to the majority of his questions. After a mere twenty minutes it was time for my cross-examination.

I got to my feet and tried to haul up a smile for the man who had just gifted me yet another death threat.

'Detective Inspector Linford, during the defendant's original interview, was she represented by a solicitor?'

'Yes,' he said. 'The lady sitting behind you. Ms Roth.'

'Before the interview commenced, did the defendant have a meeting in private with her solicitor?'

'Yes.'

'And when the interview commenced, did the solicitor confirm that, on her advice, Miss Meadows was going to answer "no comment" to any question asked?'

'She did. I made it clear to Miss Meadows that it was her choice, irrespective of the advice she'd received, whether or not she answered any questions or offered an explanation. I also explained that if she later relied on anything given in evidence, which she hadn't already raised in my interview, then the jury would be entitled to draw whatever inferences from her silence they deemed appropriate.'

'Did she answer any questions?'

'Only one or two, in so far as she claimed to have no idea how the drugs ended up in her car.'

'Regarding access to drugs in Wormwood Scrubs, based on your inquiries, would you say that they were rife?'

'That appeared to be the case.'

'Were they rife before Miss Meadows started working there?'

'I think that would be fair to say, yes.'

I nodded, running my hands along my own robes. 'Detective Inspector Linford, do you know a young man named Omar Pickett?'

'My Lady!' Garrick bellowed, leaping up. 'A matter of law has arisen.'

'Yes, Mr Garrick, I see that,' she replied. 'Does it have to be dealt with in absence of the jury?'

'I've no objection to the legal matter being dealt with in front of the jury,' I noted. 'I've nothing to hide from them.'

'It's not about having something to hide,' Garrick spat, and then glanced to the panel. 'As Mr Rook well knows, legal matters should be resolved in the jury's absence.'

The judge asked the jury to leave us while the matter was resolved, and I did my best to look perplexed as they filed out of court. When they were gone, Garrick returned to his feet.

'My Lady, Omar Pickett is a paid police informer who has waived public-interest immunity as to his status and was due to give evidence in another courtroom in here this week. What relevance he, or his relationship to DI Linford, has to this case can only be none.'

'Maybe the detective inspector should wait outside,' she replied.

Linford needed no second invitation, and he withdrew from the court.

'Mr Rook?' she continued.

'My Lady, Omar Pickett is indeed a paid police informant who set up the drugs raid to which Mr Garrick is referring. I believe that these dealers knew they were being set up, and they had every intention of going into Wormwood Scrubs to expand their criminal operation. The defence say that this gang monopolised the drugs trade within the Scrubs by poisoning thirteen inmates, which they did only days after arriving as a way to spread terror into those loyal to the former empire inside the prison. If I can establish that through Linford, then I can show to the jury that others were running the drug trade within the Scrubs.'

'All very persuasive,' Garrick conceded, 'but it misses one crucial point. Even if Mr Rook's analysis is correct, Miss Meadows could still have been the link supplying these dealers within the walls.'

'Exactly,' I agreed. 'All the more reason for me to establish through the witness that there is no link between Omar Pickett's gang and my client.'

The judge leaned back into her chair, digesting the tale, and nodded slowly. 'I will allow you a modicum of leeway on this point, Mr Rook, but I advise you to proceed with care. You are on the thinnest of ice.'

'Thank you, My Lady.'

Linford was brought back into the court, followed by the jury.

'Mr Linford,' I said, 'before Mr Garrick's interruption, I asked if you know Omar Pickett.'

'You know that I do. You also know that he was the victim of a drive-by shooting last night.'

'Goodness,' the judge intervened. 'Is he all right?'

'He is in hospital recovering from his injuries, My Lady,' Linford said. 'Thankfully, those injuries do not appear to be life-threatening.'

'How do you know Mr Pickett?' I continued.

'Omar Pickett is a low-level drug dealer, whom I first arrested back in December of last year. He is also a registered police informant, and I am his handler.'

'Among the information he gave you throughout the course of your working relationship,' I said, 'did any of it relate to another case involving members of the so-called E10 Cutthroats, a gang originally from the Leyton area of London?'

'Objection, My Lady.' Garrick was back on his feet. 'Mr Rook's fishing expedition is about to jeopardise the separate ongoing trial to which I was referring only moments ago!'

'On the contrary,' I said, 'the case to which my learned friend is referring isn't likely to see a courtroom for some time. It therefore cannot be jeopardised.'

'How could you possibly know that?' Garrick snarled.

'Gentlemen,' Lady Allen snapped, followed by an apologetic glance to the jury, 'let's proceed with decorum, shall we? Mr Rook, I'll allow you to continue, but do so with caution and keep the questions relevant.'

'Caution and relevant are my twin watchwords, My Lady. Now, DI Linford, did Pickett give you information regarding the so-called E10 Cutthroats?'

'He did,' Linford relented with a soft nod.

'Were these alleged gang members arrested and subsequently remanded in custody at HMP Wormwood Scrubs?'

'Six of them were.'

'Were they arrested for dealing drugs?'

'Yes.'

'And was that only days before thirteen inmates at that very same prison were killed with poisoned Spice?'

'Yes, I believe it was.'

'Thank you, DI Linford. How many times have you been inside the defendant's home?'

He thought about it for a moment. 'Twice. The first was back in January, when her property was searched after the discovery of the drugs in her car.'

'Did you find any more drugs or drug paraphernalia on the property?'

'We did not.'

'And was there a dog on the premises at that time?'

'No. I know she claimed to have one in her supplementary defence statement, but it wasn't there in January and it wasn't there the second time I visited on Wednesday of last week.'

'So, if she did have one, it must have lived there for a short period between those two pivotal dates. Do you know where she might have acquired such a dog?'

'She very recently claimed to have received it as a gift from Deacon Walker, a convicted drug dealer who had served time at Wormwood Scrubs while she was working there. Of course, it's difficult to ask Mr Walker for his side of the story, as he was found murdered beneath her allotment last Wednesday evening.'

Mutters around the room. 'True,' I said, 'but there's always a chance of speaking to the man he bought it from, isn't there?'

Linford frowned. 'I don't follow.'

'Are you familiar with a man named Jacob Werner?'

'Yes ...' His eyes narrowed suspiciously. 'Jacob Werner bred fighting dogs at a disused launderette in Croydon. But we only discovered that this weekend, when his body was found on the premises.'

I leaned forward, hands on our row, startled. 'I beg your pardon?'

'The results of his post-mortem haven't been released yet, but it appears that Jacob Werner was beaten to death at a launderette owned by his cousin, the man who discovered his body.'

'And the dogs?'

'Dead. All of them.'

I must've fallen quiet, because the next thing I knew Lady Allen was staring down at me and saying my name. 'Mr Rook? Do you have any more questions?'

'No,' I said. 'Thank you, DI Linford.'

That was the end of the prosecution's case, and though Garrick closed with a flourish that took us into the afternoon, I was too distracted to pay much attention.

'Mr Rook,' Lady Allen said, 'do you want to begin the defence's case today, or would you prefer to wait until first thing in the morning?'

'The morning. I would prefer to have a clean start in the morning, My Lady.'

'Very well. We will adjourn until ten thirty tomorrow.'

I left court to find a message from Percy instructing me to come into chambers to collect a new set of keys, as the locks had been changed this morning. I left Zara on the Tube home, and alighted at Chancery, intending to slip in and out of chambers as quickly and quietly as possible. Any sort of fanfare was the last thing I needed.

When I turned up to the clerks' room at the back of reception, however, I found Rupert Stubbs waiting for me there. Worse still, upon my arrival, every clerk except for Percy stood up and walked out in silence, closing the door behind them.

Rupert turned an empty chair towards me. 'Have a seat, Elliot, and lose the hat.'

His tone wasn't quite as grave as I'd been expecting, but it still caused me to swallow loudly as I accepted his invitation. He began to pace the room then, while Percy watched with his loafers raised on a neighbouring chair and a tight, unimpressed expression on his face.

'I see that it has been another fascinating twenty-four hours in the life of our newest QC,' Rupert said.

'I have to admit,' I replied, 'it's been a bit much, even for me.'

'A bit much,' he said, flashing a raised eyebrow in my direction as he floated past. 'Let's discuss your most recent accomplishments, shall we? You took it upon yourself to place a witness into hiding, and then secreted the address away in chambers. A witness, it should be added, who is not even involved in one of your own cases, but in that of another barrister's pupil. This move incited a vicious attack on our caretaker to make way for an impostor who broke into your room, stole said address, and then shot the witness outside the supposedly safe house in which you'd hidden him. Not only that, but you have now been given an Osman warning of your own.'

I sighed. 'Look, I know that these things always seem to happen to me, but I'm only trying to do my job.'

'Your job,' Rupert said. 'Tell me, Elliot, do you remember the barrister's code of conduct?'

I glanced to Percy for support, but all he did was shrug.

'I'm a little rusty …' I said.

'A barrister must promote and protect fearlessly and by all proper and lawful means the lay client's best interests, and do so without regard to his own interests or to any consequences to himself or to any other person. In short –' Rupert came to a stop and surveyed me from across the room. 'Well done, pupil. I'm proud of you.'

'That may be so,' Percy added irritably, swinging his shoes down to the carpet, 'but I don't think the same can be said for DI Linford's opinion of you. He says that you should concentrate on your own job and leave him to do his.'

'When did you speak to Linford?'

'He called earlier to discuss the circus you left behind last night. It seems our temporary cleaner's application, mere hours before the incident, was more than just a serendipitous coincidence. They're struggling to trace him, but he says it's only a matter of time.'

'I bet he says that.'

'Elliot,' Rupert said, reclaiming my attention, 'if you need somewhere to stay while this Osman warning is hanging over your head, then you're welcome to one of my spare rooms.'

I shook my head. 'I appreciate the concern, but I have to get home to the dog.'

'You?' Percy said. 'A dog?'

'Yes,' I said. 'She's a fighting dog I stole after flooring a breeder who works for the same county lines drug dealers that ordered the shooting of the witness last night.'

'Oh forget it!' Percy snapped, bringing his feet back up onto the neighbouring chair. He reached across his desk, retrieved a couple of new keys and tossed them at me. 'You know something, Rook, you don't always have to be such a sarcastic old twat.'

With keys in tow, I returned to the Underground and went home. On walking from the station to my front door, however, the single sheet of paper folded in my pocket seemed to gain weight. At one point I heard a moped in the distance, and the instant of terror almost brought me down to the pavement. When it came time to walk Scout, I did so swiftly and kept my eyes moving in all directions. For a while, I could've sworn that I was being tailed by a black Volvo estate, so I cut the walk short, went home and dug out an old cricket bat. Every few minutes I'd peek out of the window in the kitchenette. I filed my latest death threat alongside the last, stuffing it into the drawer with my wedding ring, and sat on the floor with the television off. I opened a bottle of whiskey and didn't bother to get a glass.

Scout curled up beside me with one eye open, watching the door, and we stayed that way until I drank myself to sleep.

29

Tuesday's alarm seemed crueller than usual, but that was mostly because it woke me up off the floor of the kitchenette, where I was still sitting with my back against the refrigerator and the cricket bat in one hand. Upon waking, I cried out and swung the bat through the air. It was going to be another long day.

By nine o'clock I was already dressed in my wig and robes, smoking outside the courthouse and waiting for Lydia to arrive. The first person I recognised stomping across the grounds was not the solicitor, however, but Zara, dressed in her oversized hoody and jeans. As she approached, I caught her looking me up and down with an almost horrified expression.

'You look like shit,' was how she greeted me.

'Thank you. What are you doing here?'

'Did you really think I'd miss your big day?'

'I wish I could.'

Lydia arrived, heels clacking along the turning circle, weighed down by her shoulder bag and the customary pile of papers under one arm.

'Right,' she said, 'what's the plan?'

'We need to convince Charli to give evidence,' I replied.

'And if she won't?'

'Then I want her to sign an endorsement to the brief confirming that I've advised against that course, but she has chosen to ignore my advice. I'd need that signature witnessed by you, her solicitor.'

'I don't get it,' Zara said. 'Why do you need her to provide evidence so badly? Isn't that just going to give Garrick an opportunity to rip her apart in cross-examination?'

'Yes, but our current sticking points are the no comment interview, and the mystery of the damn dog. So far, we haven't had anybody confirm that there was ever a dog there to begin with, which completely wrecks my theory of Deacon Walker cuckooing the property.'

'But *you* saw the dog,' Zara said. 'We both did. Can't you just say that?'

'As a barrister, I can't give evidence. It'd have to be her brother, or maybe the neighbour. If we could get one of those two to make a statement, then we could serve that on the prosecution and we'd at least have proof of the dog's existence, but I'd much rather have Charli just do that this morning.'

'Makes sense,' Zara said. 'Why is the no comment interview such a problem this time? Barber never answered a single question in his case last year. I assumed it was the standard.'

'The solicitor's advice can't be generic,' I explained. 'There has to be an understandable reason to advise a no comment interview if we're to negate any adverse inference from the jury.'

'OK.' Zara turned to Lydia. 'What was the reason in this case?'

'When I saw Charli just before the interview started, she was in a state of shock,' Lydia said. 'I asked the custody sergeant if she could see a doctor to assess her mental fitness for the interview and he declined my request. He told me she'd be interviewed regardless, so I said fine, but I'll advise her to go no comment all the way.'

'Was this conversation recorded on the custody record?' I asked.

Lydia thought about it and then shook her head apologetically. 'I don't think so. You know how it is down at the station. Everything happens so bloody fast.'

'So,' Zara said, 'the only proof the defendant has of the reason she didn't give evidence at the time can only come from you, right?'

'I am *not* giving evidence,' Lydia said, holding up a hand. This wasn't surprising: it's not unheard of for solicitors to give evidence, but it is quite unusual, and they generally don't like it.

'All right,' I said. 'Then we need to go and speak to Charli as soon as possible.'

'Count me out,' Zara said. 'This is my day off. I'll see you from the gallery.'

'In court on your day off?' I noted. 'You sound more like me every day, Rookie.'

'Oh no,' she said, dismay clouding her face. 'Don't say that!'

Lydia and I went to see if Charli had arrived yet. Luckily, she had. More often than not, the private security firms that have taken over prisoner transport arrive late to court, particularly those coming into London from women's remand prisons. Charli was being held in the closest one to Snaresbrook, which was a two-hour drive away, and they would've had to have set off early to beat the city traffic. I held my thumb against the intercom's buzzer at the cells and, after about thirty seconds, a lady finally asked if she could help.

'Solicitor and counsel to see Charli Meadows,' I answered, and we were let into the airlock system, with the door behind us locking before another opened ahead.

Charli's expression was blank when we walked into the room. Her response to my request was very simple.

'I'm not giving evidence today.'

'Charli,' Lydia said patiently, 'if you don't give evidence then there'll be no explanation or denial. You'll almost certainly be convicted.'

'I don't care,' Charli responded quietly, gazing off into nothing. 'I just want it over.'

'It wouldn't take very long,' I tried softly. 'All I'd ask you was whether or not you knew the drugs were in the car, to confirm that you had a dog, and that you replied "no comment" following Lydia's advice after she feared for your mental fitness at the time.'

'And what about the prosecutor?' Charli asked. 'Will he be so quick?'

I sighed. 'No. 'I don't imagine that he will be.'

'Why can't you do it, Lydia? You can explain the interview and you met Biggie.'

'I'm not sure it would be appropriate for me to give evidence,' Lydia grumbled, then rolled her eyes to me, clearly hoping that I'd press Charli a little further. 'What do you think, Elliot?'

'Oh, I think you'd be all right.' I smiled. 'We'd only deal with those two issues and you'd be out of the box in ten minutes, I all but guarantee it.'

Lydia's eyes widened and then narrowed, as she fumed. 'Fine,' she said impatiently, 'but the court might have to wait for me. I have another client in Court 8 for a PCMH at ten thirty. He's coming here from Pentonville and I'm not going to rush him.'

'The court will be happy to wait, I'm sure.'

'Fantastic,' Lydia snapped. 'Thank you very much, Elliot.'

With that, the conference was over. As she had another client to see, Lydia remained down in the cell area, while I went off to the public canteen to see Zara.

'She's going to do it,' I said.

'Who? Meadows?'

'Lydia.'

'Ouch.' Zara sipped at her cup of tea, fighting a sly grin. 'How'd that go?'

'I need another smoke. That's how that went.'

'Ever the charmer.'

Back outside on the steps, I checked the time.

'How long?' Zara asked.

'Fifteen minutes.'

'You ready?'

'I don't think so.' I was staring out across the grounds, smoking slowly, delaying the inevitable. The last of the morning's cars were filing through the great gates on the opposite side of the lawn. Most of the vehicles crawled up the driveway in the direction of the courthouse, merged onto the massive turning circle in front of us, and then broke off for the parking area behind the building. Others used the turning circle to drop off all manner of lawmakers and lawbreakers at the bottom of the steps. 'Something that still puzzles me,' I said, 'is why Deacon was killed.'

Zara shrugged. 'Maybe he was falling for Meadows. 'Maybe he didn't want her to be sent down for the frame-up, assuming she *was* framed. Maybe he was skimming off the top, like those blokes in Margate.'

'Maybe,' I agreed around my cigarette. 'Perhaps he was never supposed to give an Argentino to the woman already charged with smuggling drugs. Maybe he fucked up in a way we'll never understand as long as we … Zara? What's wrong?'

Zara was staring ahead as if she'd seen a ghost walking across the expansive grounds. I followed her gaze, confused, and what I saw brought the same impossible, spectral dread crawling across my flesh.

There, coming to a stop in the centre of the turning circle, was a pristine white Audi RS8, registration DM1.

The cigarette I'd been smoking dropped from my mouth.

The passenger door opened and out stepped Delroy Meadows. He leaned down, gave a grateful thumbs up through the window, and then the car was on its way, passing a parked black Volvo estate that looked oddly familiar.

'I knew it!' Zara wheezed.

'Delroy Meadows,' I said. 'All this time. Delroy fucking Meadows.'

It took him another thirty seconds to walk the distance towards us, after which he smiled; there was worry in his eyes. 'Morning, Rook. I hope today is going to –'

'That car,' I said. 'I thought that car belonged to Deacon Walker.'

'What?' He glanced over one shoulder to the car now disappearing back out of the gates. 'The Audi? You must be joking. As if Deacon could've afforded that.'

'I saw him driving it,' I said. 'He used to drive to your sister's in it!'

Delroy frowned. '*That* car? Why the hell would Deacon Walker be driving around in that? Sorry, but you've got your wires crossed there, mate.'

'Whose is it?' Zara asked, apparently trying and failing not to sound too frantic. 'Who just dropped you off?'

'Danny,' Delroy said warily. 'I did a couple of hours at the garage, so Danny said he'd drop me off.'

'Danny?' I choked.

'Yeah, you know? Danny! The Pinball Wizard …'

'Your mechanic?'

'Right. Why? What's up?'

I pointed a shaking finger towards the gate, even though the car was long gone. 'That car … *That car was –*'

'It was a beautiful ride,' Zara interjected with a strained smile. 'I have two questions of my own. How much do you pay your mechanics? And, do you need a new one?'

This relaxed Delroy into a smile, and he buried his hands into his pockets. 'I couldn't afford to pay anybody that much, that's for sure. Not with all these court fees. No, that was a gift from his old man, I think. Spoiled little brat.'

'His father.' I swallowed, catching Zara's eye. 'I'll bet that number plate cost him a few quid. The two of you share the same initials.'

'Yeah, only mine isn't quite as exotic as his.'

'No?' Zara giggled unnervingly. 'Why, what's his surname?'

'Mandamás.'

'Mandamás …' I repeated in disbelief.

'I know, don't get me started. Some name for a ginger, eh?' He stood awkwardly for a moment, and then checked his watch. 'We start in a couple of minutes, don't we? Don't you reckon we should be, like, getting inside?'

'Absolutely,' I said. 'I'll be inside as soon as I've finished this.'

I held up my empty hand, fingers clenched around nothing, my cigarette still smouldering by my feet. Delroy glanced down at it, and then to me with an expression that suggested I might have lost the plot, then he left us standing outside.

'Mandamus!' Zara gasped, almost keeling over. 'It's a legal term, isn't it?'

'Yes. The judicial command given to an inferior court, or when ordering somebody to perform a duty. In Latin, it literally means *we command*. But he didn't say Mandamus. He said Mandamás, which is Spanish.'

'As in, Costa del Crime Spanish?'

'Yes.'

'You spent a lot of time in Spain, right? Do you know what it means?'

'Yes.' I swallowed. I took a long, shaky breath. 'Mandamás translates as Top Dog.'

'Holy shit!' Zara was now bouncing in her boots. 'We need to tell Linford!'

'We do,' I agreed. 'But he's inside, and court commences in four minutes.'

'So, what the hell are we going to do?'

I marched for the doors. 'We're going to win.'

30

Garrick was already in the courtroom when I entered. He gave me a rare friendly nod as I settled into counsels' row.

'I must say, Rook, that I am genuinely looking forward to cross-examining your client this morning. For both sides, this has been quite the case.'

'I wouldn't look forward to it too much,' I replied bluntly, pouring myself a water.

The court filled quickly. Every participant seemed restless this morning, apparently eager to hear Charli's side of a story poised so impossibly against her. Despite having already given his evidence, DI Linford was sitting alongside the CPS lawyer behind Garrick, staying until the bitter end of these bizarre proceedings.

Lady Allen looked down from the bench, inviting me to commence in the usual fashion.

'Yes, Mr Rook?'

'My Lady.' I climbed to my feet. 'The defence does not call Charli Meadows to give evidence.'

Whispers swept the room.

'I see,' she replied. 'Have you warned your client that the jury may draw whatever inferences they think fit from her decision not to give evidence?'

'I have.'

'Very well. Will the defence be calling *any* evidence?'

'Yes, My Lady. I intend to call my instructing solicitor, Ms Lydia Roth, but she is currently dealing with a brief matter over in Court 8. I'm not entirely sure how long that will take.'

'I can find out easily enough,' she said, and then muttered something to the court's clerk, who picked up her phone and conducted a short, hushed conversation, before reporting back to the judge. 'Apparently,' Allen continued, 'the matter in Court 8 involving your solicitor is just drawing to an end. I'm informed that she should be here in two minutes, so rather than rise I think we'll wait for her to arrive.'

'Perfect,' I said. 'Thank you.'

I sat back down to wait. I fiddled with my cuffs and straightened my wig. The room was mostly silent. A few coughs. A sniffle here and there. Two minutes passed. Then three. Four. I noticed the judge's eyes narrow as she watched the clock.

Garrick leaned close, his tone fouler than it had been at the prospect of tearing my client to pieces. 'This is a funny two minutes,' he grumbled. 'Is she off doing her hair?'

In the circumstances, I couldn't do more than shrug. Members of the jury were watching me expectantly, which brought warmth into my cheeks. I pictured Lydia swaggering through the corridors in her usual fashion, heels clacking. No rush, Lydia. Take your time.

She was probably weighed down with paperwork, as always. The image brought a half-grin to my mouth. Tonight, I imagined, I'd search on eBay for one of those neon-green satchels that paperboys carry. The cheaper and more garish the better. I'd present it to her over our next drink. Or a child's rucksack, perhaps. I could just see her designer glasses pairing nicely with a *Star Wars* backpack full of papers.

I couldn't keep from grinning at the image, which drew a suspicious frown from the bench, so I quickly reached for my water to hide my lips behind the glass.

Yes, that'd be perfect: a child's rucksack full of papers.

I felt my smile fall away. My lips turned very cold, but not from the drink.

A rucksack. Full of papers.

Stacks of paper on a train to Margate.

Lydia's papers, always lighter after venturing down into the cells. Lydia Roth, handing papers to her clients. Legal papers folded up in their pockets and taken back to Belmarsh, Brixton, Pentonville, Wandsworth, Wormwood Scrubs.

I must've tipped the glass too far, because water was pouring all over me.

Somebody in the jury giggled.

'Mr Rook,' Allen said with a hint of concern, 'is everything all right?'

I didn't have chance to respond before doors opened behind me and the sound of heels entered the courtroom. 'The defence calls Ms Lydia Roth,' I croaked, stumbling to my feet without turning round.

Lydia walked straight into the witness box and swore on the Bible to tell the truth, the whole truth and nothing but. She was smiling politely, but she didn't look thrilled to be sworn inside the box. Her eyes were colder than I'd seen them. As always, the papers she'd been carrying were gone. Had she always looked so bare without them?

In those split seconds, I imagined the minutes ahead as if I were at a crossroads.

If my spiralling thoughts were incorrect, I might well be struck off for trying.

And if these suspicions were well founded, I might still be struck off regardless. Not for the first time, Rupert's voice came to mind.

To promote and protect fearlessly and by all proper and lawful means the lay client's best interests. To do so without regard to his own interests or to any consequences to himself or to any other person.

I clenched my shaking fists and spoke. 'Can you please state your name for the court?'

'My name is Lydia Roth.'

'And your occupation?' I asked.

'Solicitor.'

'Are you, in fact, the solicitor acting for the defendant, Charli Meadows?'

'I am.'

I swallowed. 'And were you acting for her when she was interviewed for this offence?'

'I was, yes.'

'We've heard the officer in the case, DI Linford, give evidence to the effect that Miss Meadows answered "no comment" to the various questions asked of her in interview. He claims that she had been advised to make no comment by you, is that correct?'

'Yes.'

'And why did you give that advice?'

'Well, as I said to the interviewing officer at the time, my client seemed to be in shock. I didn't think she was in a fit mental state to be interviewed.'

'And what did the interviewing officer say in response?'

'He told me that he disagreed, and that the interview would proceed as normal. I informed him in return that, if the interview did go ahead, I'd advise Miss Meadows to give no comment.'

I nodded and felt tension through my own neck. 'During your preparation for this case,' I said, 'did you ever visit Miss Meadows at her home address?'

'Several times,' she replied.

'And was there ever a dog in the house?'

'Yes, there was, about a month ago. A huge white dog. She had to lock it away while I entered the house.'

'Great,' I muttered, feeling anything but.

That was all I needed to ask. Her evidence was completed. It was time to sit down. My emotions were spiralling: here was the familiar burn of anger, the dizziness of shock, and something else altogether. Hurt.

I didn't sit down. I couldn't. I sighed and then began.

'Roth is your married name, is it not?'

'I'm sorry?' Lydia replied; if she hadn't been waiting on Garrick's questions, I suspect that she would've already had one foot out of the box. 'What did you say?'

'Your maiden name,' I said. 'What is it?'

She tilted her head, glanced around the room, and then leaned closer to the microphone as if it was just the two of us here. 'Why?'

I could feel the shake in my hands. 'What is your maiden name, Ms Roth?'

'Elliot ...' She blinked, eyelashes fluttering, but her eyes were wary now. 'What on earth does that matter?'

'Macey,' I replied for her, hearing the disappointment in my own voice. 'Is it true that your maiden name is Lydia Macey?'

She pursed her lips. 'Where are you getting this from?'

'I didn't see the similarity before,' I said sadly. 'Your hair is so much lighter than his, and of course I wasn't looking for it, but those eyes … Those green eyes …'

'Mr Rook?' The judge appeared genuinely concerned.

'Ms Roth,' I continued, 'are you related to Daniel Mandamás, also known as Daniel Macey?'

'Related?' Lydia glanced to the jury. 'I have no idea who you're talking about.'

A voice from the public gallery; it was, unmistakably, Delroy Meadows. '*What?*'

'Silence,' Lady Allen said, but her eyes were fixed on Lydia. 'Answer the questions, Ms Roth.'

'The questions are nonsense,' she said. 'I came up here to answer two questions, that is all, one about –'

'Ms Roth,' I continued, sharper now. 'Are you the daughter of the notorious drug tsar Roy Macey, a fugitive currently believed to be hiding out on the Costa del Sol?'

She laughed, but the laugh was dead. 'You're joking, aren't you?'

'And therefore,' I continued, 'are you one of the two figureheads in charge of Roy Macey's extensive county lines drug-dealing operation?'

'My Lady!' Garrick cried, hauling himself to his feet. 'I don't know what Rook is doing, but these are all leading questions!'

'They are,' Allen responded, 'but I for one am curious to see where they lead. Please continue, Mr Rook.'

'I will, My Lady, I just need a moment to figure out exactly *where* these questions do lead, as –' Then it all fell into place, and the feeling was near to bliss. 'That's it.'

'That's *what?*' Lydia spat back.

'The garage,' I said, remembering something Delroy Meadows had told me the very first time I'd seen Danny at work: *the guy's a genius with a spray gun.*

Lydia's face, once so striking, had turned the colour of old cream.

'Ms Roth,' I said, 'is it true that your twin brother, Daniel, sprays the synthetic drug known as Spice onto rolling tobacco, for sale to the general public, as well as legal papers for distribution among the local prisons, at his place of work in Hackney Wick? That place of work being the very same garage where the defendant's car was taken for its MOT mere weeks before those drugs were discovered concealed in the boot?'

Gasps across the room. From the public gallery, Delroy's voice again: 'He does *what?*'

'This is ridiculous,' Lydia replied coldly. 'You're delusional.'

'I have been.' I nodded. 'So, you're saying that if the stack of legal papers you were carrying this morning, which you presumably passed on to your client over in Court 8, were retrieved and analysed, they *wouldn't* be coated with synthetic cannabinoids bound for Pentonville?'

Her smile was like a knife now; she looked like a total stranger. 'Have you been drinking again, Elliot?'

'Not today,' I said. 'Not yet. That's all I have to ask. If you wait there, Mr Garrick may have some questions for you.'

I glanced at Garrick. He was slumped with his chin almost resting on our row.

'Mr Garrick,' Allen said, '*do* you have any questions for Ms, um, Roth?'

'N-no, My Lady. No questions.'

'In that case you are free to go,' Lady Allen said, 'but on no account whatsoever may you leave this court building until further notice.'

Lydia didn't respond. She stormed for the exit with her nose turned up high. My hands were still shaking wildly.

As soon as the doors at the back of the room had slammed shut, Lady Allen turned to her clerk. 'Find out if the van has already left for Pentonville with its remand prisoners, would you, Kate?'

'Certainly.' Another brief phone call took place before the clerk hung up and replied quietly. 'Not yet, My Lady. The van is still on the premises.'

The judge nodded, hands working at her chin, apparently oblivious to the excitable whispers now rising across the room. 'Officer Linford,' she said clearly, 'before the van leaves, it might be a good idea for you to recover those papers from Ms Roth's client. I'll issue a warrant for their retrieval. In the circumstances, I don't think we need to worry about legal professional privilege, do you?'

Jack Linford was already on his feet. 'I was thinking the same thing, My Lady,' he said, and he rushed from the room.

'Members of the jury,' Allen continued, 'I think we'd better adjourn until two o'clock to take stock. Please go with the usher.' She turned to me. 'Mr Rook, I won't address you until we return, at which point I hope to God that I have a clearer idea of what on earth is going on here.'

'Very good, My Lady,' I replied, already moving for the doors while Garrick sat staring into nothingness.

I expected to see Lydia beyond those doors. I braced myself, still not entirely sure whether I was merely horrified

315

or genuinely hurt, but the first person I saw on the other side was Zara. My head, already whirling, took a moment to process what was happening.

Zara, dressed in her hoody and jeans, was struggling against the grasp of two security personnel.

'Get off me, you idiots!'

'What the hell is going on?' I asked, storming towards the men.

At my approach, they loosened their grips slightly, but each held on to one of her arms.

'She just came running out of the public gallery and tried to rob a solicitor heading for the exit,' one of them answered. 'Don't worry, she's going nowhere.'

'It's Roth!' Zara cried, tugging against their grips. 'She's doing a runner!'

'You morons!' I roared. 'This woman is a barrister, and that solicitor is disobeying a court order not to leave the building!'

The men shared a glance – at first doubtful, and then extremely worried – and released Zara, who didn't hang around for any sort of I told you so. She went sprinting for the exit, boots sliding through the corridors, and I followed.

Lydia was already out there, standing some way off across the grounds. With the security guards close behind us, I leapt the steps and ran for the lawn. Then I heard the engine. I heard it before I ever saw it coming.

Through the gates, screaming into the grounds, was that familiar white Audi. It cut directly across the turning circle, gold alloys spitting turf behind them, and halted beside Lydia. Without a backward glance, she threw herself into the passenger seat and slammed the door.

'She's going to get away!' Zara panted, powering ahead of me.

The car was moving, but it wasn't aiming for the exit. It was speeding directly towards us.

I caught Zara by the hood with both hands and prepared to throw her aside, ready to take the fatal impact in her stead. Fortunately, I never had to. Moments before the car reached us, something came tearing around the courthouse from the left. I flinched, closing my eyes, and the next thing I heard was an almighty crash.

I opened my eyes.

The Audi was stationary, askew across the lawn, with a vaguely familiar black Volvo estate embedded into the side of it. A crowd was already streaming out of the courthouse behind us, every man and woman filming the scene on his or her phone, as Zara and I were still frozen in stunned silence.

From the Volvo, two heavyset plain-clothes officers emerged. They tore open the Audi's doors and dragged the shell-shocked twins out onto the ground. Daniel Macey appeared to be roaring with anger as the handcuffs went on, though his vocal cords never uttered a sound.

Lydia made up for that, yelling what must've been every obscenity known to both the English and Spanish languages. I couldn't help but feel a secret sorrow; seeing her like this, I felt like such a fool for having ever enjoyed her company. Zara must've suspected as much, because she gave me an awkward pat on the shoulder as we watched the scene unfold.

Then another arm landed on my shoulder, and I was surprised to see that this one belonged to DI Linford, who was beaming as if we'd just won a match in his Sunday-morning league. A third officer had appeared from the Volvo, and he was striding towards us as his colleagues held the twins flat on the ground. 'What shall we nick them for, guv?'

'Take your pick,' Linford said. 'Let's start with drugs and murder and work our way up from there, shall we?'

At this, a marked police van rolled in through the gates. I could just about hear the twins being cautioned as they were loaded into the back of it, though Lydia was still swearing furiously as blood trickled from her nose. An officer was signing the rights to her brother.

'How?' Zara asked. 'All of this! How the hell did you know?'

'Contrary to what you both think,' Linford said, 'we don't just issue an Osman warning and then leave you to fend for yourself. You've been under our protection for the past twenty-four hours.'

'Twenty-four hours?' I replied, eyeing the Volvo with dawning understanding.

'Of course, we didn't know exactly who we were protecting you *from*,' Linford went on.

'Well, there's nothing like leaving it until the last second, is there, Detective Inspector?'

Linford laughed. I couldn't quite bring myself to laugh with him.

PART FOUR

OLD BOYS

31

'Have your cases always been like this?' Zara asked. We were circling Eagle Pond, the massive expanse of water covering the northern quarter of Snaresbrook's grounds. It was almost two o'clock, and I was nearly out of cigarettes. I'd arrived with a full pack.

'They didn't used to be,' I told her. 'Not until you came along.'

'Maybe we're bad influences on each other.'

'Almost certainly,' I said.

She smiled. 'Well, you're not in an ambulance this time, which is good.'

'Yes. Every cloud, I suppose.'

'At least Lady Allen will remember me,' Zara said. 'What do you think will happen with Charli? Should we go and see her or something? Tell her what's going on?'

'I can't tell her what's going on when I have no idea myself. We never covered this at Bar school.'

'No,' she said, 'I guess not. What do you think will happen now?'

I shrugged. 'Let's go and find out, shall we?'

Garrick wasn't in the courtroom when we arrived, but Linford was. He came towards us grinning. I wondered if he'd stopped grinning once at any point over the past few hours.

'How?' I asked. 'How did you know?'

'Well,' he said, 'getting shot tends to break a young man's loyalties.'

'Omar Pickett,' Zara said. 'He talked?'

'Sang is more like it. Everything he'd heard about these so-called Macey twins running things and a garage in Hackney Wick, the poison at the prison, you name it. He didn't know about Deacon Walker's death, of course, but he did claim that earlier this year, right before the raid at the Alex, a couple of his gangmates were sent to those allotments on Low Hall Lane with an unusual errand. Something he didn't think much of at the time.'

'Which was?' I asked.

'To plant a certain weed behind the fence there. Looks as if they were playing the long game on this, using Charli Meadows to cover their arses before this ever began. We've had eyes on Roth all morning. To tell you about it this morning, and to take Pickett's statement officially, would've brought about a legal obligation to contact Israel's solicitor, and with his solicitor being Roth, well ...'

'Israel?' Zara asked. 'Did Omar mention Andre?'

'You could say that.' He was beaming. 'We've been busy over the last couple of hours, Ms Barnes. Searches of the Meadows garage have dredged up hundreds of pages of legal papers stored in Danny's personal locker. Front sheets relating to Lydia Roth's cases set on top of blanks. We've also recovered the papers from her client over in Court 8, which follow the same pattern: one true case paper on top of a bundle of blanks. They haven't been analysed yet, but I'd bet your earnings they're coated. Forensics have also found traces of organic plant material on the grinding tools in Danny's locker. We don't know anything for sure yet, but they're saying the traces are purple in colour and incredibly toxic.'

'Wolfsbane,' I said.

He nodded. 'That's not all. Lady Allen issued us with a fresh European arrest warrant for Roy Macey.'

'Great,' I said, 'though I'm not sure what use that will be when Interpol have been hunting him for the past twenty years.'

'That's the best part! We've already found him!'

'Roy Macey?' I asked in disbelief.

Zara gasped. 'I don't believe it! Where was he?'

'Right here in London,' Linford chuckled, 'sitting on his daughter's mantelpiece.'

'What?' I said. 'Her mantelpiece?'

'His ashes!' Zara said. 'Don't tell me he was dead to begin with?'

Linford nodded. 'For years, we reckon. They used his name as a sort of …'

'A brand,' I said. 'They used their father's name like a brand.'

'Exactly.' He shook his own head. 'I've got to say, I didn't see this coming when I arrested Omar Pickett three months ago.'

'What about the Cutthroats?' Zara asked. 'They'll be looking for revenge.'

'Maybe,' he said. 'We'll keep an eye on things for now, but without the Maceys holding them together, I imagine they'll go back to their old ways soon enough. Stabbing and shooting each other for a few yards of extra territory. I'd avoid E10 if I were you.'

'And what about Charli Meadows?' I asked. 'What happens now?'

'I've briefed Harlan Garrick. I think you'd better hear it from him.' Linford checked his watch. 'I think it's time.'

At that moment, Garrick blundered in through the doors and collapsed into his seat without meeting my eye. Zara slipped to the back of the room as Lady Allen returned to the bench and the court was called into session.

'So, gentlemen,' she said, looking every bit as perplexed as I was feeling. 'What do we do now?'

I showed my hands; I had nothing.

Garrick stood slowly, apparently forcing himself upright. 'My Lady, a great deal has been happening since court rose a couple of hours ago.'

'Yes,' she said, nodding, 'I have seen my lawn, Mr Garrick.'

'Quite.' He coughed into his fist. 'I have been fully briefed by Detective Inspector Linford. For operational reasons, I cannot repeat everything he told me, but for the purposes of this trial ...' He hesitated, swallowing something unpleasant. 'My Lady, I have been instructed by DI Linford – instructions that have been confirmed by the Crown Prosecution Service at the highest level – that we are to offer no evidence against the defendant, Charli Meadows, in this case.'

I laughed out loud; just one burst, which sent a visible shudder through Garrick's body.

From the dock behind me, a single sob answered.

'All right,' Allen said. 'Well, since the defendant is still in the charge of the jury, we had better get them in for their verdict.'

The jury was brought into the room and, once seated, Allen addressed them.

'Members of the jury,' she said, 'you were in court this morning to witness the extraordinary scenes. As a result of this, and of other matters resolved by subsequent inquiries, the prosecution have decided to offer no evidence against Miss Meadows. While this is a decision I wholly agree with, I cannot legally release the defendant as she is in your charge. I am therefore going to appoint one of your number to stand up and return a verdict of not guilty. Juror Number 6. As you are in the foreperson's chair, you will have the honour. Stand up, please.'

The elderly Caribbean lady in chair number 6 rose to her feet, looking confused.

'So,' Allen smiled, 'do you the jury, as directed by me, return a verdict of not guilty in this case?'

The juror nodded. 'Um, yes, My Lady. Not guilty.'

'Perfect. Then I formally return the verdict of not guilty. Does that conclude our business for the day?'

'Not quite,' Garrick sighed. 'As My Lady knows, Miss Meadows has also been remanded in custody in relation to a large number of offences including several murders. In relation to those matters, I am to inform the court that she is no longer a suspect and, from now onwards, Miss Meadows's status will be as a witness for the prosecution. It follows that there is no longer any reason for her to be remanded in custody. Charli Meadows may be released.'

A voice – her brother's – roared from the gallery. 'Yes!'

'Very well,' the judge replied, turning to the dock. 'Officer, please release Miss Meadows.'

The dock officer – with all eyes now upon him – blushed. 'Apologies, My Lady, but she'll have to go downstairs to be processed before she's released.'

Allen's eyes flared. 'Miss Meadows is an innocent woman of good character facing no criminal charges. Under what authority do you purport to keep her in custody while she is, as you call it, processed?'

The dock officer shrank on the spot. 'I'll need to check with my supervisor.'

'You will not,' Allen scalded. 'You will open the dock gate and release Miss Meadows immediately or I will have you remanded in custody for contempt of court.'

That did it. The dock officer opened the gate. Charli Meadows rose to her feet, paused for a moment and closed her eyes. Then she stepped down out of the dock and proceeded to walk straight out of the courtroom to scattered applause from the public gallery.

'Well.' Lady Allen sighed, leaning back into her chair. 'I think that concludes our business for today. Thank you for your assistance, everybody. It has been ... unusual.'

The usher led the jury out as soon as the judge retired. Eventually, after everybody else had filed out in dribs and drabs, only Harlan Garrick remained in the room while I packed away the case papers.

I could hear some sort of incessant grinding, and it took me a moment to realise that the noise was coming from his teeth.

'I'm still not entirely sure what happened today,' he said, 'but may I say that your performance in this case has been utterly shambolic.'

'You think so?' I replied. 'I'm not sure that Charli Meadows would agree with you.'

'Yes, I think so. Your conduct has been an embarrassment to the Bar, and I've a good mind to report you to your head of chambers.'

'Be my guest. Only, when you do, you ought to ask him to remind you of the barrister's code of conduct. I suspect you could use a reminder.'

He gathered his papers into his arms and, in a sweep of silk, began to walk to the doors. 'You have an answer for everything, don't you, Rook?'

I couldn't resist. 'Only one.'

He turned back, glowering. 'Which is?'

I grinned. 'I count that as two-one to me.'

And then he was gone.

Charli was waiting outside the courthouse when I emerged. Zara was there with her, pointing out the destruction on the lawn, waving her arms around and doing her best to replicate the experience in a mature fashion.

'So this dickhead's just, like, driving straight at us! And I'm like, *shit*, then this cop car comes and *smash*! The car goes spinning across the grass, everybody's screaming, people coming out onto the steps with their phones and that, filming it all ...'

Charli looked bewildered, and she seemed grateful for the distraction when I came walking down the steps. 'Mr Rook.'

I nodded a greeting. 'Welcome back to the real world, Charli.'

'Thank you,' she said, offering her hand. 'I'm not sure if you ever really believed in me, but I can never repay you for what you've done. I don't expect there are many barristers that would risk their careers, let alone their lives, for any client.'

I shrugged it off and shook her hand. 'I can't imagine how relieved you must be feeling.'

'I don't even know myself,' she said. 'I mean, I will, in time. It's just ... shocking, you know? I just want to get back to my kids.'

'Of course.'

She hesitated. 'What *did* happen to my dog?'

'I don't know,' I admitted. 'Maybe they'd realised the significance of that breed, and its ties to Werner, being found in your allotment after all. Maybe they knew that, without the dog's body, you'd be hard-pressed to explain any burial to begin with. Either way, they must've disposed of it elsewhere, but we'll likely never know where. I think it's probably best not to think about it.'

She nodded, eyes flooding.

A cheer boomed from the doors behind us and Delroy came leaping down the steps. He caught his sister in a bear hug, scooped her up high and spun her round in a circle. Charli sobbed. Zara and I watched. Attempts on our lives be damned; the effort had, as always, been worth it.

Delroy glanced over, crying a little himself, and grinned. 'So, does this mean I can get some of those legal fees back now that she's been found not guilty?'

'I'm sure you can probably get your solicitor's fees back,' I said, 'given the circumstances, but I'm sorry to say that some wise chap in government has decided that innocent people can no longer recover their legal fees.'

'In that case, I'll have to try and make it back by overcharging on a couple of repair bills. There's this Jag in at the minute, they say the owner's some sort of legal genius, but I don't think he's all that much.'

I laughed. 'How are you getting on with that?'

'Oh, pretty good. The garage is still being turned upside down by coppers as we speak, and my only employee has been arrested for mass murder.'

'I'll expect it in the morning then, good as new.'

'Yeah, right.' He slapped his sister on the back. 'In the meantime, I know three kids who are about to have the best night they've had in a long time. I'll be in touch, Rook.'

'Whenever you get around to it,' I said. 'For now, go and celebrate.'

'We will,' Charli said. 'Thank you. Both of you. Thank you.'

Zara and I stood together, watching the Meadows twins walk those grounds, arm in arm, towards the exit.

'Right,' I said, 'I think we'd better get out of here too, before somebody tries to invoice us for that lawn.'

'I can't.' Zara sighed. 'Linford is giving me a lift to the Scrubs.'

'Andre?'

'It'll still have to be listed in court and officially thrown out there, but I think he'd like to hear the news this afternoon, in person, don't you?'

'I do. When are we leaving?'

'*We?*' Zara shook her head. 'Not we. Not this time.'

I recoiled. Just a touch. 'Why not?'

'This is something I have to do on my own,' she said, and her expression turned a little sad. 'I didn't think it would end like this. Do you think it counts?'

'Counts?' I frowned, lost. 'Counts for what?'

'You know ...' She shuffled her feet. 'Pupillage comes to the six-month mark on Sunday and ... well, it's not exactly a win in court, is it?'

I smiled. 'It counts. A young man is going home to his family because of you. Once again, you have gone above and beyond. You've done more than any barrister of twenty, thirty, forty years' call would've done.'

'You think so?'

'Of course,' I said. 'In all the ways that truly matter, it counts.'

32

'Well, you messed that one up, Rook,' Percy said. 'You were briefed in one of the largest mass-murder cases in English history, and you successfully managed to get all the charges against your client dropped before the trial ever began. If I wore a hat, I'd take it off to you.'

I was sitting in one of Rupert's leather wingbacks on the fourth floor of our building with my eyes closed. 'It's called justice, Percy.'

'Justice doesn't pay the bills.'

Unfortunately, having just that morning collected both my car and its astronomical repair bill from Delroy Meadows, that was something I'd learned the hard way. I had been back in the newspapers though, and the requests for my counsel were once more flooding into the building. Even Isaac Reid, the convicted double murderer in Belmarsh, had been in contact about me appealing his conviction after all; it seemed that he wasn't as scared to give evidence on the true killer now that the Macey twins were behind bars.

At least one thing about Daniel Macey had been true though: he really *was* a genius with a spray gun, and my car looked better than it had done in years. The only thing that Delroy hadn't been able to source was an original 1987 Jaguar emblem. I told him not to worry; I'd quite recently come across one of those.

Now it was Monday 26 March, the first day I'd physically come into chambers since the incident at Snaresbrook the previous Tuesday. I was hoping that the fallout might've died down by now, but it had taken me almost ten minutes to fight my way through the frenzied pupils on the ground floor.

Percy was sitting in a matching wingback on the opposite side of Rupert's room. I opened my eyes and watched Rupert as he busied himself. On his desk was an open bottle of cognac. Beside it were eight glass tumblers.

'How's Ernie, Rupert?' I asked. 'I hear you went to see him over the weekend.'

'Quite well, all things considered,' he replied, pouring a few fingers of amber liquid into each of the glasses. 'Grateful for the card. Embarrassed by the collection. You know how Ernest is. The hand is healing quickly, but he's impatient. He wants to come back to work already.'

'Good,' Percy said. 'The corner lamp in my room blew last week, and I've been sitting down there in semi-darkness.'

Just before I had chance to call him a useless toff, there came a knocking upon the door and I sat upright. My entire body clenched. It was time.

There were forty-five junior barristers at Miller & Stubbs, along with four Queen's Counsel. Two of these silks were, of course, Rupert Stubbs and me. The others were Hugo Darby and Alan Booth, who were leading the short procession of men now filing into the room. Immediately behind them were two of our longest-standing clerks, Nigel Goody and Francis Keene, followed lastly by Charles Stein, Zara's pupil-master.

Every member of our current tenancy committee, present and correct.

It was a room full of middle-aged white men. That made me nervous. I tried not to think about the crushing defeat I'd already seen on Zara's face when I left her sitting in my room on the way up here.

'Good afternoon, gentlemen,' Rupert began, handing out the drinks while each man chose one of the various scattered seats. 'You all know why we are here. Today marks six months since Miss Zara Barnes was invited into chambers for pupillage. Ordinarily, of course, this committee would have voted on whether or not to accept her as a pupil in the first place, but we didn't quite get the chance with this one.'

'No,' Percy added rather resentfully. 'We didn't get chance because Rook, who has never before been interested in acting as a member of this committee, took it upon himself to offer her the place after I'd already turned her away.'

A disapproving grumble rippled through the room.

'Yes,' Stein noted, 'then he dumped her onto me.'

'True,' Rupert said, coming to rest on the edge of his desk, 'though that hardly matters now.' He took a sip from his own glass and smacked his lips together. 'Since establishing this set with Aston Miller, I have been proud to share my name with some of the greatest legal minds this country has to offer. The decision to offer tenancy here is never taken lightly. Now, since he is our newest silk, Elliot has been invited onto this committee along with his fellow Queen's Counsel. However, given his relationship with this pupil, I do wonder if he is in any sort of position to make an objective judgement.'

'Definitely not,' I said. From my glass, I took a mouthful. 'I'm not going to waste your time by sitting here and pretending that my vote might be swayed. You know me.

333

You know how I feel. I believe the girl would be a credit to chambers.'

Rupert nodded. 'Then I shall follow that up with my own observations. Since Barnes arrived here as a pupil, there has scarcely been a peaceful moment. Putting the two of you together, Elliot, is quite obviously a recipe for disaster. You have been beaten in the street. Hospitalised. Almost arrested. Your car has been destroyed. There have been at least two attempts on your life, and the drive-by shooting of a witness. You have behaved not so much like a silk, but more as some sort of maverick sleuth. I'm not sure chambers can handle much more excitement. On the other hand, the two of you do end up getting the job done, some-how.' He paused, rolled his eyes and shook his head. 'Does anybody else have a case to make? Charles, she has been your pupil ...'

He shrugged. 'I've had no concerns.'

The room was quiet.

'That's it?' I asked.

'What else is there? She comes in and works. In future it might be nice if I could get a pupil that I see more than the occasionally fleeting glimpse once or twice a week, but I've no complaints about her work.'

'Very well,' Rupert said. 'Does anybody have anything that they'd care to add?'

All eyes rolled to our senior clerk, who was fiddling with his silver cufflinks. He gave up, lifting his chin, and across the room I braced myself for a low blow.

'There've been many clerks to come out of the Peck household,' he said. 'Clerking is in our blood. To some, a clerk is a glorified receptionist, but if the justice system is a machine, and barristers are cogs, then clerks would be the oil keeping it all going. Of course, one day we will be obsolete. There are now software packages to invoice fees and we have emails instead of conferences. But I believe it is tradition that keeps our justice system the greatest in the world. Court dress, oaths, swearing by almighty God. Tradition. Now, I've said many times before that we hire by names, grades and calibre. At Miller & Stubbs, we've always set a precedent and, frankly, this Barnes doesn't fit in with our traditions. She's – different.'

I was glowering, but he didn't notice. He took a slow mouthful and this time savoured the taste.

'And yet, I would trade fifty barristers of the finest pedigree for another two of her. She has intellect and drive, courage and grit. That's a good enough pedigree, even for me.'

'Hear, hear!' I cried, lifting my own glass.

Percy smiled. 'We could all learn a lot from Zara Barnes. I say aye.'

Rupert nodded. 'Aye.'

Stein concurred, lifting a single finger. 'Aye.'

The word was repeated around the room as Zara Barnes was unanimously voted into chambers.

'Elliot,' Rupert began, 'I assume that you will want to go down and tell her the news? Elliot?'

But I was already running down to the room on the third floor that was now, properly, ours.

A Note on the Authors

Born into a coal-mining family, Gary Bell was an apprentice mechanic, production line worker and door-to-door salesman before being arrested for fraud in his mid-twenties. After taking his exams at night school, he went on to study law as a mature student at Bristol University and has now spent over thirty years at the Bar, before becoming a QC specialising in criminal defence in 2012.

Scott Kershaw is the author of three novels. Prior to becoming an author, Scott worked as a professional chef for several years, and travelled the Continent as a music journalist.

A Note on the Type

The text of this book is set in Linotype Sabon, a typeface named after the type founder, Jacques Sabon. It was designed by Jan Tschichold and jointly developed by Linotype, Monotype and Stempel in response to a need for a typeface to be available in identical form for mechanical hot metal composition and hand composition using foundry type.

Tschichold based his design for Sabon roman on a font engraved by Garamond, and Sabon italic on a font by Granjon. It was first used in 1966 and has proved an enduring modern classic.